HELLHOUND
ON MY
TRAIL

HELLHOUND ON MY TRAIL

J.D. RHOADES

Copyright © 2017 by J.D. Rhoades
Cover and jacket design by 2Faced Design
Interior designed and formatted by E.M. Tippetts Book Designs

ISBN 978-1-943818-23-5
eISBN 978-1-943818-66-2
Library of Congress Control Number: 2016952317

First hardcover publication February 2017 by Polis Books, LLC
1201 Hudson Street, #211S
Hoboken, NJ 07030
www.PolisBooks.com

POLIS BOOKS

Also by J.D. Rhoades

I got to keep movin', I got to keep movin'
Blues fallin' down like hail, blues fallin' down like hail
And the days keeps on worryin' me
There's a hellhound on my trail
Hellhound on my trail...

-Robert Johnson

CHAPTER ONE

A S THEY LOWERED HER FATHER'S body into the ground, Kathryn Shea raised her eyes and scanned the crowd who stood silently in the rain, watching. *How many are really here to pay their respects,* she wondered, *and how many to make sure the old bastard's actually dead?*

She created a mental map with a quick glance across the rows of seated dignitaries as she took her seat beneath the funeral home tent. She knew who everyone was, where everyone was sitting, and what that meant. *That one,* she thought, picking out a face from the mental photograph, *is here to be seen. He'll try to maneuver himself into a photo op with me, the grieving daughter. Not going to happen. That one,* she thought, picking another, *wants my father's seat. Also not going to happen.*

*

She could tell the service was ending by the cadence of the words, without really registering their meaning. She put her hand on the stick-thin arm of her mother sitting next to her, knowing what was to come.

The crack of the gunshots sent a shiver through the old woman's body, and she made a small whimper of fear and dismay. "It's okay, Mother," Kathryn murmured. "It's okay." Another barked set of orders. Another ripple of gunfire. A louder moan came from the old woman's throat. Kathryn tightened her grip in warning. *God damn it*, she raged inwardly. *Don't you dare make a spectacle out of this.* Her mother looked down at Kathryn's fingers digging into the paper-thin skin of her forearm, then back up, her eyes uncertain. A third crack of gunfire. This time the old woman was silent, perhaps unsure of whom or what she should be more afraid of.

Kathryn saw the flag being taken reverently from the coffin and folded just so by a Marine who barely looked old enough to shave. He brought the folded flag to them as they sat beneath the canopy and out of the rain, taking no more notice of the moisture dripping from his dress cap than he would have of a gentle summer sun. He knelt before the old woman, who stared at him, eyes wide and uncomprehending. "On behalf of the President of the United States," the young man murmured, "the United States Marine Corps, and a grateful nation, please accept this flag as a symbol of our appreciation for your loved one's honorable and faithful service." He held the flag out to the old woman, who hesitated, then reached out for it with shaking hands, skin shriveled and barely covering the bones.

"Let me, Mother," the daughter whispered as she reached out and took the flag. "Thank you," she said softly to the kneeling Marine. The young man nodded, stood up, saluted, then swiveled as if on brass gimbals and returned to his line. There was a brief moment of confused silence, then the crowd began to murmur and shift in their seats. Finally, a few brave souls rose to their feet, followed gratefully by the rest. The daughter stayed put, but she nodded to the man in the perfectly pressed and starched chauffeur's uniform standing in the rain a few feet away. He nodded back and advanced under the canopy.

"We're ready to go, ma'am," the man said kindly to the old woman in the chair, who was looking around in confusion. She blinked at the familiar face, then smiled, rising on his offered arm. Kathryn turned away, knowing that her mother would be quickly hustled home, cared for, and, most importantly, out of her way. There was work to be done.

She saw a junior Congressman from Iowa sidling toward her, one she'd sorted out before as no use. She maneuvered deftly to put a former White House Chief of Staff now serving as a lobbyist between them.

"Kat," the former Chief of Staff said to her, taking both of her hands in his and kissing her on the cheek. "We're so sorry for your loss. Your father was a great man. A great American. And a good friend to me and Margie."

Such a good friend, you couldn't keep your hands off his sixteen-year-old daughter's ass on that "fact-finding trip" to Belize, she thought behind the wall of her perfect smile. "Thank you, Carl," she said, giving his hands a squeeze before pulling away. "Give my love to Margie. And Cassie, of course." *When Cassie gets out of rehab,* she thought. She slid away through the crowd, accepting condolences, hugs, and air-kisses.

Finally, she spotted the man she'd been looking for, leaning against a limo, holding an umbrella over his head. He was thin and gray. His hair was gray, his suit was gray, even his eyes were a washed out gray color. No one seemed to notice him or engage him in conversation; he was a man who seemed to fade into the background even as you were staring straight at him. She worked her way toward him through the crowd of alleged well-wishers. He approached and met her with the umbrella.

"You're handling the crowd well," the gray man murmured. His name was Frederick Cordell, and he'd made a career out of being both invaluable and invisible as an adviser to rich and powerful men. He'd made several kings before, never a queen. He looked forward to the challenge.

"Thanks," Kathryn said. "I don't suppose you have a drink in that car of yours."

"I have several drinks in this car of mine." Cordell opened the door for her. She slid gratefully inside, ignoring the dismayed shouts of "Kathryn!" "Kat!" from the crowd still milling about her father's graveside. For a moment, she allowed her iron composure to slip, but only to the extent of leaning her head against the tinted glass and closing her eyes. Cordell sat in the seat beside her and watched. His pale eyes never seemed to blink. He made a motion to the driver up front and the limo pulled smoothly away from the curb, the privacy shield rising soundlessly. After a few moments, Kathryn opened her eyes. Cordell handed her the martini he'd been building from the limo's compact wet bar.

"Thanks," she said, taking the glass, then a sip. Her eyes closed again, this time in pleasure. Cordell continued to watch. After a moment, she opened them again. "So," she said.

"I don't know," Cordell interrupted, "if I ever fully expressed to you my admiration for your father."

"Thank you," she said. She took another sip, then tipped the glass up and drank deeply.

"He was a great American."

"He was a ruthless, merciless son of a bitch," she whispered.

He smiled. "That too."

"Mmm." She held out the glass for a refill. "So where are we?"

He opened a folder that had been sitting on the seat next to him. "We've got firm commitments from about half the county party chairmen."

She chewed at a thumbnail, still looking out the window. "Only half?"

"Half is excellent this early in the cycle. We should go ahead and announce. Soon, maybe as early as Monday. While you've still got..." He trailed off.

She looked back at him. "While I can still use the sympathy over my father's death. Go ahead and say it."

He met her stony gaze without flinching. "We *are* using 'carrying on the Shea legacy' as a campaign theme."

She looked back out the window at the rain. "I'll let you know."

He nodded, clearly deciding to let the matter drop for the moment. After a few seconds, Kathryn spoke again. "It's too bad Clifton couldn't be here. Any news on his condition?"

This time it was Cordell's turn to look out the window.

"What?" she asked.

He turned back to her. "Mr. Trammell," he said with a cold smile, "is circling the drain."

"Cliff Trammell," she said, her voice as icy as his smile, "may not have gotten the recognition my father did, but he's served his country honorably his entire life. So you could show a little more respect."

"Yes ma'am," he said. "Mr. Trammell's condition continues to deteriorate. He's not expected to live out the week."

She snorted. "He'll surprise you. The man's tough as oak."

"Yes ma'am. There is one matter that may be of concern."

"The son."

"Yes ma'am. One of Mr. Trammell's old...I guess you could call him a protégé...met with Trammell at the hospital yesterday. He then went to Trammell's house, entered, and exited twenty minutes later carrying a briefcase. He then went immediately to Reagan International Airport and took a flight to Phoenix, Arizona. That's the closest airport to where the son is living."

"So. Trammell's decided to try and make contact with the son he abandoned forty-some years ago."

"It would seem so. My sources tell me that, since his diagnosis, Mr. Trammell's apparently expressed a great deal of remorse over certain events in his life. Abandoning his son in particular."

"It's not that event I'm concerned about," Kathryn said.

"Ma'am?"

"Do we have any idea what's in that briefcase?"

"No ma'am." Cordell paused. "At least I don't. Do you?"

"I might." She tapped her fingers against the door handle, lost in thought. "Do you have people on the ground in Arizona?"

"I took that precaution, yes, ma'am."

"People you trust?"

He nodded.

"I don't want that suitcase delivered."

He nodded again. "I didn't think you would. I've already taken steps."

She arched a perfectly trimmed eyebrow at him.

"Nothing serious," Cordell assured her. "It'll look like an everyday mugging of a tourist. They'll take the briefcase. And the courier's wallet and watch, just for show. Do you want it brought back to you?"

"Yes," she said. "Unopened. Is that clear?"

"Yes, ma'am," he said.

"I mean it."

"It won't be opened except by you. But…" He hesitated.

"You're about to tell me that you'll be able to serve me better if there are no secrets between us."

He spread his hands. "It happens to be true."

And if what I fear is in that briefcase, Kathryn thought, *and you get hold of it, the knife that my father's oldest friend held to his throat for years will be in your hands, Mr. Cordell, and held at mine. Not. Going. To. Happen.* "I'll think about it," she said.

"Yes, ma'am."

She leaned back and finished the second martini. She felt the warm glow spreading through her. "What was the son's name again?" she asked.

Cordell spoke without hesitation. "Jack Keller."

CHAPTER TWO

Jack Keller was stacking glasses behind the bar when he heard the heavy thud against the front door. It wasn't a knock; it sounded as if someone or something heavy had been thrown against the solid oak. He straightened up and drew in a quick gasp of breath. The bullet wounds in his chest and back had mostly healed, but from time to time they reminded him they were still there. He paused before moving again, hating the apprehension of pain that made him hesitant. Then he heard the shout. It was a wordless cry of fear and pain, high-pitched enough that Keller couldn't tell if it came from a man or a woman. He covered the remaining space between the bar and the front door in three long steps. Another shout came from outside as he fumbled with the deadbolt. He yanked the door open, this time ignoring the sudden stab of pain in his chest muscles.

The blast of desert sunlight after the cool dimness of the bar's interior made him throw up his hand and squint against the dazzle.

Through the glare, he saw a man sitting in the hard-packed brown dirt of the tiny strip of parking lot between the bar and the highway. The man was dressed in a light brown suit, now covered in dust from the parking lot. He was clutching a slim black briefcase to his chest. The skin on his balding head glistened with sweat. His glasses were askew and he looked up at his two assailants in terror.

There were two of them, one white, one black. The black guy was dressed in black jeans and a tight white T-shirt that showed off his gym-rat physique; the white one wore khaki cargo shorts that displayed tree-trunk legs and a black tee with the sleeves cut off. He was the one who was reaching down toward the man on the ground, who pushed himself backward with his feet.

"HEY!" Keller barked. The white guy stopped, straightened up, and looked at him. He didn't respond, just nodded to the black guy who had already started toward Keller.

"Get back in the bar, man," the black guy was saying, holding both his hands out in front of him in a warding gesture. "This ain't anything you need to worry ab—"

Keller interrupted him by grabbing the man's right wrist with his left hand and pulling him forward. The man stumbled slightly, directly into the path of the right cross that Keller threw at his jaw. He was fast, however, and Keller's punch was slowed by the pain in his chest muscles. He rolled with the punch, then yanked his hand free and drove forward hard. His big arms wrapped around Keller and his forehead slammed into Keller's nose. Keller grunted with the pain and they fell to the ground.

The man rose up and turned to his partner. "Hurry the fuck up!" he grated, and pulled back a fist for the punch that would put Keller's lights out. Before he could deliver it, Keller heard a dull ringing sound, like a muffled bell. The man screamed in agony and rolled off, clutching at his arm. Keller struggled upright to a sitting position, the blood streaming down his face.

A young woman with short brown hair was standing a few feet away. She was holding an aluminum baseball bat in one hand and a shotgun in the other. As Keller got to his feet, she tossed the shotgun to him. He caught it with one hand and racked the slide with one quick practiced movement. The sound seemed abnormally loud in the sudden shocked quiet.

"Y'all need to get gone from my property," the woman said. "And take your trash with you." She gestured at the man on the ground, who had stopped howling and was glaring at her with murder in his eyes. Keller could see the ends of bone nearly breaking through under the skin on his arm.

"And while you're at it," Keller said to the man still standing, "give that guy his briefcase back."

The man holding the briefcase looked back and forth between them. "This doesn't concern you."

"What part of 'my property' don't you understand, shithead?" the woman snarled. She glanced at Keller. "Jack, honey, would you mind shootin' this asshole for me?"

Keller raised the shotgun. His nose was throbbing, the blood still flowing and sticky on his upper lip, but it was the blood pounding in his temples that he felt the most.

"You won't shoot me," the man holding the briefcase said. "I'm not armed." His words were more confident than his expression.

"This is the West, bubba," Keller said. "And I'm the one with the broken nose and blood all over me. I don't think the sheriff's going to spend much time deciding if shooting a couple of muggers was justified. Now give the man his stuff back. I'm already annoyed, but if I have to wait any longer to get some ice on this nose, I'm going to get *really cranky*."

"All right, all right!" the man said. He dropped the briefcase in the dirt. He gestured to the man on the ground. "Can I help my team...I mean my friend there up?"

Keller stepped back. He didn't lower the shotgun. "Sure." He and the woman watched as the white guy helped his partner to his feet. The man in the suit had staggered to his own feet and retrieved the briefcase. The three of them watched as the two men got into a nondescript beige sedan and drove away. Keller saw the man with the broken arm give one last angry glance at them before they turned onto the desert highway and drove away. He also noticed the rental plates.

The woman took a deep breath. "Sorry for your inconvenience, sir," she said to the man in the suit. "We're not open yet, but can I offer you some water?"

The man was dusting off his clothing. "Thank you," he said, his voice shaking a bit. He looked at Keller. "Would you be Jackson Keller?"

Keller was still looking at the car dwindling in the distance. "Depends on who's asking." He lowered the gun as he decided they weren't turning around. The man in the suit walked toward him, then stopped as Keller swiveled to face him. The shotgun was still held loosely down by his side, but Keller apparently looked as if he might still use it.

"My name is John Maddox," the man said, his voice quivering slightly. "I work for...I mean, I'm an aide to..." He looked at the woman. "Look, can we have this conversation inside? It's blistering out here."

The woman's eyes narrowed. "My name's Julianne Stetson," she said. "My friends call me Jules." She gestured behind her at the neon sign over the door, not currently lit, that said HENRY'S. "This is my place. And whether or not you have that water outside or inside depends on what your business is here."

Maddox pushed his glasses up on his nose. "I understand your reluctance. It's been an...interesting morning."

No one spoke. Finally, Maddox took a deep breath. "Okay. Mr. Keller, I have a request. From your father."

Keller's eyes narrowed. "My father? What the fuck is this?"

"Jack," Jules said.

"Mr. Maddox," Keller said, "my father abandoned my mother and me before I was born. I've never met him, never heard from him, and don't actually even know his name."

"His name," Maddox said, "is Clifton Trammell. And it's not exactly true that he abandoned you." He raised the briefcase. "Look, I have some documents in here that will prove what I have to say."

"So what?" Keller said.

"Your father wants to see you. To meet you."

Keller walked to the open door of the bar. "I don't want to see him." He turned back. "Tell him if he wanted to see me, he should have asked forty-seven years ago."

"He's dying, Mr. Keller," Maddox said.

Keller stopped for a moment. Then without looking around, he said, "I don't care," and walked back into the cool darkness.

CHAPTER THREE

JULIANNE AND MADDOX STOOD AND stared at each other across the parking area. She broke the silence first. "Well, you might as well come in."

Maddox looked doubtful. "I don't think I'd be welcome."

Her jaw tightened. "Goddamn it, this is my place, not Jack Keller's, and when I say someone can come in, he can damn well come in. Now what's your pleasure?"

"Um…I'd love a coffee."

"Coffee we got. Come on." Without looking at him, she walked back into the bar. "Close the door behind you," she said over her shoulder. He hesitated for a moment, then followed.

The frigid air conditioning inside washed over him, feeling so sweet he had to close his eyes. When he opened them again, the only person he saw behind the bar was Julianne. She'd laid the baseball bat on the bar and was drawing a cup of coffee from a large silver urn off to one side. "What do you take in it?" she said to him as he took a barstool.

He placed the briefcase on the stool next to him. "Black will be fine."

She nodded and slid the heavy ceramic mug across the bar. As he picked it up, she asked, "So, what's the deal here? How come Jack's daddy waited all this time to try and talk to him?"

He stopped, the cup halfway to his lips, then took a sip. When he was done, he asked, "Are you, um, Mrs. Keller?"

She laughed. "Not hardly." Then the smile fell from her face.

"I'm just asking because...well..."

"It's a family matter. I get it. But Jack ain't got no family. His daddy knocked his mama up, then ran off. His mama dumped him off with his grandmamma, then went and drank herself to death. Everyone else in his life..." Her voice had taken on a bitter, angry note, and she stopped.

"You seem to care a lot about him," Maddox observed.

She looked away. "I guess. But maybe if you tell me what this is about, I can get him to talk to you." She gestured at the briefcase. "Like, if there was a million dollars in there. Or a lottery ticket."

Maddox laughed. "Sorry. Mr. Trammell devoted his life to public service. He has an estate, and a death benefit, but..." He trailed off, suddenly embarrassed.

She frowned. "It went to his *real* family." That bitterness was back.

"I'm afraid he didn't really have one of those, either."

She shook her head. "You're not makin' a real good case here, Mr. Maddox."

He looked down uncomfortably at his cup. "I'm sorry. But it's important that I speak with..."

"So who is this guy, anyway?" she interrupted. "All his mama told him is that he was a sailor at the naval base in Charleston."

Maddox nodded. "At the time of Mr. Keller's birth, that was true. He was a lieutenant in the U.S. Navy."

"And after?"

Maddox paused. "He's led a life of service to his country."

"You said that. Still pretty vague."

"I know," Maddox said. "But a lot of what he did…it was important work. Necessary. But confidential. Let's leave it at that."

"And all that time," she said, "his own son was strugglin' to make his way in the world. Never knowing why his daddy didn't want him." She sighed. "I might be able to get Jack to change his mind, but I don't think I want to. You seem like a nice person, Mr. Maddox, but your boss seems like kind of a dick. You want some more coffee?"

Maddox nodded and held out his cup. As she poured, he said, "You should know that this is something that's weighed on Mr. Trammell's mind all his life."

"And he's decided now," a voice said from the doorway, "on his deathbed, to try and ease his conscience." Keller stepped into the room. He was holding a towel filled with ice to his nose. The towel was pink with blood. "Sorry, Mr. Maddox," he said, "but I'm not interested."

Maddox stood up from the barstool. "Your father…"

"I don't have a father, sir," Keller snapped. "If I had, he would have at least let me know he was alive before this. And you can tell him I said that."

"I see," Maddox said. "Well. That's disappointing." He straightened his tie.

"Before you finish your coffee," Keller said, "and head back to… where did you come from, anyway?"

"I flew out of Washington, DC."

"Another good reason not to go back with you. But maybe you can tell me who those two guys were who were working you over."

Maddox shook his head. "I never saw them before. Just muggers, I guess."

"No," Keller said. "Those guys were military. Or ex-military."

Maddox's brow furrowed. "How would you know that?"

Keller shrugged. "It was obvious. The haircuts. The way they worked together. And one guy started to refer to the one with the broken arm as his 'teammate.' That's a giveaway." He pointed at the briefcase. "What's in that briefcase that a couple of ex-military guys who are trying really, really hard not to look military are willing to rough you up for?"

Maddox looked at the briefcase and sighed. "It's…something that Mr. Trammell said I should only show to you as a last resort." He looked up at Keller. "It concerns what happened to you in the war."

The room went still, only the soft hum of the cooler behind the bar breaking the silence. Keller slowly lowered the bloody, ice-filled towel from his face and set it on the bar. He didn't look at Maddox. "Get out," was all he said.

Maddox was opening the briefcase. "Okay," he said. "I will." He took a large white envelope out of the case and laid it on the bar.

"Take that with you," Keller said, his voice hoarse.

Maddox didn't answer, nor did he pick up the envelope. He turned to Jules and reached into his jacket pocket. "Thanks for the coffee. How much do I—"

"I said "GET OUT!" Keller bellowed. He slid off the barstool and headed for Maddox, fists clenched, his face dark red with rage.

"Jack!" Jules said. Keller stopped in his tracks, breathing hard. "On the house," Jules said to Maddox. "But he's right. Your invitation just got revoked. Get out. And don't come back."

"I won't," Maddox said. "But I'll be in the motel across the street until noon tomorrow. Room Sixteen. If you change your mind—"

"Mr. Maddox," Jules said, laying her hand on the bat which still rested on the bar. "I ain't gonna tell you again. Get out of my place."

He just nodded, picked up his briefcase, and left. Keller went back to the bar and sat down, staring straight ahead. He picked up the waterlogged towel and pressed it back to his nose.

"Here," Jules said, "put some more ice in that." She walked around behind the bar and gently took the towel from him. When she'd refilled the makeshift bag with ice from the well behind the bar, she noticed Keller looking down to where the envelope lay.

"Not marked," she said softly. "You want me to throw it away?"

He didn't answer. She reached out and ran a gentle hand through his hair. "Your hair's gettin' longer," she murmured. "It's been short since I known you. But it looks—"

He broke in, his voice low. "If I don't see what's in there, I'll never get any sleep for thinking about it."

"You barely sleep now," she said sadly. She moved closer and put her arm around him. "I'll stay with you if you want."

He slowly reached up and put his left hand over hers where it rested on his right shoulder. "Thanks. That'd…that'd be good."

She rested her head on his left shoulder. "I won't run out on you, Jack," she said. "Not like…" She stopped, not wanting to say their names.

"They didn't run out on me, Jules," he said. "I drove them away."

She wiped her eyes with the back of her free hand. "Well, you ain't drove me off yet, Jack Keller," she said. "And I figure I've seen you at your worst."

"No you haven't," he said quietly. "Not by a long shot." He took her hand and kissed it. "But thanks." He looked down the bar, surveying the envelope as if it were a poisonous snake. He picked it up and weighed it in his hand. Then he undid the metal fastener and dumped the contents of the envelope onto the bar.

They stared for a moment at the DVD in the plastic case that lay there. There was no label and no indication of what was on it.

"There's a DVD player in the trailer," he said, referring to the ancient camper behind the bar where Jules had been letting him stay. "But I don't even know how to work it."

"I do," she said. "You ready to see this now?"

"No," he said, "but let's do it anyway."

CHAPTER FOUR

THE PICTURE ON THE SCREEN of the old and battered TV was jumpy and indistinct, showing little but a gray haze. A set of graduated lines like the marks on a ruler ran across the top of the screen; across the bottom were confusing sets of numbers and letters. But it was the middle of the picture that drew the eye, where a set of white crosshairs met in the dead center. The crosshairs moved across a landscape that was featureless and blurred. The sound that came out of the tinny speakers was a high-speed thudding noise like a maniacal drumbeat on a sped-up tape. It was broken up intermittently by squawks of radio static.

Jules leaned forward, frowning, and reached for the set where it rested on the tiny dining table inside the camper. The TV and the DVD player they'd dug out of the storage locker and hooked to it took up most of the table's surface. Jules had squeezed in next to Keller on the narrow bench seat facing the TV.

"Don't," Keller said as Jules started trying to adjust the set.

"This picture's terrible," she complained. "There's no color."

Keller's voice seemed to come from far outside himself. "It's supposed to be black and white."

"What is it?" Jules said.

"It's a gun camera. From a helicopter. I've seen them before."

As if joining the conversation, the static resolved into a tinny, distorted voice. "Gunslinger two-six, this is Greentree Actual, do you copy? Over."

It took her a moment to make the connection to the stories he'd told her. "Oh, my God," she said. Her hand moved swiftly to the on-off switch. He was quicker. He grabbed her wrist before she could kill the TV, so hard that she cried out. "Leave it." His voice was tight and furious.

"Greentree, Gunslinger two-six," another voice, this one with a distinct country twang, came from the set. "We copy. Over."

"Jack," Jules whispered, "you're hurting me." He relaxed his grip slightly, but didn't release her until she pulled away. She shrank away from him, her eyes wide and fixed on his face.

"Gunslinger," the first voice said, "Jumbo reports a pair of Iraqi scout vehicles headed north, approaching gridline three-seven-zero. You got eyes on them? Over."

The crosshairs moved faster, scanning over the bleak and empty landscape. A bright white blob shot across the field of view, then the viewfinder scanned back, slowed, and finally found its target: a single, blocky shape that glowed distinctly white against the gray void.

"That's an infrared sight," Keller said. "Warm objects show up bright white."

"Greentree," Gunslinger two-six said, "I got one vehicle, repeat, one, stationary, about a half click from the gridline. Over."

"Must be them, Gunslinger," Greentree's confident voice came back. "Light 'em up. Over."

There was a brief pause. "Request confirmation, Greentree,"

Gunslinger two-six said, the uncertainty in his voice clear even through the radio distortion and static. "I've got eyes on one unit. I say again, one unit. You said there were two. Over."

"Ah, roger, Gunslinger, there were. They must have split up. Or the one you're looking at broke down. Take the shot. Over."

On the screen, a smaller white dot had detached itself from the vehicle and was trudging across the desert. Keller let out a low, tortured groan.

"Jack," Jules said. "Is that…you?"

Keller didn't answer.

"Please," she said, and there were tears in her voice. "I was wrong. You shouldn't watch this. Please don't watch this."

Still no answer. Keller was so tense he was practically vibrating. Jules slid out of the seat and backed up against the stove of the camper's miniature kitchen, her eyes going back and forth between the TV and the seat where Keller was hunched over, eyes fixed on the screen, his arms folded across his chest as if he was trying to hold his insides in.

"Greentree," Gunslinger two-six said on screen. "Request confirmation there are no Blue units in area. I got a bad feeling—"

"Gunslinger," the voice barked, "I said take the fucking shot. Over."

Another voice broke in, this one with a working-class Boston accent. "C'mahn, man. Do the fuckah and let's go home."

Keller's fists were resting on the tabletop, clenching and unclenching as if looking for a neck to snap. Jules was sobbing now. "Jack, *please*."

The crosshairs wavered over the target. "I can't get a lock."

"Try goin' to black hot," the Boston voice said. The picture wavered for a moment, then the shades reversed. The warm vehicle was now black against the pale desert, and more distinct. The crosshairs steadied, then there was a bright flare and the picture shuddered. "Missile away," the voice of Gunslinger two-six said.

"Good lock, good lock," the Boston voice said. "C'mahn, c'mahn…" There was a sudden bloom of darkness across the screen, a rapidly spreading black flower. An unidentified voice whooped. "Good kill! Good kill!"

Keller felt a rush in his head, like the hot desert wind or the howl of the missile that had come out of the night to destroy his tiny command. *Burning, they're burning…* In his mind, echoing down the long dark tunnel of his memory, he could hear the screams of the men in the Bradley Fighting vehicle, *his* men, as the thinly armored machine went up in flames.

"Burn, baby, burn!" the Boston voice said, bubbling with excited laughter.

Keller screamed. He reached out and grabbed the small television in both hands. He tried to stand up with it, but the table restricted his motion. Eyes wide, he twisted his body, flinging the TV as hard as he could. Jules had already fled from the space where the television crashed against the stove, trailing the wires that had pulled out of the DVD player. The set exploded in a shower of glass and sparks as the tube burst. Jules stumbled out the door of the camper, sobbing in terror. Keller slid from behind the table, his boots crunching in the debris from the shattered television set. He picked up the DVD player with one hand and flung it across the short length of the camper, where it smashed against the curved wall over the alcove where the bed was. He fell to his knees, heedless of the pain where the shards of glass cut through his jeans, and howled like an animal. The stench of cooking meat was in his nose and the screams of the dying slowly trailed off. Then there was nothing. He knelt there, staring, the roaring in his head blotting out everything else.

CHAPTER
FIVE

I T MIGHT HAVE BEEN MINUTES or hours when Keller came back to himself. He was still kneeling, glass and pieces of plastic cutting into his knees. Julianne was crouched down in front of him, holding a cell phone to her ear. "Yeah," she was saying. "He's right here. Okay." She held the phone out to him. He looked at it stupidly, as if he couldn't remember what it was. "It's Lucas," she said. "He wants to talk to you."

Slowly, Keller reached out and took the phone. He hesitated another moment, then put it to his ear. "Lucas," he said, his voice as dry and rough as sandpaper.

The rumbling voice of Dr. Lucas Berry was like the soothing noise of ocean surf. "Sounds like you're having an interesting day, Sergeant."

Keller licked his dry lips. Jules handed him a bottle of water. Her eyes never left his face, but the fear was gone, leaving only concern. He took a sip of the water, then a larger gulp. "Yeah. You could say that." He took another swallow. "So how much did she tell you?"

"Just the basics. Some guy shows up and gets roughed up in your girlfriend's parking lot by what looks like military, or ex-military, muscle. He claims to have a message from your dying father, then drops off what looks like the gun camera video from 'ninety-one. The video from the helicopter that killed your men and nearly killed you. After which you seem to have had what we in the mental health biz call an 'episode.'"

Keller rubbed the cool, sweating bottle against his forehead. "Yeah." He looked up at Jules. "Sorry." She put a hand on his arm and squeezed.

"You know, Jack," Berry said, "you might have checked in with your therapist before putting yourself through something like that."

Keller rose to his feet, setting the water on the table and trying to brush the debris off his pants with his free hand. "You're not officially my therapist anymore, Lucas. You're two thousand miles away, for one thing. And we're not in the Army."

"Point taken. How about talking it over with your old friend Lucas who cares about you, then?"

Keller grimaced. "Yeah. I probably should have done that. I wasn't thinking. Sorry."

"No need to apologize. Just tell me what you feel. Right now. Quickly. Don't think about it."

"Empty," Keller said. "Hollowed out."

"Do you feel like hurting yourself? Or anyone else?"

Keller did think about that. "I'm not real crazy about this Maddox character right now, to tell you the truth."

"That response is within normal limits."

"What?"

"It means I can't say as I blame you. You need to tread carefully around this guy, Jack. I don't know what his agenda is, or whatever this person claiming to be your father has in mind, but this whole thing has a bad smell about it. I'd stay the hell away."

"Yeah," Keller said. "I probably should."

"But you're not going to, are you?"

"No. He said my father might have some answers. About what happened to me. And why."

"How and why would he have those answers? Have you thought this thing all the way through, Jack?"

Keller gave a short, bitter laugh. "Do I ever?"

"No," Berry said. "How's that worked out for you?" Before Keller could answer, he sighed. "Never mind answering. Just do me a favor. I know it's useless to tell you not to go, so I won't. But keep in touch. I'm going to do some digging while you're on your way. See what my old Army contacts know about this Trammell and this errand boy of his."

Keller felt a lump in his throat. "Thanks, Lucas," he said. "You're a good friend."

"Yes, I am. And Jack?"

"Yeah?"

"Take care of yourself, okay?"

"I will." He broke the connection.

Jules was looking at him across the table. Tears were glistening in her eyes. "You're gonna go, aren't you?" she said in a small voice. "Again."

He nodded. "I have to, Jules."

"And I can't come with you."

"This is something I have to—"

She broke in. "No, I mean I can't go. I have a business to run." She reached out and put a hand over his. "Just come back, okay?"

He took her hand in both of his. "I will."

She sighed and shook her head. "I wish I could believe that."

"I came back last time."

She grimaced. "Yeah. You came back beat up, shot all to hell, and… well, you know." She held up a hand to stop his reply. "Just be careful. Take care of yourself."

"Lucas said the same thing."

"And he's right. Like it or not, Jack Keller, you're important to people. People like me." She stood up. "Now, before you go talk to this Maddox, find a broom and help me clean up this mess you made."

CHAPTER SIX

"**I** SEE," CORDELL SAID INTO HIS cell phone. "And how is the man who was injured?" He nodded as he listened to the reply. "Very well," he said finally. "Sit tight. Await further instructions." He cut the connection. The only sign of his anger was a slight tightening of his lips. The person who he had just talked to would never hear from him again. He'd failed, and soon he would realize he'd been discarded, frozen out. He'd most likely need to start looking for another line of work. The world in which he and Cordell operated was not one that forgave failure. It was why the first thing one did in case things didn't work out is find someone else to blame. It wasn't personal, and it wasn't just business; it was survival.

Cordell looked through the doorway of the dining room, into the living room of the large house in northern Virginia where Kathryn Shea lived. All he could see from his vantage point was the back of her head. He squared his shoulders and walked into the living room.

She didn't look up at him as he entered, but continued staring into the fireplace. There was no fire. A large leather chair that had been one of her father's favorites seemed to embrace her now. She loosely held a rocks glass with a single ice cube remaining in one hand. Earlier in the evening, she had switched from martinis to straight bourbon. That was never a good sign.

Cordell took a seat on the couch that sat at a right angle to the chair. Her head turned slowly to take him in. Her eyes were dull and glassy, but when she saw the look on his face, they seemed to sharpen. "Well?" she said.

Cordell knew better than to try and sugar-coat bad news. "Mr. Trammell's emissary reached Mr. Keller."

Kathryn turned away and looked into the dark, cold fireplace. She raised the glass to her lips, then looked at it in annoyance as she noticed for the first time that it was empty except for the rapidly melting cube of ice. Cordell leaned over and took it from her hand. He hoped she wouldn't ask for a refill.

"Tell me what happened," she said. She enunciated every word with the extreme care of the very drunk.

"The people who were supposed to take the briefcase were late. They tried to do it in the parking lot of the bar where Keller's been working. He and the bar owner, a young woman, came out and stopped them. One of them was injured when the bar owner broke his arm with a baseball bat."

Kathryn looked back at him, her dark eyes widening. "The woman? A *woman* broke your man's arm?"

"Not my man, per se. An independent contractor. But yes."

She let out a brief snorting laugh. "Maybe you should have hired her."

He ignored the jibe. "Trammell's man, a former operative named Maddox, went into the bar. That's all we know at this time."

"We don't know if he gave Keller anything."

"No." He hesitated. "There are certain resources I could be using to learn more at this time. But using them could be…problematic."

"Then don't tell me about them," she said. "But use them. Use any means necessary." She saw the look on his face and nodded. "Yes, Mr. Cordell, I am completely aware of what those words mean. But I need to know what Maddox gave Keller. And I don't want Keller talking to Trammell. It's a matter of national security."

"Ms. Shea," Cordell said, "this would be a lot easier if I knew what it is you are so…" He almost said "afraid," but quickly corrected himself. "Concerned about Mr. Trammel, or his representative, giving to Keller."

She stood up, a little unsteadily, and took the glass back from him. "Cliff Trammell can spill his guts when he gets to the Pearly Gates," she said, "not before." She smiled grimly. "Not that that'll get him in. Probably just the opposite. Cliff Trammell is one man who the truth will definitely not set free." She walked, a little unsteadily, to the sideboard where a half-full bottle of Blanton's Gold Edition and a sweating ice bucket sat. She picked up the tongs from the bucket, hesitated a moment, then set them back down. She turned to face Cordell. "I'm going to bed," she said. "Feel free to use the guest room."

Cordell stood. "Good night, Ms. Shea," he murmured. "And thank you."

She nodded and left, staggering slightly as she went through the door.

Cordell watched her go. For a fleeting moment, he considered following her up the stairs, up to the lavish bedroom he knew sat at the top of them. He had always kept a cool professional distance from his clients, but there was no denying the impact that Kathryn Shea had on him. She was undeniably beautiful, and there was something about that iron control she kept over herself that made a man want to break through it, tear down those walls, to conquer…

He shook his head. No time for that. There was work to be done.

Some very long strings would need to be pulled, and it would be very bad for everyone if anyone saw the hand pulling them. He took out his cell phone again.

CHAPTER SEVEN

THE DESERT SANDS MOTEL STOOD across the desert highway from Henry's. The place had been built in the mid-'70s, and it showed the wear and tear of forty-plus years of desert wind and sand. The motel made a razor-thin profit catering to a clientele of tired truckers, cheating spouses, transients, and drunks who staggered across the highway from the bar after a night of overindulgence. It had been sold a few months ago to a family-owned company headquartered in Bangalore, India. The new managers had repaired the battered sign out front and slapped a new coat of paint on the place. The only effect was to make it look like a beaten-up old motel with fresh paint on it. Maddox's dust-covered rental car stood out in the sparsely populated parking lot.

Keller knocked on the door of Room 16. It was 11:45 in the morning. He hadn't gone directly over as he'd planned. Julianne had convinced him to sleep on his decision. She'd hung the "closed" sign on the bar door to let him know she'd be sleeping on it with him. They hadn't gotten much sleep, however. Near dawn, after they'd made love for the third time, she'd told him, "I ain't doin' this to try to make you stay. I just want you to know you got someone to come back to." That had been the only time his resolve had wavered. By sunup, however, the itch to be moving forward became irresistible. He gave Julianne one last, deep kiss and headed across the highway. He didn't look back.

Maddox opened the door. "Mr. Keller," he said. He didn't seem surprised.

"Okay, you bastard," Keller said, keeping his voice as level as he could. "Tell your boss I'll see him."

Maddox nodded. "I understand you're angry at your father—"

"You don't understand shit," Keller broke in. "I ought to kick your ass."

Maddox held up his hands in front of himself and stepped back slightly. "I'm only the messenger, Mr. Keller."

Keller didn't advance on him, although he wanted to, badly. "Bullshit. You sprung that gun camera video on me. Had you seen it?"

Maddox put his hands down and shook his head. "No. I swear to you I haven't. Only a very few people have."

"Like my *father*." The last word sounded like a curse.

Maddox nodded. "Like your father, yes."

"And he knew what the effect on me would be. Worse, he's probably had it for years. Or at least known about it."

"That, I can't answer. I don't know any specifics. I do know that he can give you the names and the current locations of the people responsible. Both for the incident and the cover-up. But I don't know how long your father has known."

"And just how would he know this?"

Maddox moved back into the room. Keller could see he had his suitcase open on the bed. As Maddox began placing socks and a shirt back into the case, Keller entered.

"Clifton Trammell," Maddox said, "has worked in, let's say,

sensitive positions for the United States government for his entire adult life. In his position" — he shrugged, then bent down to zip the suitcase shut — "you learn things."

"What position?"

Maddox went across the room to a dresser that looked so battered it might have been thrown down a flight of stairs. "That is a question you'll need to ask him." He took an envelope off the top of the dresser and held it out to Keller. "Our plane tickets are in here," he said. "We'll need to get going to make the flight. I hope you're — "

Keller didn't reach for the envelope. "I'm not going anywhere with you, Maddox."

"What?"

"I'll get there on my own."

Maddox lowered his arm, his brow knitting with puzzlement. "But...but why?"

"Because I don't trust you."

Maddox's jaw tightened with anger. "Fine. But you need to know there's not much time."

Keller hesitated. He wasn't sure he wanted the answer to the next question. He asked it anyway. "What does he have?"

"Pancreatic cancer," Maddox said. "Stage Four. He could go at any time." His mouth twisted. "And if it makes you any happier to hear this, yes, he's in a great deal of pain."

"No," Keller said. "That doesn't make me happy." He didn't want to tell Maddox that for one brief shameful moment, it had.

THE MAN WHO SAT ACROSS the Formica table from Cordell was lean and gaunt. His black hair was peppered with gray and cut close to his skull. He had sunken brown eyes and the permanent squint of a man who'd spent most of his life in the sun, looking at people over the sights of a weapon. His birth name was Arlen Riddle, but he rarely used it. He wasn't using it now, and he clearly was unhappy when Cordell called him by it.

"I thought our business was done the last time I did a job for you people," Riddle said. His voice was low and raspy, with a hint of Texas accent in it.

Cordell took a sip of his coffee. He looked around the nearly deserted diner to make sure there was no one eavesdropping. "I'm afraid not. We have another situation requiring your skills. And your discretion."

"Discretion," Riddle muttered. "Christ."

"We could always give the job to someone else," Cordell said. "But then our arrangements regarding your...activities would need to be reviewed."

Riddle had gone from the Marine Corps' elite Force Recon Company to a job with the Drug Enforcement Administration's Foreign Deployed Advisory and Support Teams. The FAST teams had engaged in direct action across the globe against some of the world's most dangerous drug traffickers. They often operated independently, with minimal government oversight. There were many temptations to cross legal and moral lines, and Arlen Riddle had fallen prey to more than one of them. By the end of his tenure with DEA, it was growing harder and harder to distinguish the activities of Riddle and his team from those of the people he was originally sent to take down. The drug traffickers, with their usual flair for dramatics, had given him a nickname: *El Perro del Infierno*. The Hound of Hell.

Once Riddle's activities had been uncovered by people at the top (meaning they'd gotten too brazen to ignore), some of his superiors wanted to try him, convict him, throw him in a cell and let him rot there until the Last Judgment. Some were angry and disgusted enough to suggest just turning him over to the cartels he'd been robbing product and money from and letting them deal with him.

Cordell had been advising the DEA head in his under-the-table lobbying campaign for Director of Central Intelligence when he'd found out about the incipient scandal. He'd persuaded all concerned that a public trial would not only destroy everyone's career, but would cripple the DEA for years. As for the other alternative, such a thing could not be considered. Cordell had saved Riddle's freedom and his life, but now he owned the man and his talents. Both men knew it as they regarded one another across the table. Only one was happy about it.

"So," Riddle said, "what's the job?"

Cordell pushed a manila envelope across the desk. "The information you need is in there. There's a man named Jack Keller. He's in Arizona, near Phoenix. He's going to be trying to contact his father here. It's important that that not happen."

"So…" Riddle said. He left the word hanging in the air as he picked up the envelope and opened it. "What exactly are you saying?"

Cordell smiled. "Use your best judgment as to how to proceed."

Riddle pulled a pair of photographs out of the envelope and looked at it. It was a black-and-white mugshot showing a blond man with a square face and jaw and long hair pulled back in a ponytail. "Is this Keller?"

Cordell nodded. "That picture is several years old. He's cut his hair since."

Riddle grunted and slid the first photograph behind the second. This photograph was in color. It was shot from long range, using a zoom lens. "This would be the father, then."

"Yes."

"Why's he in a wheelchair?"

"He's sick. Cancer."

Riddle pulled out a thin sheaf of documents from the envelope. He riffled through them casually, then slid them back in, along with the photographs. He folded his hands on the table and looked at Cordell, his eyes narrowed. "So let me get this straight. You want me to go to Arizona, find this guy Keller, and stop him from seeing his dying father."

"That's not all," Cordell said.

Riddle's lip curled. "Of course not. What else do you want me to do? Kick a baby down a flight of stairs? Drown a little girl's kitten in front of her?"

Cordell ignored the gibe. "We want to find out what Keller's father may have already told him. Or given him."

Riddle leaned back. "Ah," he said, "I'm starting to get it."

Cordell said nothing.

Riddle went on. "Dying old man wants to confess his sins to his son. But you, or whoever you work for, want those sins unconfessed."

Cordell took a sip of his coffee. It was strong, stale, and bitter. He made a face and set it back down. "I don't know that I believe in sin."

"I'm sure that makes life easier for you." Riddle picked up his own coffee for the first time and drank. He didn't seem to mind the taste. "So you think Keller may have already gotten something from his father. What?"

Cordell rubbed his temples. "I don't know."

"You don't know."

"I honestly don't. It's some sort of object. I think."

"That doesn't give me a lot to go on, Mr. Cordell."

"I know. I'm trying to find out. As soon as I do, I'll let you know."

"Or maybe I can make this Keller tell me." Riddle grimaced. "I don't like it. But I guess I don't have much choice, do I?"

Cordell said nothing. The answer was obvious.

Riddle sighed. "Okay. How much lead time does this Keller have? Is he already on a plane here?"

Cordell shook his head. "No. However he gets here, it won't be by plane. That'll give you time to intercept him. You may even be able to catch up with him at this desert bar."

Riddle raised an eyebrow. "How can you be so sure he won't come by plane?"

Cordell signaled for the waitress. "I'm sure."

CHAPTER EIGHT

KATHRYN SHEA ROLLED OVER AND buried her throbbing head in the pillows. The night before was a series of shattered fragments in her memory. She shuffled through them quickly. One phrase she had used in talking to Cordell leaped out at her.

By any means necessary.

She'd told him she knew the implications of that phrase, and she did. As her father's daughter, she knew them better than most. But in the cold light of day, did she really want to unleash everything that phrase could mean? Could there be a way to resolve matters with Cliff Trammell short of the kind of dangerous game she'd been so willing to set in motion last night?

She sat up in bed and picked the phone up off her nightstand. It took her a moment to remember the number, but she punched it in. Her hands were shaking as she did so. That wasn't a good sign, but she pushed the thought aside.

The phone rang three times before someone on the other end picked up. "Kathryn," the voice said. It was a voice roughened with age and turned ragged by relentless agony, but she would recognize it anywhere.

"Uncle Cliff," she said, trying to keep her voice bright.

Trammell chuckled, the sound quickly collapsing into a wet, racking cough that took a good thirty seconds to resolve. "Come on, Kat," he gasped at the end of his spasm, "we can cut the bullshit. You're not a little girl anymore. "

No, she said to herself, her grip on the phone tightening, *I'm not.* Before she could speak again, he continued, his harsh voice softened somewhat. "I'm sorry I couldn't make the funeral."

"That's all right," she answered. The words, banal and meaningless, helped steady her. "Daddy would have understood. He knew you were his friend."

"Friends." The word seemed to amuse him. "People like your father and I...we don't have friends. You know what I mean."

She did. She knew it well. But she didn't answer.

"We have colleagues," Trammell went on. "We have drinking buddies. Rivals. Sometimes blood enemies."

She swallowed, the dryness in her mouth and throat nearly making her gag. "And what was my father to you, Cliff?"

That chuckle again. "All of the above. Of course." His voice turned serious. "Which brings me to the reason I'm sure you've called."

"Yes," she said. The next words stuck in her throat.

"My son."

Her grip tightened on the phone. "Yes."

"You want to know if I'm going to give him a certain object."

She closed her eyes. "Yes."

"Maybe I already have. Have you thought about that?"

"Why would you do that?" she demanded. "What good would it do anyone to give...the object...to this Keller person?"

"I don't know," Trammell said. "What harm would it do?"

"If he chose to make it public, it would destroy my father's reputation," she said. "And you know it."

"Yes," Trammell said. "And it would surely put a crimp in your own candidacy as well."

She couldn't answer this time. The shaking in her hands had gotten worse. "Jack Keller's a nobody," she said, trying to keep the desperation from her voice. "No one will listen to him if he tries to…"

"Kat," he broke in, his voice exaggeratedly sorrowful. "You are *so* not the negotiator your father was."

The words struck her like a blow to the face. She sat there speechless for a moment, feeling the blood throb in her temples. "If that's the way you want it, then," she whispered, "so be it." Before he could answer, she cut the connection. She dialed Cordell, her fingers punching furiously at the numbers.

Cordell answered on the first ring. "Yes?"

"The object I'm concerned about," she said, "is a film. A reel of sixteen-millimeter film."

"Sixteen-millimeter?" Cordell sounded puzzled. "Who still uses…"

"No one," she interrupted. "It's an old film. It may have been transferred to video or even DVD. But Trammell has the original. It…" She hesitated. "It belonged to my father. I want it back."

"I see," Cordell said. She waited for the next question. It didn't come. "Thank you for confiding in me."

"Just find out if Keller has it. Or has seen it."

"What if he has?"

"Then we need to make sure he never tells anyone else about it. Completely sure."

"Understood," Cordell said. "I'll see to it. Don't worry. And Ms. Shea?"

"Yes?"

"I won't view the film without your express permission. Nor will anyone working for me. You have my word."

"Thank you," she said, even though she assumed he was lying. She'd have to deal with that problem when and if it arose. She cut the connection.

CORDELL PAUSED AND HELD THE phone down by his side as he thought about what to do next. A roll of 16-millimeter film, she'd said. That was a medium that hadn't been used in a while, at least not widely. So whatever was on it must be old. From her father's early career. Maybe even before he'd gone into politics, back when he had been in the military.

"Vietnam." Cordell said it out loud. His research had disclosed that the future Senator Michael Shea and Clifton Trammell had met when the two of them were serving in Vietnam in the late '60s. Shea's career had actually begun with an iconic photo of him as a young Marine lieutenant carrying a crying Vietnamese infant in one arm while the other held the hand of the boy's seven-year-old sister as he led them away from their burning village. The village, the accompanying news story told the public, had been torched by the Viet Cong after the village elders were tortured, then crucified on bamboo crosses for giving aid to the Americans. It was a rare public relations coup in a war which had been offering few of them in those dark days. Amid growing disillusionment and exhaustion after years of war, Michael Shea became a symbol of why we'd supposedly gone to war in Southeast Asia in the first place.

Cordell had been unable to find any photographs or film of Clifton Trammell from that era. At all. He might as well have not existed.

"What did Trammell catch you doing?" Cordell muttered under his breath. Drugs? Hookers? He shook his head. Speculation was useless at this point without data or information. He dialed the phone again. Riddle answered. "Yeah?"

"The object you're looking for is a film. An old one. Sixteen-millimeter. It may have been transferred to DVD or videocassette."

"What's on it?" Riddle said. "And if you tell me that's on a need-to-know basis, I'm bailing."

"I honestly don't know. But if you find the film, seize it. If anyone has seen it, make sure they don't tell anyone else about it."

"Don't, or can't?" Cordell didn't answer. "Stupid question," Riddle muttered.

"Yes," Cordell said. "It was. Don't ask it again." He broke the connection.

CHAPTER NINE

Jack Keller hadn't been in a civilian airport since 1991. At that time he'd been a prisoner, in the custody of two MPs escorting him back from Kuwait. They'd been polite, professional, but wary, clearly wishing they were traveling on a more secure military aircraft. All that was available, however, was one of the civilian airliners drafted into service to transport military personnel during the crisis. Keller himself had been silent, docile, wrapped in the numbness that had enveloped him since the desert and which he had not yet learned to name.

In the present day, it seemed, everyone was a prisoner in the airport. Keller stood in a long line of stoic people shuffling slowly through the winding queue that led to the first security checkpoint. They reminded him of inmates lining up for meals or delousing. He had been in line for almost an hour, but no one complained, no one looked at the faces of their fellow travelers or at the uniformed and bored guards processing everyone. Keller reached the first checkpoint and handed the agent his driver's license and boarding pass. She glanced up disinterestedly at him, then handed them back. He shouldered his carry-on bag and moved on to the next stage. As he queued up to run his the bag through the metal detector, another uniformed agent walked up to him. This one was a large, broad-shouldered black man with a big belly and a shaved head.

"Jackson Keller?" the man said.

Keller was in the middle of slipping off his running shoe. He looked up. "Yeah. I'm Jack Keller." He immediately registered something was wrong. The man was standing just a little too far away, as if he was trying to stay out of Keller's reach. "Would you mind coming with me, Mr. Keller?" he said.

Keller slipped the shoe back on. "What's happening?"

The agent held out his hands as if trying to placate him. "Nothing's wrong, sir," he said. "Just stay calm."

"I am calm," Keller said. "I'm just..."

The agent's voice rose with stress. "You need to come with me, sir." He was motioning frantically to someone. Keller looked and saw a pair of uniformed Maricopa County Sheriff's deputies hustling over. One was older, with a fringe of gray hair beneath his cap; the other looked like he hadn't graduated high school.

"Easy, buddy," Keller said, "I just don't want to miss my plane." Other passengers were looking at him for the first time. A short guy with a backwards ball cap and a shaggy neck-beard raised a cell phone and snapped a picture. Keller shook his head. As he did, the deputies arrived and took up positions on either side of the TSA guy. "Okay, okay," Keller said. "Whatever. Lead on." He reached down to pick up his bag. The deputies tensed. One reached for his weapon and Keller saw that he'd unsnapped his holster. He straightened back up, very slowly. "What," he said to the TSA guy, "you want to carry my bag?"

The three looked nonplussed for a moment; the older of the two deputies motioned to the bag. "Go ahead and pick it up," he said.

Keller picked up the bag, keeping his eyes on the cop as he did so. The trio was clearly nervous, and in Keller's experience, nervous cops were something to worry about.

"This way," the TSA guy said. He turned and walked away. Keller followed. The two cops fell in on either side of him. Keller heard the crowd behind him erupt in conversation.

They led him down a short corridor to an office with no windows and nothing on the walls. The only furniture was a cheap wooden desk and three chairs, one behind the desk, two before it. "Wait here," the TSA guy said.

"I'm going to miss my…" Keller began, but the TSA guy left, closing the door behind him. Keller went to follow him and saw one of the deputies standing in the hallway. "You need to get back in the office—" Keller closed the door on the "sir" that the officer didn't mean anyway. Keller sat down and waited. No one came. He checked the time and gritted his teeth. He waited some more. Finally, he took his cell phone out of the bag and dialed Julianne's number. She answered after a couple of rings. "Hey, hon."

"Jules," Keller said, "something really weird's going on."

Her voice sharpened with concern. "What?"

"I just got pulled out of line at the airport and shuffled into an office. Now some sheriff's deputy who doesn't look old enough to wipe his own ass is holding me in here."

"They…what? Why?"

"I have no idea," Keller said. "But I don't like it."

"Me either," she said. "I'm turning around."

"Don't. No sense in you ending up in the same room."

At that moment, the door opened. A man walked in, dressed in the same bright blue TSA uniform as the man who'd stopped him. This agent's uniform, however, fit as if it was tailored. He had close-cropped gray hair and a goatee. He frowned at the sight of Keller talking on his cell phone. "I'm going to have to ask you to put away the phone, sir," he said. Keller considered making an issue of it for a split second, then casually stuffed the phone into his shirt pocket. He didn't break the connection, hoping that Jules could hear everything.

"You mind telling me what this is all about?" Keller said.

The man gave him a tight, professional smile, devoid of any warmth. "I'm Agent Aldridge," he said. "We just got a red flag that popped up when you went through security. We wanted to check it out."

"A red flag? What the hell does that mean?"

The smile never wavered. "Tell me, Mr. Keller," Aldridge said, "have you been overseas recently?"

Keller thought for a moment about his recent foray into Mexico, but he didn't see any need to share any more than he had to with this bureaucrat. Besides, Mexico didn't exactly count as overseas. "No," he said, "not since 1991. And that was with the Army."

"Ah," the man said, and nodded. "The Army." He didn't say anything else. He and Keller continued to stare at one another.

"Okay," Keller said at last, "if that's all that you needed to know, I'm going to be—"

"I'm afraid we can't let you board that plane," Aldridge broke in.

"What?" Keller said. "Why?"

Aldridge gave him a look that was unconvincingly apologetic. "It seems your name came up on a list."

"A list? What kind of list?"

Aldridge shrugged. "A list that says you're not allowed to fly on a plane in American airspace."

Keller shook his head in disbelief. "A no-fly list. I'm on the no-fly list."

Aldridge put his hands up in front of him in a warding-off pose. "No, sir. There is no such thing as a 'no-fly list.'"

"There's just a list that says I can't fly."

Aldridge nodded. "Exactly."

Keller resisted the urge to grab the man and shake him until that artificial smile fell off. "You mind telling me why I'm on the list?"

"Oh, we don't know that," Aldridge said. "We're not privy to that information."

"Look," Keller said, "I paid for that ticket, and now you're saying I can't use it, but you can't tell me why. Do I at least get my money back?"

"I don't know, sir, you'll have to take that up with the airline."

"God damn it." Keller picked up his bag and moved toward the door. Aldridge moved to block his way.

"Wait a minute," Keller said. "Am I under arrest?"

Aldridge looked pained. "Oh, no, sir," he said. "But I'm going to have to ask you to stay here."

Keller's eyes narrowed. "And what happens if I say no, I'm not staying?"

Aldridge looked stern and his voice took on a martial tone. "You need to stay here, sir."

"I'm getting tired of this game," Keller said. "If I'm not free to go, then I'm under arrest, and get me a fucking lawyer. If I'm not under arrest, get the fuck out of my way."

Aldridge looked smug as he reached for the radio on his belt. He was on familiar ground here. Even if the so-called "subject" was doing nothing actually wrong in the first place, resistance, even to petty bullying, was always a crime. Before he could raise the mic to his lips, Keller pulled his own cell phone out of his shirt pocket. "You getting all of this, Julianne?"

The reply came back, small and tinny, yet distinct. "Every word, honey."

Aldridge froze. "You....you're recording this?"

Keller had no idea if Jules' phone had that capability, but he knew one thing every bad cop feared most was being recorded. He decided to bluff. "No, but my girlfriend on the other end of this line is. Every word. So like the song says, Agent Aldridge...should I stay or should

I go?"

Aldridge's mouth opened, then closed. Finally, he stepped aside. "You may go. But you're not getting on that plane, Mr. Keller."

"Guess not," Keller said with a cheerfulness he didn't feel. He picked up his bag and walked toward the door. Aldridge hesitated a moment, then stepped aside as Keller strode past. The deputy in the hallway gaped at him, then glanced at the doorway where Aldridge stood, looking grim. Neither one made any move to stop Keller as he walked down the corridor and back out into the airport lobby. He stared at the long line of passengers trudging through the queue, toward the concourses that now might as well be on the moon for all his ability to reach them. He pulled his cell out of his shirt pocket again and spoke into it. "I guess I need you to pick me up."

"I'm almost back at the bar. I'm gonna stop and use the ladies' room, then head back. I'll be there in a little bit." Her voice brightened "So, I'm your girlfriend now?"

Despite his anger and frustration, Keller had to smile. "Yeah. Let's go with that."

R IDDLE STOOD IN THE PARKING lot of the bar and looked it over. A handwritten paper sign on the heavy wooden door said "CLOSED FOR FAMILY EMERGENCY." He tried the handle anyway with one gloved hand. As expected, it was locked. He glanced across the desert road at the dilapidated motel. He saw no signs of life or movement there, but he ruled out trying to pick the lock in such an exposed location. He walked around to the back of the sand-scoured old cinderblock building. A rusting camper trailer sagged on its tires next to a shed that looked near collapse. Both blocked the sight lines to the back door. That door's lock yielded to his picks in moments.

He stepped into a dimly lit storeroom lined with shelves. A dented ice machine grumbled and sweated in one corner. Moving silently, as much by habit as by any idea that someone might be present, he moved to the doorway of the storeroom. It led to a short hallway. Directly across the hallway, a desk piled high with various papers took up almost all of a tiny, untidy office. Riddle performed a quick and unsubtle search, picking up and tossing papers and catalogs onto the floor as he determined they were no use to him. He wasn't concerned about covering his tracks. There was no film reel or canister in the office. There was what looked like a side table against the wall, covered with a tablecloth. When he lifted the tablecloth, he saw the heavy green metal door of an old-fashioned safe. Riddle leaned over and tried the handle. Locked, of course. He straightened up and stared at the safe. There were any number of ways to get into a locked safe like this, but they took time. The most efficient way, he'd found, was to find someone who knew the combination and "persuade" them to open it. But there was no one around.

He heard the rattling of the front door, then the squeak of hinges as someone entered. Riddle snapped the office light off. He drew his pistol from his waistband holster and waited just inside the door to the barroom. Maybe this was someone who could be persuaded.

CHAPTER
TEN

JULIANNE CLOSED THE CELL PHONE connection, smiling as she did so. For the first time in a while, she felt good about what was happening between her and Keller.

There was something about him that both compelled her and scared her a little at the same time. She knew he was capable of violence. When he'd first started coming into her bar, she'd taken notice of the good-looking stranger, but the hectic press and bustle of serving the crowd of regulars that seemed to find their way to her place on a nightly basis had pushed him to the back of her mind.

Then one night, a trio of bikers had turned ugly, hassling other customers and busting up furniture. When she'd tried to throw them out, they'd pinned her against her own bar, as the other customers watched helplessly, and told her she was going to be their property from then on. They hadn't been paying any more attention than anyone else to the quiet man who'd sat in the corner night after night, silently drinking his beer. Until, that is, that man got up, opened up one biker's face to the bone with a beer bottle, fractured another one's forearm with a barstool, then beat the third one so badly he had to drink his meals through a straw for months.

When the deputy sheriff had finally arrived, he'd taken stock of the situation and promptly arrested Keller as the last man standing. Julianne had bailed him out, persuaded the magistrate, an old friend and customer of her late father, not to formally charge him, and offered him a job as bar-back and occasional bouncer. He'd moved into the trailer behind the bar, and soon after, into her bed. She hadn't had anyone there for a long time, and sometimes she asked herself what she was doing for letting this strange, mostly silent man into her life. Even the sparing glimpses he'd given her into his past had let her know that his had not been a peaceful or settled existence. The last time he'd left, he'd come back with bullet wounds and, she knew, a heart shattered by another woman. That still stung, and it made her more than a little ashamed of herself for taking him back. His dark and silent moods had gotten worse, and the way he'd exploded in rage at the video had shaken her. But he'd never raised a hand to her and she knew in her heart he never would.

She thought about the night before, how safe she'd felt wrapped in his arms in the camper trailer's tiny bed. The thought of that, and what they'd done when they weren't resting, made her smile again and shiver a little with remembered pleasure. Maybe he was turning the corner. Maybe things were going to work out.

The smile turned to a frown as she saw a black SUV parked in the lot in front of the bar.

"Damn it," she muttered. "What part of 'closed' don't you get?"

She got out of her dusty and dented pickup and walked over to the SUV. Empty. Her frown deepened. She walked to the front door and tried it. Still locked. The key slid easily into the lock and she stepped inside and stood still, listening.

The place was dim and quiet, only the neon beer lights behind the bar providing illumination. There was nothing to indicate anything amiss, but something felt wrong. Slowly, walking as lightly and quietly as she could, she crossed to the bar. "Hello?" she said into the dimness. There was no answer. She looked around, still puzzled.

A man stepped out of the door to the back rooms. He was holding a pistol pointed at her.

"Don't move," he said.

She froze, a shock of fear running through her as she saw the gun in his hand. She raised her own hands hesitantly. "I already been to the bank," she said. "There ain't much money in the register, but you can have what's there. Just go."

"I'm not here for the money," the man said. He was standing in the shadows. It was hard to make out his features. "Where's Jack Keller?"

"He ain't here. He's out of town." She swallowed nervously, trying to fight the fear down. "What do you want with him?"

"I need to know if he received a package lately."

She thought of the DVD that Maddox had brought. She considered just telling him about it. She didn't know any reason not to. Except he was holding a gun on her, and that didn't mean anything good for Jack. "I don't know what you're talkin' about," she said.

"I think you're lying," he said. "People who lie to me learn to regret it. Sometimes it takes a while, and sometimes they have to go through a lot of pain, but they always regret it." He raised the gun. "Come here."

"Okay, okay," Julianne said. Her mind was racing. "Yeah, he got a package. It's in the trailer. Out back. Where he stays." She nodded toward the bar. "Spare keys to the trailer are under the register."

He stepped back slightly. "Get them."

"Okay. Can I put my hands down?"

"Yes."

As she passed him, she glanced at his face. His sunken cheeks and burning, hollow eyes made him look like some kind of junkie. He didn't make any move to keep her from looking at him. She felt her knees going weak. He didn't care if she saw him, and that meant he didn't intend to leave her alive to identify him. She slipped behind the bar and reached beneath the register, taking a deep breath as her fingers closed around the handle of the baseball bat there.

T HE GIRL'S MOVE WAS SO obviously telegraphed, Riddle might have felt sorry for her had all the pity not been burned out of him years ago. He was inside the arc of the swing before she'd gotten the bat out from under the counter. He wrapped her right arm under his left and pulled her to him, jamming the gun up under her chin. Their faces were inches apart, close enough for him to smell her sweat. Her eyes were wide with fear. She was still game, however; she tried to bring a knee up into his groin just as he pulled her closer and turned slightly to take the blow on his upper thigh. He jammed the barrel of the gun painfully beneath her chin, grinding metal against bone until she cried out. "Drop the bat," he said through clenched teeth.

She hesitated for a moment; then he felt rather than saw her arm relax and heard the clunk as the bat fell onto the counter. He stepped back, never taking the gun or his eyes off her. He reached over with his left hand and groped for a moment before he found the bat and hefted it. "I ought to shove this up your ass," he grated. "I still might. Now where's the film?"

"I don't know what—"

He interrupted her by thrusting the end of the bat into her stomach, hard. The breath went out of her as she doubled over, hands clutching at her midsection. She fell to her knees, whimpering in pain. He slid the gun into its holster and shifted the bat to his right hand. She looked up at him with tears running down her face. "Please," she whimpered, "it's where I told you. In the trailer out back."

"I think you're lying," he said, and brought the bat down onto her left shoulder. He heard the crack of bone just before she screamed in agony. He raised the bat again. "Told you you'd regret lying to me," he said, "but you're going to start telling me the truth. Eventually."

CHAPTER ELEVEN

Keller STOOD ON THE CURB and looked down the road that led to the terminal. The road was packed with taxicabs, town cars, and people's personal vehicles. He didn't see Julianne's truck anywhere. He frowned, took out his cell phone, and punched in her number. His frown deepened as the call went to voicemail: "Hey, it's Jules, leave a message."

"Hey," he said. "I'm still at the airport. Call me and let me know if you got held up." He slid the phone back in his pocket. She probably just got delayed, he thought. But he still felt uneasy for reasons he couldn't clearly identify. He waited a few minutes, then called again. Straight to voicemail. He broke the connection and dialed the number of the bar's landline. No answer. He dialed the only other number in the area he knew.

Someone picked up immediately. "Desert Sands Inn, this is Chuck, can I help you?"

Keller was glad that it was the older son of the dour man who ran the hotel who was on duty. He didn't think Mr. Patel cared very much for him, and Mrs. Patel had a shaky command of English at best. But he'd always found nineteen-year-old Charuvinda, who'd Anglicized his name to "Chuck" when working the desk, to be cheerful and helpful.

"Hi, Chuck, it's Jack Keller."

"Oh, hi, Mr. Keller," Chuck said. "What can I do for you?"

"I can't get Julianne on the phone. Can you look and see if her truck's parked outside the bar?"

"Sure thing." There was a pause, then Chuck came back on the line. "Yes sir, her truck's out front. Along with another one. A black SUV."

"Huh. Okay. Thanks, Chuck."

"You want me to go over and tell her to call you? Her phone might just be dead."

He thought about it for a moment. "No," he said. "Your old man will be pissed if you're not on the desk. I don't want you to get in trouble."

"I'll be fine," the young man assured him. "Really. It's no problem. It's always slow in the afternoons."

"Thanks, Chuck," Keller said. "But no. Have a good day."

"You too, Mr. Keller."

Keller broke the connection. Maybe she'd gotten a visit from a vendor, like the beer distributor. He could wait.

RIDDLE LOOKED DOWN AT THE body of the girl, broken and bleeding on the floor behind the bar, but still breathing shallowly. He held a silver DVD in one hand, turning it idly, watching it reflect the colors of the beer lights behind the bar.

She'd told him where it was quickly enough. Then, after a few more blows, she'd told him where to find the safe combination. None of it had earned her any mercy. There was none to be earned. She couldn't be allowed to live and identify him.

Her breathing had grown more labored as he watched, and he heard the rattle he'd heard so many times before as death closed in on her and her airways filled with the fluids she no longer had the strength to swallow. He considered finishing her off with the bat or the gun, but he hesitated. Something about these moments held a fascination for him, a macabre interest in the body's last losing struggle with the inevitable. He so rarely got the chance to savor it. As he watched, the girl gave one last heaving breath, then the air went out of her in a rush and she was still.

"Okay, then," he said softly. He looked at the bat in his hand. It was covered in blood, with bits of hair stuck here and there in the rapidly coagulating fluid. Looking down at himself, he realized he had gotten a fair amount on himself; there were red spots and smears all over his pants, shirt, and leather jacket.

"Shit," he muttered, and dropped the bat on the floor. He needed to get out of there. He'd wasted time watching the girl die. An inspiration came to him. He picked up the bat, still dripping with gore, and walked out the back, making sure that some of the blood dripped along his path. He shuffled his feet, trying to smear any footprints, and noticed that he was leaving a long trail of blood on the hardwood floors. He continued in this way out the back door and back into the trailer. Once inside, he dropped the bat next to the small bed, turned, and left. The false trail probably wouldn't confuse a thorough and determined investigation, but he was betting whatever backwater sheriff's department they had out here wouldn't mount one with a quick and easy solution so near to hand: unstable vet with a violent past beats girlfriend to death, then flees town. At worst, it'd give him time to disappear. As he came around the building, he kept the SUV between him and the motel across the street as best he could. He didn't look back as he drove away.

At 4:45, the first of the regular customers, a former ironworker now on disability named Tom Buske, walked in. He stopped for a moment, startled by the quiet. Then he caught the coppery smell of blood in the air. He approached the bar slowly, not wanting to get closer, but knowing he had to see if anything was wrong. He looked behind the bar and felt his stomach trying to leap into his throat. He managed to just make it out the front door before he vomited, falling to his knees as he emptied his lunch of Spaghetti-O's and white bread into the parking lot. It was Charuvinda Patel who called the sheriff's after looking out the office window and seeing a man on his knees outside the bar, looking as if he was having some sort of seizure. That call would later earn the young man a smack on the back of the head from his father and a lecture about minding his own business.

A county sheriff's deputy answered the call, discovered the body inside, and quickly called for backup and an ambulance. The elected sheriff himself arrived a half hour later, talked to a few members of the rapidly growing crowd of customers, and immediately came to the wrong conclusion. A BOLO order went out to immediately pick up Jackson Keller and bring him in for questioning in the murder of Julianne Stetson.

CHAPTER TWELVE

Now Keller was truly worried. He'd tried to call Jules again and had gone straight to voicemail. He didn't know how to get back. The bar was an hour and a half away. A cab driver would laugh in his face if he tried to get a ride that far. He didn't have a credit card to try and rent a vehicle. He couldn't go forward and he couldn't stay where he was. Finally, he called the Desert Sands again. This time it was Mr. Patel who answered. "You will stop calling," the man said in his precise but heavily accented English. "You have caused enough trouble."

"Trouble?" Keller's heart was pounding in his chest. "What trouble? What's happened, Mr. Patel?"

"The police are looking for you," the man snapped. "I hope they find you. You should go to prison for what you have done to that nice girl."

"What I've done!?" Keller shouted, ignoring the people on the sidewalk who were staring and starting to edge away. "What are you talking about? What happened?" But the old man had hung up. "God DAMN it!" Keller barely kept himself from dashing the phone to pieces on the concrete.

"Hey, buddy," an airport security guard hailed him. "There's no loitering here. Move along."

Keller tried to keep his voice level. "My ride…the person who was supposed to pick me up…hasn't shown. And now I think something may have happened to her."

"Not my problem, pal," the guard said, his sweaty moon-pie face showing nothing but disdain. "Move it."

The dismissive tone infuriated Keller. His fists clenched, almost involuntarily, with the desire to pound the pudgy little rent-a-cop's face in. He was actually starting toward the man when he noticed the van parked at the curb.

It was the standard white airport transit van, like any one of a thousand others shuttling people from hotel to airport and back again. The driver was at the back door, unloading luggage for the small gaggle of travelers standing on the curb, heads down over their phones. Before he had a clear idea of what he was doing, Keller was running toward the open driver's side door of the still-idling van.

"Be with you in a moment, sir," the stocky, balding driver called out as he placed the last roller-bag onto the curb. Then, "HEY!" as Keller slid into the driver's seat, tossing his carry-on into the passenger side. He didn't bother to close the door as he put the van into gear and stepped on the accelerator. The door swung wildly to and fro, the side mirror showing a crazily oscillating image of the driver stumbling, trying to catch up with the interloper who was stealing his van.

Keller clutched the wheel tightly with a sweat-slick right hand and frantically groped for the door with his left as he accelerated. Horns honked and tires squealed when he suddenly swerved, the van lurching into the travel lane. He was only dimly aware that what he was doing was not the product of clear or rational thinking. He just knew he needed to get back to the only home he had, to find out what had happened to Julianne. Once he got that settled, he'd figure out what to do about getting the van back to its owners. He kept glancing at the rearview mirrors to see if anyone was pursuing. No one was, but it was just a matter of time. The driver was probably in the airport terminal at that moment reporting the theft.

He'd made it to the freeway before he saw the first police car, and it was going the other way, on the other side of the median, lights flashing and sirens screaming. He kept below the speed limit, trying to be as inconspicuous as possible, until he'd gotten well away from the airport. At that point, he put his foot as hard as he could on the accelerator, heading for home and dreading what he would find when he got there.

"WE MAY HAVE A PROBLEM," Riddle said to Cordell over the phone.

"I didn't hire you to tell me about problems," Cordell snapped back. "I hired you to solve them."

Riddle's voice was tight with strain. "I think I've solved one problem. I have that shipment you requested."

Cordell looked out the window of his office. The view over the Potomac River was shrouded in fog. The cloak-and-dagger language was probably unnecessary. There weren't a lot of people who'd dare to tap Cordell's phone, but he appreciated the care Riddle was taking. "Good. So what's the problem?"

"There was some breakage."

Cordell sank into his desk chair, rubbing his temples. "Is it repairable?"

"No."

This *was* bad news, Cordell thought. Deaths created investigations and there was no telling where those might go.

Riddle went on. "But I think we can shift liability for it to our competitor. At least in the short term."

"That's good. Because the people backing our competition don't have a lot of staying power. He's not well financed. If you can keep the competition out of the running for, say, a couple of weeks, our problem may resolve itself."

"It would probably be better to take them off the board permanently."

Cordell's brow furrowed with concern. He wondered if the man was getting a little too bloodthirsty. But then again, from everything he was learning about this Jack Keller, he might be a continuing problem. "Use your discretion," he said finally.

"Understood." Riddle broke the connection without saying goodbye.

Cordell frowned at the phone. He knew the man was rough around the edges from spending so much time in the world's darker places, but there was no need to be rude.

CHAPTER THIRTEEN

A FEW MILES INTO THE DESERT, Keller felt the adrenaline rush begin to subside, like a tide going out. *This was a mistake,* he thought. Then: *What the hell was I thinking?* He looked down at his hands. He noticed they were shaking and wet on the wheel. It was as if they belonged to someone else. He pulled the van over to the side of the road. The desert stretched out on either side, nothing visible but the scrubby, wind-gnarled creosote bushes and cholla cactus. He released the wheel and leaned back, taking a deep breath to steady his nerves. He needed to talk to someone. Taking out his cell phone, he glanced at the screen. Jules hadn't called back. He hit the button for the only other person he knew to call.

"Lucas Berry," the deep, strong voice came through the phone's tiny speaker and Keller immediately felt calmer. "Lucas," he said.

"Jack? What's wrong, son?"

"I'm sitting by the side of the road in the desert. I…I stole a van. At the airport."

"Yes, I'd say that's a problem. Are you hurt?"

"No. I'm okay."

"Doubtful. Tell me what happened."

Keller filled him in, starting with the incident with airport security. He finished up with "And I couldn't reach Jules. I tried calling the motel, and the guy who runs the place said I should be in jail for what I'd done. I think something's happened to her, Lucas. I didn't have any way to get back. No one would talk to me. So I..." He trailed off.

"Hmmm." Berry's response was so perfectly familiar, Keller almost laughed. After a moment, Berry went on. "Sounds like someone's fucking with you, Keller. It's stressing you."

"Yeah. You could say that." A thought came to him. "Did you find out anything about—" He almost said my father, but changed it at the last second to "this Trammell character?"

"No," Berry said, "and that's weird. We know the guy was military, but my buddy at the records center in St. Louis can't find a trace of him. What's even weirder is that the day after my phone call, I got a visit from two guys in dark suits from CID at Fort Bragg. At least that's where they said they were from."

Keller sat up straighter. "What did they want?"

"They wanted to know what my interest was in Clifton Trammell. I told them the truth. I was looking him up on behalf of a patient. They got a little pissy when I refused to tell them who."

"They didn't know already?"

"I got the impression they didn't even really know why they were being sent to ask. They seemed a little irritated in general about the whole thing."

Keller shook his head. "What the hell is going on, Lucas?"

"We can figure a couple of things for sure. Trammell is, or was, some kind of spook. The kind that the government doesn't want anyone to even know exists."

"You think that's why my name's on the no-fly list?"

Berry paused. "If that's the reason, and it's not just a garden variety Homeland Security snafu, then someone with a very long reach wants to keep you far away from him. I suggest you do what they want."

Keller clenched his jaw. "I don't like being fucked with like this, Lucas."

"I know. That's what worries me. This is fuckery on a higher level than you've ever had to deal with. And, given your situation at this moment, I think we can agree your decision-making skills are not what they should be."

This time, Keller did laugh. "Understatement of the year. So what do I do now?"

"As a medical professional, I need to tell you to return the stolen property and accept the consequences of your self-destructive actions."

"And as my friend?"

A longer pause this time. "How soon can you get back here to North Carolina?"

Keller rubbed his eyes. "I don't know. Remember I'm driving a stolen van, without a lot of cash on me to fill the tank. And..." He stopped as he looked in the rearview mirror.

"And what?"

"And a police car just pulled up behind me and hit his lights. Shit."

"Okay, Jack, what I'm about to tell you is very important. Don't try to run."

There were two men in the car, and they got out at the same time, one from either side.

"Give me some credit, Lucas. I'm not going to try to outrun a police cruiser in an airport van. I may be crazy, but I'm not stupid."

The trooper who came from the passenger side left his door open and crouched slightly behind it, his weapon pointed at the back of the van. The other draped his gun hand over the front of his own opened door and raised a microphone to his lips.

"Okay, give me some info," Berry said. "What agency or what county are they from?"

"YOU IN THE VAN," a voice boomed over the police car's loudspeaker. "THIS IS THE MARICOPA COUNTY SHERIFF'S DEPARTMENT."

"Offhand," Keller said, "I'd say it's the Maricopa County Sheriff's Department."

"Okay. Just sit tight. I'll let them know I know where you are and that I expect you to stay healthy."

"GET OUT OF THE VEHICLE," the voice said. "HANDS IN THE AIR."

"How are you going to do that?"

"Leave the line open. Tell them I want to talk to them."

"NOW. OUT OF THE VEHICLE." Even over the distortion and static of the loudspeaker, Keller could hear the strain in the voice.

"Lucas," he said as he opened the driver's side door, "these guys already have guns on me. If I get out of a stolen vehicle with a dark object in my hand, they're going to blow me away."

"Good point. Leave it on the seat or the dash, then. Don't break the connection. Tell them there's someone who wants to—" But Keller had already laid the phone on the seat. He slid out of the vehicle, raising his hands in the air as his feet hit the ground.

"TURN AROUND. FACE AWAY FROM ME AND GET ON YOUR KNEES."

Keller slowly sank to his knees. The rough gravel by the roadside dug into his kneecaps. He was facing west, into the lowering sun. He squinted against the glare and wondered for a moment if this was going to be the end. If his life was truly being manipulated by forces powerful enough to reach out and stymie him from a thousand miles away, it would be relatively simple to have him gunned down in a roadside arrest. All someone would have to do is claim that he...

His thoughts were interrupted by the sound of feet approaching quickly, crunching in the rocky soil. "On the ground!" a voice snapped. "Hands behind your back!"

He began lowering his arm to break his fall and something hit him in the middle of the back, knocking him to his face in the sand and gravel. He fought down the temptation to roll over and begin fighting back. He had barely started to put his hands out when he felt his right wrist being grabbed and wrenched behind him. He gritted his teeth against the pain and felt the cuff being snapped around his wrist. "I'm not resisting," he grated. "I'm not resisting." The words seemed to have some effect, as the grip on his left arm became firm but not brutal. The officer helped him to his feet. A hand on his shoulder turned him around.

The cop who stood before him was short and muscular, dressed in dark brown uniform pants and light khaki shirt. He had light olive skin and eyes hidden behind the inevitable mirror shades under a dark-colored ball cap with the sheriff's logo on it. His nametag read ALVAREZ.

"What's your name, sir?" Alvarez demanded in a loud, aggressive voice that completely negated any effect of the "sir."

"Jack Keller," Keller responded. "ID's in my back pocket." He glanced over and saw the other cop, a bareheaded older man with thinning gray hair, holding his weapon steadily on him several feet away.

"Uh-huh," Alvarez said. "You got anything in any of your pockets that I need to know about? Any needles? Weapons? Sharp objects?"

"No, sir." He stood impassively as the younger cop fished the wallet out of his back pocket and flipped it open. The license in the front compartment made him squint. "North Carolina?" he said. "You're a long way from home."

Brother, you have no idea, Keller thought. "Yes, sir," was all he said.

Alvarez stepped back slightly. "Mr. Keller, you're under arrest for theft of means of transportation. You have the right to remain silent.

Anything you say…"

Keller took a deep breath as the familiar litany went on. If they meant to execute him by the side of the road, they probably wouldn't be reading him his rights. It wasn't an execution. It was just an arrest.

"I say something funny, sir?" Alvarez snapped.

"No. No." Keller realized he was smiling. "I just thought… never mind." He gestured with his chin toward the vehicle. "By the way, someone's on the phone in there. He wants to talk to you."

Alvarez looked baffled. "What?"

"The phone. On the seat. There's someone on it who wants to talk to you."

Alvarez looked at his partner, who looked just as confused as he did. The gun, however, never wavered. He sidled over to the open door, never taking his eyes off Keller. Finally, he stole a glance into the interior of the vehicle. He reached in and picked up the cell phone. For a moment, he stared at it as if it was some sort of alien artifact.

"Go ahead," Keller said, "say hello."

Alvarez scowled, but put the phone to his ear. "Hello?" His scowl deepened as a voice came over the line. "This is Deputy Alvarez of the Maricopa County Sheriff's Department. Who is this?"

The look of irritation returned to one of bafflement at the response. "Who?" He listened for a moment, then tried to reply. "Listen, Mr. Berry…okay, Dr. Berry…we're…sir…"

Keller tried to repress another smile. When Lucas ramped up his delivery, using that voice that Keller had once told him sounded like it ought to be coming from a burning bush, he was pretty much unstoppable, even by a cop two thousand miles away. Finally, Alvarez gave up. "Yes, sir. Right. We'll make a note of it." A pause. "You're welcome, Dr. Berry." He cut the connection and looked at the phone again as if he couldn't quite comprehend what had just happened. He shook his head and turned back to Keller. "Okay," he said, clearly struggling to get back into his comfort zone, "mind telling me where you were going with this vehicle?"

"Deputy Alvarez," Keller said, "so far you've acted pretty human in a tense situation. So I'm not trying to disrespect you when I tell you I'm not saying a damn thing without a lawyer."

"Well, I'm not trying to tell you not to get one," Alvarez said, "but you know, once you lawyer up, there's not a lot we can—"

"Do to help me. I know. I've heard this all before, Deputy. And I'm still not saying anything without a lawyer. You're a professional, I'm... well, let's just say this isn't my first rodeo. So let's get in your car and get this show on the road, okay? And could you tell your partner there to quit pointing that gun at me? I'm sure he's getting tired, and I'm not bucking you."

Neither Alvarez nor his partner were used to this much rationality from a criminal suspect. Truth be told, Keller wasn't used to it himself. He wished he could thank Lucas for talking him out of a state of mind that would have ended in an ass-kicking or worse. He didn't resist as they put him in the back of the patrol car. As they were pulling away, however, he leaned forward. "Hey," he said. "I need you guys to do me a favor."

"Shut up, asshole," the older cop who was driving said.

"Warren," Alvarez told him, "chill. This guy's a veteran."

"How the hell do you know..."

"The guy on the phone told me." He turned to speak to Keller. "Iraq, right? The first one."

"Yeah," Keller said. "You?"

"Too young for the first one. Spent the second one walking the edge of the DMZ in Korea." He sounded almost regretful. "So what did you want?"

"I was trying to get back to where I was living. My girlfriend was supposed to pick me up." He didn't see any reason to tell the cop why. "She didn't show, and I couldn't reach her on the phone, so I tried to call the people across the street. The old guy who lives there said something had happened. I need to find out if she's okay."

"Gimme the address," Alvarez said. Keller did. Alvarez got on the radio. "Dispatch, this is Unit Twelve. Request information on any incidents in District Two, repeat, District Two."

The radio crackled back. "Stand by." After a long pause in which all Keller could hear was the sound of the cruiser's tires on asphalt and his own heart beating in his ears, the radio came to life again. "Twelve, say again the name of your suspect in custody."

"Keller," Alvarez replied with a puzzled glance back to the back seat. "Spelled Kilo-Echo-Lima-Lima-Echo-Romeo."

"Stand by." After a moment the dispatcher came back. "Unit Twelve, Ten Twenty-Five Headquarters, Detective Sergeant Ross, CID, reference Code Four Five One."

"Code Four Five One?" the driver said. "What the fuck?"

Alvarez didn't answer. He looked at Keller in the back seat. All of the warmth had gone out of his eyes.

"I have a feeling I know what Code Four Five One means," Keller said.

Alvarez shook his head. "What the hell did you *do*, Keller?"

Keller didn't answer.

CHAPTER FOURTEEN

THE DETECTIVE THAT MET THEM at Headquarters was unusually well-dressed for a homicide cop. In Keller's experience, most of that breed wore a coat and tie only grudgingly. Detective Ross's suit looked tailored, and his tie was knotted perfectly. His gray hair was professionally cut. Even his mustache was trimmed just so. He entered and took a seat across the table from Keller in the interview room, his cold blue eyes studying Keller's. He was carrying a manila envelope in his hand. He didn't speak. Keller knew the game; wait for the suspect to blurt something out and hope that it was either something incriminating or something a good prosecutor could spin that way. Usually, Keller could outwait anyone. These were not usual circumstances. He broke the silence first. "I'm pretty sure I asked for a lawyer."

Ross still didn't answer. He reached into the envelope and pulled out a set of photographs. His eyes never left Keller's as he put them on the table. Keller didn't want to look down, but he finally did. What he saw made his breath catch in his throat. He tried to remain stoic, but the sight of Julianne's ruined face and battered body made him close his eyes.

"We found the murder weapon in your trailer," Ross said in a low, even voice. "It had her blood and her hair all over it."

Keller sucked in a deep breath and looked back up. "One, I didn't kill her. Two, I want a lawyer."

"If you didn't do it…" Ross began.

Keller finished for him. "Why do I need a lawyer? Come on, Detective, we both know that script. The guy that didn't do it needs a lawyer as bad as the guy who did. More, probably. Now let's move this along." *So I can get on the trail of whoever did this,* he thought but didn't say.

Ross didn't answer, just stared at him. Keller stared back. It was so quiet he could hear the ticking of Ross's wristwatch. Finally, the detective shook his head and gathered up the pictures. "Okay, wiseass," he said as he stood up. "You had your chance."

"Not really," Keller said.

"What?"

"I never had a chance. But you have a nice day, Detective."

Ross slammed the door as he went out. Keller sat silently, hands still on the desk, no expression on his face. He knew there were people behind the mirror of the interrogation room. He wasn't going to let them see or know what he was feeling. The grief, the regret, and most of all the rage would stay locked behind his eyes until the time came to release it. That day would truly be a day of reckoning for someone.

THE NEXT TWENTY-FOUR HOURS PASSED slowly, as all hours do in lockup. Keller shared a cell with a silent, tattooed Latino who probably wouldn't have spared three words for him even if he'd had any English. That gave him more time to think than he liked. He lay on his bunk and stared into space, trying some of the relaxation exercises Lucas had taught him just to keep himself from pacing the cell like an animal in a cage. Day dragged into night, the only sign of that passage being a barely edible dinner of a single bologna sandwich and water, then lights out. Keller didn't sleep. His cellmate snored like a chainsaw with a bad muffler.

In the morning, after a breakfast of powdered eggs and watery milk, a pair of guards came to take Keller to his first court appearance.

The spectators and defendants awaiting their own turns looked up with interest as he was brought into the courtroom, shuffling in his leg shackles. He noticed that one of them was writing furiously in a notebook. *Press*, he thought. *Great. That's all I need.* He kept his face impassive. After a short pause, the judge, a slim Asian man with glasses, called his name and Keller stood.

"Jackson Keller, you are charged with theft of a means of transportation, assault with a deadly weapon with intent to kill inflicting serious injury, and first-degree murder. Given the nature of the charges, the court will record a plea of 'not guilty,' unless you object."

"No objection, sir," Keller said.

"Without objection, then, we move on to the issue of counsel."

A voice spoke up from behind him. "I'll be entering an appearance for Mr. Keller, Your Honor."

He turned slightly. A petite woman in a gray suit was striding up the aisle as if she owned the building. As she got closer, Keller got a better look at her. She appeared to be in her mid-fifties, her straight blond hair cut short and lying close against her head like a helmet. She was deeply tanned, with laugh lines around her eyes that made Keller instantly want to like her. He resisted the temptation. He regarded lawyers as a necessary evil. He'd only met two in his life that he actually liked. One of them was back in North Carolina, and the other was dead.

The judge looked surprised. "Ms. Alford," he said. "We haven't seen you around in a while."

"I've been enjoying retirement, Your Honor," the woman said.

"Approach, please," the judge said. As she strode to the bench, she whispered out of the corner of her mouth to Keller, "I'll be right back."

"I'll be here," Keller said dryly. He noticed that the briefcase clutched in her right hand was battered and cracked. It looked like something that had been left in the desert for forty years. He thought there must be a story connected with it.

The judge extended a hand as Alford reached the bench. She took it and the two shook hands like old friends. They had a brief conversation that ended with the judge chuckling. She stepped back and went back to stand beside Keller, who towered over her.

The judge returned to formality. "Will you be making a motion for bail, Ms. Alford?"

"Your Honor," Alford said, "given the nature of the charges, we'll reserve that motion for the time being. We do, however, request a probable cause hearing."

The prosecutor, a young man who looked too young to be a freshman in college, much less an assistant DA, stood. His prominent Adam's apple bobbed nervously as he said, "Your Honor, the State intends to go to the Grand Jury on these charges in lieu of preliminary hearing."

Alford didn't look happy, but she nodded as if this was bad news she'd been expecting. "Very well, Your Honor." She reached out and gave Keller's elbow a squeeze. "I'm a friend of Lucas Berry," she murmured. "Hang on a sec." She turned to the deputy who was approaching to take him back. "Deputy"—she squinted at the nametag on his shirt—"Rojas...hey, are you related to Pete Rojas? Retired from the PD a couple years back?"

The deputy stopped, looking uncertain. "Yes, ma'am," he said. "He's my uncle."

"Awesome. Tell him Erin Alford says hi and I hope he's enjoying his retirement. Ft. Lauderdale, wasn't it?"

He nodded. "Yes, ma'am."

"Lucky guy. I'm envious. Hey, can I have five minutes with my new client here?" Without waiting for an answer, she took Keller's elbow and began steering him out the side door into the corridor.

"Wait...I..." the deputy started to protest.

Alford released Keller's elbow and spread her fingers out like a child showing his age. "Five minutes. I swear." They were in the corridor now and she nodded toward an open door. "You can stand outside the conference room door." She smiled, steering Keller in the direction she wanted him to go.

"Well...okay."

"Thanks, Deputy, I owe you one."

Inside the tiny conference room was a small round table with two chairs. As soon as the door closed, Alford dropped the charm and became all business as she took a seat. "Okay. First rule. You—"

Keller sat down as well. "Say nothing to anybody. Not even a friendly cell mate."

She looked annoyed at the interruption, but nodded.

"I didn't kill her," Keller said.

She nodded again. "Well, that helps."

"You don't believe me."

"Mr. Keller, it doesn't matter what I believe. What matters is what the State can get a jury—"

"I've heard that speech, too."

She snatched up the briefcase and stood up. "Well, good, since you've got it all figured out—"

"She took me to the airport. I must have been there when she was..." He choked on the word, the impact of what had happened closing his throat.

Alford's expression softened and she sat back down. "Okay," she said. "Sorry. We got off on the wrong foot. Something to remember,

Mr. Keller. I don't like being interrupted. It makes me testy."

"Sorry," Keller said. "I'm a little tense myself."

She chuckled. "Understood."

"So…you've been retired."

She leaned back and studied him. "Yes," she said without expression.

"Mind if I ask why?"

Her face still registered nothing. "I didn't screw up in some spectacular way that got someone convicted, if that's what you're worried about."

"Well, maybe a little."

She snorted. "Only lawyers in movies retire over silly shit like that. In fact, the real screw-ups seem to hang on forever. I retired because I could."

"You did that well?"

She gave him a wry smile. "Partially. I also married money."

"Good for you. So how do you know Lucas?"

The smile widened. "I'm supposed to be the one asking questions."

Keller didn't smile back. After a moment, her face became serious again. "You don't know if you trust me."

Keller didn't answer. She sighed. "Fair enough, I guess." She leaned back in her chair. "We met in the Army. I was a JAG lawyer. He was a witness in one of my cases. I was defending a young sergeant charged with assaulting a superior officer. I was trying to establish that my client had diminished capacity as a result of combat-related post-traumatic stress disorder from the Panama invasion."

"And Lucas helped you with that?"

She shook her head. "I wish. He was a rebuttal witness for the prosecution. He absolutely gutted my case. He said my guy didn't have PTSD at all. As you might have noticed, he's pretty impressive. When he stepped out of the box I wanted to throw myself off a cliff."

"And yet you're friends."

"Yeah. The evening after the hearing, Lucas called me up and asked me out to dinner." She raised a hand at Keller's look. "Just to tell me some things he thought I needed to know. It was all business. Over one of the best seafood dinners I ever had, he gave me a crash course in post-traumatic stress disorder. Then, at the end of the night as we were paying our separate checks, Lucas made an offhand comment. 'Look at Spheeris's record.' Spheeris was the captain my guy had slugged. Knocked his ass in the dirt, as a matter of fact."

Keller was becoming intrigued despite himself. "So what did you find?"

"When I started poking around, people started coming out of the woodwork wanting to talk to me. This Spheeris guy was a nightmare. His unit had been on training maneuvers prior to shipping out for the Gulf. Every simulated engagement, he'd gotten his people wiped out. Couldn't navigate, couldn't manage simple deployments, and even in basic exercises, he froze and couldn't make the easiest decisions. If he'd been sent to lead a combat unit, he'd have killed more people than the Iraqis."

"So you put Spheeris on trial."

"Wouldn't have done any good. You can't hit an officer, even if he is a total screw-up. But I let a few people know what I knew and what kind of evidence I could put up. The right people found out about it. Even though it wouldn't have gotten me a Not Guilty, no one wanted the embarrassment. Not then, especially. Captain Spheeris was quietly reassigned somewhere he couldn't do any damage—at least not get his people killed—and my guy got a plea for time served, loss of a stripe, and a reduction in pay. Last letter I got from him, he was alive and well and running a snowmobile repair shop in Michigan. Pretty wife, two kids."

"Good job," Keller said.

Alford smiled tightly. "So, you trust me now?"

"More than I did a few minutes ago."

As if on cue, the deputy began tapping on the door. His voice was muffled by the heavy wood. "Ms. Alford?" Alford picked up her briefcase and stood. "Good. We'll talk again."

"We need to," Keller said. "There's more to this."

She nodded. "No doubt. First thing I'll do is have someone check the surveillance cams at the airport. Maybe we'll get lucky and put you there at the time of the...at the relevant time."

"Ms. Alford!" The deputy's voice was more insistent now.

"One second," she called back. "Anything else you want to know?"

"Yeah," Keller said. "This seems like an awful lot to do for a casual acquaintance. Even one that helped you with a big case."

She smiled. "Lucas Berry is a good man, Mr. Keller. And we were friends long after that one incident. I trust his judgment of people. And if he says you deserve help, then help you will get." She opened the door and beamed at the deputy. "Thanks, Deputy Rojas," she said. Then she turned back to Keller. "It doesn't look like it now, Jack, but you're a lucky guy to have friends like Lucas Berry."

"I know," Keller said. "Thanks."

CHAPTER FIFTEEN

I T WAS ANOTHER DAY BEFORE Keller saw Alford again. Even through the scratched and milky Plexiglas window that separated them, he could see that she looked troubled and uncertain, a far cry from the confidence bordering on cockiness she'd shown earlier.

"You look like you've heard some bad news," he said.

She set her battered briefcase down on the narrow shelf on her side of the window and took her seat. "I've heard some news I don't understand at all."

"Did you get anything from the surveillance cameras?" he asked.

"Not yet," she said. "They've been requested. I took the liberty of telling Ross about them."

He frowned. "The detective?"

"Yeah." She nodded. "He's a hard-ass, Mr. Keller, but he's a good detective. Unlike some of those guys, if there's something that's going to bust up his case, he's going to want to know about it sooner rather than later. And he can move the request along faster than I can."

"So if he gets it, what then? I get out of here?"

She shook her head. "This is where we get to the part I don't understand. There's a federal detainer on you."

"A what?"

"A federal hold. Even if they dismissed the murder charge, they have to hold you here for the feds."

Keller sat back in his chair. "Son of a bitch," he whispered. He resisted the temptation once again to slam his hand down on the table or pound on the glass. "Son of a BITCH!"

She was looking at him intensely. "You got some kind of federal warrant you want to tell me about, Mr. Keller?"

He fought to get his anger under control. "No," he said. He remembered Lucas's words: *This is fuckery on a higher level than you've ever had to deal with.* He hadn't wanted to tell Alford about where he'd been going, about the man who claimed to be his father, about his mysterious and sudden appearance on the no-fly list. For one thing, he figured, telling your lawyer you thought you might be the victim of a government conspiracy would mean wasting a lot of time getting court-ordered psychiatric exams. He barely believed it himself. For another, the whole subject of his alleged father was something he wasn't going to share with anyone. Except Julianne, and she was...his mind veered away from that thought. He took a deep breath. He'd do what it took to get out of here and go after whoever had killed Jules.

"Okay," he told Alford. "This is going to sound crazy. But hear me out."

She raised an eyebrow. "I'm listening."

He told her everything. About Maddox, about the gun camera DVD, about the no-fly list. When he was done, she didn't respond at first. When she spoke, her voice was thoughtful. "If it hadn't been for the federal hold, I'd say that was just another crazy-ass client story. But you make it sound almost plausible."

"Gee, thanks."

"So you have any way I can reach this Maddox?"

He shook his head. "He was staying in the motel across the highway from the bar. But I get the feeling he's the type who's only going to be found if he wants to be."

"How about your father?"

Keller tried not to snap at her. "I don't know if he's my father."

"I don't know why anyone would lie about that," she said. "But fine, let's just call him the putative father at this point."

He thought of the number Maddox had given him to call when he reached DC. "I got a number. It's written down. But it's in my bag. They took it when I was brought in.

"Not a problem," she said. "They'll have you sign a form to release your belongings to me. I'll get the number."

"What good will calling him do? I doubt he'll even talk to you."

"I don't know that. And maybe, if he's who he says he is, he can help me figure out who's pulling these strings."

He nodded. He hated the idea of relying on this man who claimed to be his father for anything. But getting out of here was the primary goal.

"So," she said, looking at him appraisingly. "We get these charges thrown out. You walk out of here a free man. What then?"

He returned her gaze. "I don't know. Maybe I go see this guy Trammell. See what his game is."

"It looks a lot like there's someone pretty high up who wants to keep you from doing that. Someone who's willing to kill an innocent girl then try to frame you for it. That person might come after you again."

"Yeah," Keller said. "They might."

Something in the look on his face made her eyes widen. "That's what you want to happen, isn't it?"

Keller shrugged. "If it happens, it happens."

"And then what?"

Keller didn't answer.

"You know," she said, "if you tell me you've committed a crime, that's covered by attorney-client privilege. But if you tell me you're *going* to commit one, like, say, murder, it's not. I have to do what I can to stop it, including telling the proper authorities."

"Really?" Keller said mildly. "That's interesting."

She sighed. "Okay, I'll stop asking questions I don't want to know the answers to."

"Good idea."

"I will, however, advise you against killing people, even if they did kill your girlfriend."

"Thanks," Keller said. "I appreciate your advice."

"Sure you do. But I have the feeling you're not going to take it." She stood up. "Okay. I'll keep you posted."

"Ms. Alford," Keller said as she started to turn away. She turned back. "Thanks," he said. "I really do appreciate what you're doing for me. I'll do anything I can to pay you back."

She nodded. "I'll be happy if you just don't do anything stupid."

Anything except that, he thought.

IT'S ME," RIDDLE SAID OVER the phone. "Did you get the package I sent?"

"Yes," Cordell answered. "The DVD."

"Is it what you were looking for?"

Cordell looked at the silver disc sitting on top of the FedEx envelope it had come in. "I'll know after I review it. Just sit tight and wait for further instructions." There was a pause on the other end. "What?" Cordell said.

"Our competition may be back in the game. He lawyered up. The liability issue we talked about may not be as strong as we'd hoped."

Cordell rubbed his eyes. "Any chance he'll be back in business soon?"

"Maybe. Unless I do something else. Maybe force him into early retirement."

The meaning was clear. "No," he said. "This isn't Colombia. Too much breakage raises eyebrows."

Cordell heard the man sigh. "Understood. I'll keep you posted."

"I mean it. Stand down until further notice."

"Roger that." The words were innocuous, the tone bordering on insubordination. Cordell clenched his teeth in frustration and picked up the DVD. It was almost time for the meeting with Kathryn Shea. He hoped that this was the object she was looking for and he could cut Riddle free. He was starting to look more and more like a loose cannon.

CHAPTER SIXTEEN

SHE SAT IN THE LIVING room, watching the incident on the DVD play out on a wide-screen TV in one corner. The picture was blurred and indistinct, but the voices over the radio left no doubt as to what had happened. After the spectacular explosion of the Bradley, the whooping and celebration was cut short by an unidentified voice over the clear channel. "Gunslinger, Gunslinger, this is Jumbo. This is Jumbo. Cease fire. Repeat, cease fire. Reports of friendlies in the area. Cease fire."

The silence was only a few seconds, but it seemed to stretch for minutes broken only by the throb of the chopper's rotors in the background. Finally Gunslinger Two-six's voice came clearly over the now-hushed channel. "Fuck. Me."

Kathryn turned the television off with the remote control held in her left hand. She took a sip of the drink in her right. She didn't speak.

"Was that what you were looking for?" Cordell asked from the couch.

She raised the glass again, stopped it halfway to her lips, then held it away from her face and studied it for a moment as if expecting it to reveal something to her. A grimace crossed her face and she put the glass back down. "No. It wasn't."

"Well," Cordell said. "That's…unfortunate."

"Yes, it is."

Cordell was clearly trying to keep himself under control. "I have to point out that if you'd been a bit more clear about what it was we were looking for in the first place, we might have saved ourselves…" He stopped himself, then began again. "A good bit of trouble."

"Trouble?" Kathryn said.

"Nothing you need concern yourself with."

She stood up and walked to the window. "Tell me what it is that we *did* just see."

"I'm not sure," Cordell said. "But we do know that Jack Keller served in the first Gulf War. Something happened. We're not sure what. He was a squad leader. Apparently a good one. Then he lost his squad. The experience seems to have unhinged him. He was given a medical discharge."

"How did he lose his squad?" She gestured at the television. "Or did we just see that?"

Cordell nodded, looking thoughtful. "That may be it. What happened to his men…well, there are gaps in the record."

"The kind of gaps you get when someone's covering up the kind of negligence that leads to men being killed by their own side?"

Cordell's nod was more definite. "That's the best theory that fits the data."

She turned away from the window. "So whatever is going on between Cliff Trammell and his son may have nothing to do with me or my father."

"If you say so," Cordell said.

"I do. So. We leave Keller alone."

Cordell took a deep breath. "It may not be that easy, ma'am."

She frowned. "What do you mean?"

"Maybe you should let me handle it. It may be best that you—"

She interrupted him. "Is Keller dead?"

"No."

"But?"

"Someone else is. And Keller's been charged."

"Did he do it?"

"Kathryn—"

"Tell me, Mr. Cordell, or get out of this house and don't come back."

"Fine," Cordell said, the anger breaking through. "But my advice to you is that there are things it's not in your interest to know."

"I'll be the judge of that."

"No. Keller didn't do it. There was an accident retrieving this video. Someone was killed. It wasn't anything we intended. But Keller was charged."

"Will the charges stick?"

Cordell shook his head. "It doesn't sound like it. Except maybe a vehicle theft. He stole a van trying to get back to the—"

"So, let me sum up," she said. "We have an unstable person with a history of violence, in jail for a crime he didn't commit. And he may get out. When he does, he's likely to want some payback from the people responsible. Which means you. And by extension, me." He started to answer, but she raised a hand to silence him. "You're right, Mr. Cordell. I don't want to hear any more. I just want this mess cleaned up. However it needs to be done. I don't want to have to sleep with one eye open the rest of my life."

"Yes, ma'am."

She turned back to the window. "Have you ever read *Macbeth*, Mr. Cordell?"

He had been walking to the door, but the question stopped him. "I vaguely remember it. From college."

"It seemed like a simple plan to Macbeth and his wife. A quick and easy assassination and hey presto! Macbeth is King of Scotland." She turned back to face him. "But that one killing led to another. And that led to another. Murder on murder, until Macbeth was at war with most of Scotland and the very forest was marching against him."

"That makes for a good play," Cordell said. "But that won't happen here."

"I hope not," she said. "I certainly hope not."

C ORDELL WALKED OUT OF THE room, shaking his head. He began to wonder if signing on with Kathryn Shea had been a mistake. On paper, she had everything: she had the name recognition, she could articulate a strong conservative message without seeming far-right crazy, and she was incredibly photogenic. But he was discovering a disturbing dark streak in her. It wasn't just the drinking, although he would have to keep an eye on that. Her obsession with her father's old friend Trammel was beginning to border on mania. *What does he have on you, Kathryn?* He resolved that he would find that out. But for now, there was a loose end to tie up. She was right. It was unfortunate, all things considered, but this Keller could be a threat down the road in so many ways. It had been Riddle's screw-up but now was not the time for the blame game. Now was the time to clean up the mess and move on. He pulled out his cell phone and hit the speed dial for Riddle's number.

He answered on the first ring. "Yeah?"

"I just spoke with the home office," Cordell said. "We've decided that driving our competitor out of business is the only option."

"Understood," Riddle said. "His doors will be shut by close of business Friday."

"Good. Thanks."

"It'll be easier if he's out and about. I assume it was you that put the lien on our competitor."

Cordell was puzzled. "The…lien?"

"The *federal* lien."

"Ah." Having Keller subjected to a federal hold might have been overkill. But Cordell had wanted to be extra sure that the man would stay under lock and key. "I'll take care of that."

"And I may need access to funds."

"I'll have someone contact you with instructions for accessing a line of credit." He took a deep breath before going on. "It's vitally important that our name be kept out of this."

"I don't even know who the principal is. I assume it's not you. And I don't much care who it is, as long as the money's there." Riddle broke the connection.

Cordell put away the phone and thought about what Kathryn had said. *One killing led to another, murder on murder.* He shook off the chill that ran down his spine. There was that dark streak of hers again. He wasn't going to take counsel of his fears. It was still early in the game. Once this Keller was dealt with, it'd be a straight and smooth path to the US Senate. And after that? Who knew?

CHAPTER SEVENTEEN

"I'VE GOT SOME GOOD NEWS," Alford said to Keller through the glass. "I've got some puzzling news. And I've got some bad news."

"Start with the good news," Keller said.

"The surveillance videos came through. They show you were clearly at the airport during the time frame of the murder."

Keller felt a weight being lifted from his shoulders. "So the charges are going to be dismissed?"

"The murder charge, most likely. Ross is still trying to figure out a timeline where his theory that you did it works. He says he wants to talk with the medical examiner again, since the actual time of death is a window of a couple hours. But he's losing his faith in that scenario. He's unhappy, but it's like I said. He's a tough son of a bitch, but he's a realist. He's not the kind of cop who wants to put the wrong guy in jail just to close the case. Not in a murder where that'd mean the real killer's still walking around loose. "

"Good to know there's a few honest cops left."

She nodded. "More than you think."

"So how long?"

"A day, maybe two."

"Good. And the bad news?"

She sighed. "Well, Mr. Keller, those surveillance recordings are kind of a mixed blessing. They do show you stealing that van. You've still got a bond on that."

"How much?"

Alford grimaced. "Fifty thousand right now."

"Fifty…"

"Now that the murder charge is going away, we'll be in good shape to make a run at getting that modified. Or do you know anyone that could put up ten percent to pay a bondsman?"

"Ten percent? Isn't it usually fifteen?"

She shrugged. "There's a lot of competition in the area."

He thought for a moment. "No," he said. "I don't know anyone who can do even that."

"How about Lucas?"

Keller shook his head. "I'm not asking him for money. He's done so much already. I've still got to figure out a way to pay you."

"We'll work it out," she said. "Right now, I'm mostly working *pro bono*. A favor for an old friend. Plus, I'd forgotten how much fun this can be." She saw the look on his face and flushed. "Sorry. I know it's not fun for you."

"No," Keller said. "But it's okay." He recalled what she'd said earlier. "So what's the puzzling news?"

She frowned. "That federal hold I told you about? The one that came out of nowhere? It's been withdrawn."

"What? Why?"

She shook her head as if she could hardly believe it herself. "I have no idea. The assistant US Attorney I called to find out about why the thing was there in the first place isn't calling me back."

A level of fuckery you haven't previously experienced. "Maybe someone now wants to make sure I get out."

Comprehension dawned on her face. "To get to you."

"Maybe. Did you call that number?"

She nodded. "Yeah. No one answered. And no voicemail."

"They didn't recognize the number. Maybe if you call from my phone."

"How would they know your number?"

"What the hell, they know everything else about me."

"Would your father," she began, then saw the look on his face and corrected herself. "Sorry, your *putative* father put up your bail?"

"I don't know," Keller said, "and I don't care."

She sighed and stood up, picking up her briefcase. "Okay. I'll let you as soon as there's any more news."

Keller stood up as well. "Thanks again for everything."

Her face was troubled. "You're welcome," she said. "I just wish I didn't have this feeling that I'm not really doing you any favors by trying to get you out. I mean, that's my job. But I feel like I'm setting you up for something terrible to happen. And I don't want that."

"Me either," Keller said. "But don't worry about it. I'll be fine."

She looked at him for a moment without speaking, her expression still uncertain. Then she turned and left.

IT WASN'T ALFORD, HOWEVER, WHO brought him his next piece of news. It was a burly, taciturn guard named Rodriguez who opened Keller's cell door the next morning and said, "Keller. Come with me." The tone was brusque but not aggressive, which was normal for Rodriguez.

Keller got up from the bed. "What's going on?"

"You're getting out." Rodriguez gestured impatiently. "Hurry up, man, I got shit to do."

"Out?" Keller said. "Did they reduce my bond?"

"No. Someone paid it. You wanna get out of here or not, homes?"

"Yeah. Yeah, I want to get out."

"Well, come on, then."

He followed the guard through a succession of doors, out to Administration, where a bored-looking female officer returned his belongings to him and had him sign the proper forms while Rodriguez stood by impassively, arms folded across his chest. As he went through the papers, Keller casually asked, "So who was it that paid the bond? This was kind of a surprise to me."

Rodriguez shrugged. "They don't tell me nothin', man. All I can say is you're one lucky guy. Come in here on a murder charge, walk out a couple days later. 'Cept for the auto theft charge. An' someone sprung you pre-trial on that. You must have friends in high places."

"Maybe not friends," Keller said. Rodriguez didn't answer, but when Keller looked up, he saw a troubled look in the guard's eyes. "What?" Keller said.

Rodriguez looked away. "Nothin'."

Keller finished the last of the paperwork, picked up his bag, and followed the guard out to the final door to the outside. As Rodriguez unlocked the door, Keller tried one last time. "You heard anything I need to know about, Rodriguez?"

Rodriguez hesitated before turning around. "Look, Keller," he said, "I don't know you. But you didn't give me no trouble. You ain't got tats like a gangbanger or a biker. And no one's said anything about you bein' mixed up with the cartels. If you was, we'd hear about that." He grimaced. "The cartel boys get handled with kid gloves." He clearly didn't like the practice.

Keller shook his head. "No on all counts."

Rodriguez nodded, apparently satisfied. "Well, you didn't hear this from me. But when we found out that someone paid your bond, my boss went in his office and made a phone call. He locked the door. That usually only happens when someone on the outside needs to know to be waitin' for some dude to get out. And I ain't talking about someone's mama." He looked around to make sure no one was listening. "All I'm sayin' is, you watch your back, Keller."

"Thanks," Keller said as he picked up his bag. "I will." Rodriguez nodded again and swung the door open. Keller stepped out into the bright sunlight, wondering if he was stepping into a pair of crosshairs.

The giant red-brick jail loomed over him, with the street a few yards away. The street was busy, with cars rolling past at a steady pace. Keller realized he had no particular place to go and no real way to get there. He reached into his bag and pulled out his cell phone, then into his back pocket to get the business card he'd stashed there. He pressed the buttons, hoping he got through on the first try. He had almost no battery charge left.

"Erin Alford," the voice on the other end answered.

"It's Jack Keller," he said. "I'm out."

"Out?" she said. "How? Did you change your mind and call Lucas?"

"No. Someone put up the bond. Don't know who."

"That's...weird."

"The guard who let me out said someone made a phone call right before I was released. He didn't know to whom. But he seemed to think it was worth warning me about."

"Shit," Alford said. "You still at the jail?"

"Yeah. Right outside."

"Stay there. I'll be there in about a half hour. Stick close to the front. I don't think anyone will try anything that close to the jail itself. At least I hope not."

"Me, too," Keller said.

The half hour felt more like half a day. Keller scanned every vehicle carefully as it rolled past, wondering if one was going to swerve, open its windows or doors, and start spitting lead. Finally, a low-slung Mercedes convertible pulled up. The vehicle's top was down and

Alford was behind the wheel, wearing a scarf over her hair and dark glasses. Keller threw his bag in the back as he got in.

"Nice ride," he said, "but I don't know if I'd be driving around with the top down with me in the car. From what that guard said, someone might try a shot at me."

"If they did," Alford said as he pulled away, "it's not like the soft top would stop a rifle round. Look in the glove box."

Keller opened the latch. He stared for a moment, then pulled out a stubby pistol with what seemed like an absurdly short barrel.

"Beretta Nano," Alford said. "Part of my wife's collection. She says it's easy to conceal. It's a lot of fun to shoot, but watch the long trigger draw, it'll pull your aim right."

Keller stared at her. Alford noticed his expression and chuckled. "Is that look because your lawyer's handing you a gun or because the one who told me to give it to you is my wife?"

"Maybe a little of both," Keller said.

Alford laughed again. "You should meet Becca. I told you I married money, right? Among other things, Becca owns a controlling interest in Liberty Arms."

Keller had spent most of his time in the past couple of years living at a one-horse crossroads in the desert, but you would have to be farther away from civilization than that not to know the name Liberty Arms. Their commercials and billboards were everywhere across the Southwest. Most of them featured a fierce-looking woman with curly brown hair holding a rifle at port arms across her ample chest over the slogan "The right to buy weapons is the right to be free." Apparently, the message had taken hold. There were Liberty Arms stores dotted across the Southwestern landscape.

"Thanks," Keller said. He couldn't think of anything else to say.

"So," Alford said, "where to?"

Keller thought about it. The bar Julianne had run and the trailer behind it was the only home he'd known for a while, but he didn't know if he could bear to go back there.

Alford seemed to sense his hesitation. "Look, come stay at the house for a day or two. Get your bearings. We've got plenty of room."

"No," Keller said. "I can't ask you to—"

"You can't go back where you were," Alford interrupted him. "At least not yet. For one thing, I need to see if it's still an active crime scene."

"Right."

"And Becca wants to meet you. Once she heard you might be the target of a government conspiracy…" She stopped. Keller said nothing, just looked at her. "I didn't mention specific names," she said.

"Good."

"But…well, I talk about things that worry me with Becca, okay? And she listens. That's what a partner is for."

"It's okay," Keller said. "I'm not mad. So how much does she know?"

"Not everything. But she's totally willing to believe there's someone in the government out to get you. And she's chomping at the bit to help."

Keller felt more than a little uneasy at Alford's idea. His recent experience in South Carolina had given him more contact that he ever wanted to have again with cults and conspiracy theorists. He was also uncomfortable with the idea that Alford's partner was planning to adopt him as a sort of pet project. Still, he needed some time to get his bearings, as Alford put it, and a safe place to do it in.

"Okay," he said. "But I'm not going to impose on you more than a day or two."

She nodded. "That's fine. And that will give me some time to find out who's behind bailing you out." She shook her head. "This case just gets weirder and weirder."

"Yeah. That happens to me a lot."

CHAPTER EIGHTEEN

THE HOUSE WHERE ALFORD LIVED with her wife was far out in the desert, near the tiny Gila Bend Indian Reservation. Keller couldn't tell how big the property was, but they'd begun passing the same line of wrought-iron spike-tipped fence running along the highway for at least a mile before Alford turned in at a large double-sided gate. An iron archway spanned the top of the driveway. Keller looked up and saw that there were Greek letters wrought into the arch.

"What do those say?" he asked.

"*Molon Labe,*" Alford said. She looked a little embarrassed. "It's Greek."

"I figured," Keller said. "What does it mean?"

She put the car in park and turned to him. "You know the story about the three hundred Spartans, right? They made a couple of movies about it."

Keller vaguely remembered lying on Julianne's couch with his head in her lap as she flipped through the channels. He recalled a movie with a bunch of men in leather diapers, capes, and swords, and a lot of shouting. She had paused to watch for a few minutes, making jokes about the costumes and the shouting before she went back to surfing. The memory of that night, when he'd felt totally like a normal person doing normal things, caused him to draw in a deep shuddering breath. "Yeah," he said after he'd gained control of himself. "I didn't see them."

"Me either. But the story's pretty classic. The tiny Spartan force standing off the whole Persian army, holding the pass of Thermopylae against impossible odds...anyway, when the Persians pull up, their general rides out and yells to Leonidas, the Spartan king, 'Greeks! Give up your weapons.' Leonidas waves his spear at the Persians and yells back, '*MOLON LABE.*' Come and take them."

"So," Keller said, "it's like that 'you can take my gun from my cold dead hand' thing."

The gate had begun to swing open, parting in the middle to let them through. It must have been triggered by someone in the house he could see several hundred yards away. "Yeah," Alford said. "Is that a problem?"

"No," Keller said. "It's just that when you yell out what a badass you are and put a sign about it over your door, I've found that there's no shortage of people who'll take you up on it."

Alford put the car in gear and started up the long gravel drive. The gates swung noiselessly shut behind them. Keller looked back over his shoulder. Through the iron bars, he saw a black SUV slow down, pause directly across the road from the gates, then speed up and drive away. He frowned.

"What?" Alford said as she saw the expression on his face.

"Someone's checking the place out."

"We get that all the time," Alford said. "But I'll let Becca know. She can put extra people on."

"People?" Keller said. But by then they were up to the house.

It was a low-roofed, single-story structure, sprawling out across a slight rise that gave it a commanding view of the emptiness all around. There seemed to be more windows than walls in the building, but the floor to ceiling glass panes were set back below the overhang of the flat roof so that they shielded the interior from the worst of the midday sun. The driveway split just before they reached the house, forming a circle around a gravel area with a bubbling fountain in the middle. A water feature in this desert, Keller thought, meant someone wanted to show off how much money they could spend. On the far side of the circle, the drive led under a *porte cochere* that covered a set of broad steps ascending gently to the heavy wooden double front doors.

There was a woman waiting on the steps. She was tall, with curly light brown hair that spilled to her shoulders. Her face, with its high cheekbones and strong jaw, looked forbidding until she smiled at the sight of Alford behind the wheel. Alford stopped the car and got out. The two women embraced. "Welcome home, babe," the tall woman murmured. She broke the embrace and turned to Keller. Only then did he recognize her as the woman from the Liberty Arms billboards. She stuck out her hand, looking Keller up and down in a way that let him know he was being sized up. "Mr. Keller," she said in a warm contralto. "I'm Rebecca Leonard. Welcome to Liberty Hall."

He took the hand and shook it. She had a firm grip. "I want you to know, Mr. Keller," she said, "that you're safe here. We take our freedom and our rights very seriously, and we do what it takes to secure them."

"Thanks," Keller said as he released the hand. He was getting a very strange vibe from this woman. It reminded him of someone; he couldn't put his finger on exactly whom. At the time, however, he didn't have much choice but to trust her. "I appreciate your taking me in. Especially on such short notice."

She smiled again, this one more formal than the one she'd graced Alford with. She gestured toward the house. "Marta will show you to your room."

As if responding to a hidden signal, the door opened and a short, severe-looking middle-aged Latina in a maid's uniform stepped out. She smiled at Keller and gestured him inside. He reached in the back of the Mercedes and picked up his bag. The maid held out her hand, still smiling. "I've got it, thanks," he said. The maid's smile slipped a notch. "Please," she said, with more insistence than entreaty. Keller handed the bag to her. "This way," the maid said. She turned and walked inside, with Keller following.

Inside, the decor was sparse, with chrome and black leather predominating. One of the few softening influences was the huge painting of a desert flower that hung in the hallway that the maid was leading him down. Keller stopped, impressed with the lush curves and vibrant colors of the painting. The maid noticed his hesitation and came walking back down the corridor toward him, hefting Keller's bag in one hand as if it weighed nothing. "Georgia O'Keefe," she said, with as much pride as if it had been hanging in her own home. "Very good painting. Very famous."

Keller just nodded. The maid gestured to him to come along and led him further down the hall.

The bedroom she led him to had the same black leather and chrome decor. The bed looked large and luxurious. Right now it was as inviting as any bed he'd ever slept in. A wall of windows looked out upon the desert, but there were thick curtains that could be drawn across them. There was a strange quality to the view, a blue haze in the windows as if the house was somehow underwater. He walked over and rapped on the glass sharply. He turned to the maid. "Bulletproof?"

She nodded. "*Sí*. You are safe here."

Maybe, Keller thought. But the place still made him uneasy. Marta opened a door. "Bathroom is in here, if you want a shower." Her tone implied that she thought he needed one.

"Thanks." He sat down on the bed and began pulling his boots off. She wrinkled her nose and closed the door. As Keller pulled off his socks, he realized how tired he was. He lay back on the bed. His initial impression was correct. It was a very comfortable bed. He fell asleep before he could stop himself.

RIDDLE SAT AT THE SIDE of the highway, by the iron fence bordering the Leonard property. In the distance, the house caught the light of the lowering afternoon sun and glittered like a jewel in the desert. He shifted the toothpick in his mouth and considered. The place was well-protected, but not invulnerable. The biggest problem was the owner. Keller was nobody, a small-timer with no connections and no value. But the rich lesbian who owned this place was another matter. He'd done his research. She didn't just have money, she had political connections, and her partner had even more. If they ended up being collateral damage, there might be scrutiny.

He grimaced. It was a different world than he'd grown up in, when people like that mattered. Still…the germ of a plan was coming to him. He recalled some of the information in the dossier that Cordell had given him. This Keller seemed to have a real talent for pissing people off. Those people could be useful. He picked up his cell phone and dialed. The first person he dialed gave him another number, which led him to a third party who gave him yet another. The person at that number told him to leave a message and that someone would call him back. That was progress, he figured. He started the car and drove away, back toward the city of Phoenix.

CHAPTER
NINETEEN

KELLER AWOKE WITH A START to the knocking on his door. He looked at the clock on the bedside table. "Shit." He'd slept for three hours. He never had gotten that shower.

The knock came again. "Dinner." It was the maid's voice. It wasn't a voice one could oppose.

"Be right there," he said. There was no answer. He pulled a clean shirt and jeans out of his travel bag and quickly changed into them.

Rebecca Leonard greeted him at the door to the dining room. She was casually dressed in jeans and a red silk blouse, and Keller relaxed slightly. For all he knew, dinner here could have been a white tie affair. "Please come in," she said with the same formal tone she'd used earlier.

Erin Alford was already seated at a large, rustic-looking wooden dining table. There was a bottle in front of her that looked like beer, but he couldn't make out the label. She started to get up as Keller came in the room, but he waved her back down. A young Latino man in a white jacket appeared at his elbow. "Something to drink, sir?"

Keller pointed. "Yeah, I'll have what she's having. Please."

"Very good, sir," the young man said, "and how do you like your steak cooked?"

Keller didn't answer at first. He was distracted by the sight of the holstered gun on the young man's hip. "Ah, medium rare," he said. The young man nodded and disappeared as quickly as he'd come. Keller took a seat. "Sorry, I kind of crashed on you."

"Not a problem, Jack," Leonard said. "We know you probably needed the rest. Jail is no place to get any real sleep."

"Yeah. Thanks again for giving me the place to regroup."

The young man appeared with the beer and a pilsner glass. "Glass, sir?" Keller looked over. Alford didn't seem to have one. "No, thanks." He took the beer from the young man's hand, but still didn't recognize the label. He took a drink. It was a good brew, full-bodied, with a slight bite to it.

"Brewed in Flagstaff," Alford said. "Becca owns the brewery, too."

"Beer and guns," Keller said. "I'm surprised they haven't made you governor by now."

"Give it time," Alford said.

Leonard smiled. "I think Arizona will have to come a long way before that happens."

The young man had returned and stood in what Keller assumed was the door to the kitchen. "Dinner will be in five minutes, ma'am."

She nodded. "Thank you, Alex." Alex went back into the kitchen.

Keller took a sip of his beer. "You expecting trouble?"

Leonard inclined her head curiously. "No more than usual, why?"

Alford spoke up. "I think he's wondering why Alex was carrying."

"Ah." She regarded him with the look a teacher might give a slow student. "The question, Mr. Keller, is why shouldn't an American citizen be carrying a firearm, as is his right?"

Keller shrugged. "Just seems a little much for dinner. After all, you don't seem to be strapped."

The gun appeared on the table in front of her so fast it was like a magic trick. Keller blinked at it, then looked up. "Sorry. My mistake."

"It was clipped under the table," Alford said. "I have one, too."

Keller took another sip of his beer. He didn't know what to say.

"Mr. Keller," Leonard said.

"Jack," he murmured.

"Jack. I'm an out lesbian living in Arizona. I'm very outspoken, some would say mouthy. I'm also rich, with a few hundred thousand dollars' worth of artwork on the walls alone. We're twenty minutes from the nearest law enforcement, even if they came at top speed, which they may or may not, all things considered. Every day, I see more senseless killings, more home invasions, more terrorists inside our country. You may think I'm paranoid. My question is, am I paranoid enough?"

Keller realized then who Becca Leonard reminded him of. Colonel Nathaniel Harland had been a highly decorated soldier who had come home from the Vietnam conflict with the unshakable conviction that civilization was at the edge of collapse. After writing a bestselling book on the subject he had taken his book money, gathered a few followers, and retreated to a camp in the Blue Ridge Mountains of North Carolina to await the end of the world. When that end had been slow to come, his followers had drifted slowly away, leaving only Harland and his adopted daughter. The daughter had been killed, but for all he knew, Harland was still up in the mountains.

At the time he'd written his book, and for long after, Harland had been regarded as a crank, a curiosity, a paranoid loon, if entertaining to read and to see on a talk show. Now, it seemed, his view of the world had gone mainstream. Keller could see the same light in Becca Leonard's eyes, an almost Messianic gleam of total assurance that she was one of the few who really understood what was happening to the world and knew what to do about it. He didn't know what to say, but he resolved to get out of there as soon as he decently could.

The silence was broken by Alex's return, accompanied by the maid Marta. They were carrying plates which they rapidly distributed to the people at the table. Keller found himself looking more closely at Marta to see if she too was armed. He thought he saw the outline of something heavy in the front pocket of her maid's apron. Keller turned his attention to the food, which was excellent. Keeping his mouth full kept him from having to provide much conversation. He noticed that Leonard and Alford didn't seem to have much to say to each other. There was clearly some sort of tension between them.

When the meal was done, Leonard turned to Keller and regarded him with that steady, disconcerting gaze. "Now," she said, as if calling a meeting to order, "would you like coffee while we discuss where you go next?"

"Sure," Keller said, although the idea of planning the next few days with this woman caused his gut to tighten.

The coffee, too, was excellent, served in heavy handmade pottery mugs. Leonard took a sip, closed her eyes in pleasure, then nodded at Alex, who nodded back and retired through the kitchen door. She looked at Keller. "There are quite a few people interested in your story."

Keller took a drink of his own coffee, keeping his face impassive. "What story is that? And how, exactly, did these people find out about it?" He looked across the table at Alford, who looked away. She was clearly not happy about the direction of the conversation.

Leonard ignored the look. "A veteran, seeking to discover the truth about what happened to him in the war, targeted by his government, denied his freedom of travel, locked up on trumped up charges...it's a pretty compelling story."

"So much for attorney-client privilege," Keller said.

Alford's voice was bitter. "And so much for thinking what I told my wife was going to stay between us."

"This is important, Erin," Leonard said.

Alford stood up and tossed her napkin down. "So was being able to trust you, Rebecca." She left the room.

Leonard sighed as if she'd just been disrespected by a wayward child who'd need a good talking to later. She turned back to Keller. "Look," he said before she could speak again. "Like I said, I appreciate the hospitality. But I'm not a cause. I just want to be left alone."

"I doubt that that's going to happen, Jack. And from what I can tell, it's not really what you want."

Keller was getting angry. "You don't have any idea what I want."

She answered him calmly. "You want the person who killed your lover. You think maybe he'll come after you again. And then you want to kill him. I can completely understand that."

It was all true, but hearing it laid out like that just made Keller angrier. "If that's true, and I'm not saying it is, that's my business, Ms. Leonard. Not yours."

She smiled grimly. "You think you can take these forces on alone?"

Keller stood up. "I'll be leaving in the morning."

She looked amused. "And going where?"

"I'll figure something out."

"Yes," she said. "That's worked out so well for you so far."

He bit back the reply that sprang to his lips and left the room. Back in his room, he sat on the edge of the bed, fuming. He just wanted to be out of there, away from people who kept interfering in his life. He got up and paced the room, trying to get himself under control. When he heard the knock on his door, he nearly yanked it open to snarl at the person on the other side, but stopped himself at the last second and pulled it open.

It was Erin Alford. Her eyes were red as if she'd been crying. She was holding another bottle of beer in her hand. "Hey," she said. "I just wanted to apologize." He didn't answer. After a moment, he stepped aside and let her in. He took the chair across the room while she walked unsteadily to the bed. She was clearly drunk. She took a long pull from the beer, then stared at the floor. "I thought I could talk over things with my wife and have it stay between us."

Keller wasn't inclined to let her off the hook. "Guess you were wrong."

She looked up at him, her face a picture of misery. "I could lose my license for this."

"Don't worry. I don't have the time to file or pursue a complaint. You'll just have to live with it."

She sighed. "You still have the charges from stealing the van to deal with. I'll see who I can find to represent you on those, if you like."

"Yeah. Sure." He stood up. "If that's all, I'm going to get that shower I missed earlier."

"Yeah. Fine." She stood up as well. "Where are you going to go tomorrow?"

He looked out the window at the desert, illuminated by the full moon. "Back home, I guess."

"Home? The bar?"

"I'll get the rest of my stuff. Then move on. I don't know where. Maybe to see this guy who claims to be my father. I don't know."

"I'll drive you as far as the bar. You shouldn't leave the jurisdiction, though. You're still under bond." Keller didn't answer. "And Jack, again, I'm sorry. Becca sometimes lets her passions blind her to the people that might get hurt."

"Yeah," Keller said. "I've already met too many people like that. Some of them have tried to kill me. So don't expect me to like her any better for it."

She walked to the door. "I'll see you in the morning." She stopped as if she were about to say something else, then took another drink of her beer and left.

RIDDLE SAT IN THE CAR by the road a half mile down the fence. He watched the lights from inside the house shimmer and glitter in the night. From time to time, he raised a pair of binoculars to his eyes and examined the place more closely. There was no way to sneak up on the house; before the sun went down, he'd spotted multiple surveillance cameras on the building itself and others scattered on the property. The people in the house would be armed, smug and complacent behind their layers of security. That would be their mistake. He had taken down people better armed and protected than these.

A light in the house went off. A light in another room went on. He was lowering the binoculars when he felt his cell phone vibrate against his leg. He answered. "Yes?"

"Tell me where this Jack Keller is," said a voice he didn't recognize, one with a heavy Spanish accent.

"You want him?" Riddle said.

"I have some business to discuss with him. I hope to have a very long conversation."

Riddle smiled in the dark. "I think we can help one another. Let's talk."

CHAPTER TWENTY

THE SUN WAS JUST PEEKING over the edge of the horizon when Riddle saw his opening. The gates swung wide and a small red pickup headed out. He caught a glimpse of the young Latino guy he'd observed working around the house. The road was long and straight; there was no need to hurry. He let the truck get nearly out of sight before he began to follow. He had an idea where the young man was going. He caught up a few miles down the road, as the truck was pulling into a small roadside market. A hand-lettered wooden sign out front advertised FARM FRESH EGGS AND COUNTRY HAM.

Riddle didn't slow down until he was a mile or so past the store, then he pulled over. He picked up the cell phone, dialed a number he'd been given the night before, and said one word into it when someone picked up on the other end: "*Vamanos.*" He closed the phone and turned his truck around. He drove back to the store, slowly. He'd timed the errand perfectly; the truck was pulling out as he approached. He fell in behind, following at a safe distance until they reached a stretch of the desert highway out of sight of the store and of the house.

Riddle pulled out to pass. He'd previously rolled down his passenger side window and laid a long-barreled .357 magnum on the passenger seat. As he pulled abreast of the red truck, he slowed slightly. As the young man turned his head to see who was passing, Riddle raised the gun, steering with his left hand, and fired. The first shot shattered the driver's side window in a spider web of glass that quickly collapsed. The truck swerved drunkenly as the startled driver nearly lost control. He over-corrected and nearly collided with Riddle's vehicle. The lurching vehicle came close enough so that Riddle had a clear shot; his second round snapped the driver's head to one side and sprayed his blood and brains across the passenger window. The truck slowed, drifted toward the center, then back toward the shoulder before shuddering to a stop.

Riddle pulled behind it and got out. As he approached the vehicle, gun held down by his side, a large black Cadillac Escalade with windows heavily tinted pulled up. A nondescript white van pulled up behind it. The passenger side window of the Caddy rolled down. Riddle tensed. A hard-faced young man with a shaved head looked out at the scene with dark, impassive eyes.

"Don't just sit there," Riddle snapped. "Help me get him out of the driver's seat."

The man didn't answer at first, then he said something in rapid Spanish to someone in the back of the SUV. A pair of young Latino men in nearly identical blue jeans and white T-shirts got out. One had the ripped muscles and crude tattoos of someone who'd spent a lot of time behind bars. The other was younger and wirier, wearing sunglasses and a blue bandanna. The three of them muscled the driver's dead weight out of the truck. They didn't react to the mess inside. "Get his coat off." In a moment, they'd stripped off the dead man's chef's coat. The shoulders and back were spattered with blood and brain matter.

As Riddle shook and snapped the coat to try and get as much of the detritus off as he could, he saw that the two were dragging the body to the side of the road. "No," Riddle said. "In the truck bed." They looked at him as if he'd lost his mind. He motioned with his head insistently. The two looked at each other, then shrugged. They tumbled the body into the back of the truck as Riddle donned the soggy chef's coat.

"*Bueno*," Riddle said.

The two looked at each other again. "We speak English, homes," Blue Bandanna said.

"Good. That'll make this easier." He quickly explained his plan. It didn't take long.

When he was finished, Jail Tats frowned. "You say this lady inside… she has lots of guns?"

"Yeah," Riddle said. "At least I assume she does. She certainly brags about them enough on TV. They're all yours when we're done. Along with Keller."

"Sure, man, sure," Blue Bandanna said. "But you know, this plan of yours…" He shook his head. "Seems more like a suicide run than anything."

"If it is, I'll be the first one who finds out. You'll have plenty of time to turn tail and run." The tightening in their shoulders and their deepening scowls let him know he'd stabbed their pride. "You in or out?"

The two men glanced as one back toward the hard-faced man in the passenger seat. He nodded.

"Okay," Jail Tats said. "We're in."

MARTA LOOKED AT THE KITCHEN clock and frowned. Alex was running late. If he didn't get back soon, the *Señora* would have to wait for breakfast. She liked it as soon as she got up. She wouldn't say anything, but her entire demeanor would let them know that she had found them wanting. Marta was too proud a woman to allow that to happen. If that boy — Alex was in his mid-twenties, but Marta still called him "that boy" — didn't move his behind, he was going to get a talking to. She walked to the front door and looked out. Through the narrow glass windows beside the door, she could see the gate at the end of the long driveway. The air above the paved drive was already beginning to ripple in the first blast of heat from the morning sun.

There. She saw the little red truck Alex was so proud of and pressed the large gray button beside the door that activated the gate. Muttering to herself, she went back to the kitchen to finish chopping the vegetables for the morning omelets. When she heard the front door open, she called out in Spanish. "You took your time about it. Bring me those eggs so we can—"

She looked up. The man standing there in the chef's coat wasn't Alex, and he was holding a gun in his hand. There was a long suppressor affixed to the barrel of the weapon. She gasped. It took her a few seconds to recall the gun in her apron, the gun the *Señora* demanded she carry, even though it made her uncomfortable and weighed her down. Those seconds made all the difference. The gun in the man's hand gave a soft cough, the soft-nosed round striking Marta in the forehead and killing her instantly.

CHAPTER
TWENTY-ONE

IN ALL HIS YEARS OF taking out heavily armed and highly motivated people, Arlen Riddle had learned one unyielding truth: All the guns in the world will not save someone if you kill them before they can point the guns at you. The secret to taking out an armed group was speed and surprise. With those on his side, one man could wreak havoc.

Before the body of the maid hit the floor, he was moving. He crossed the kitchen, into a dining room, and beyond that into a living room with huge tinted picture windows facing out across the desert. He stopped and looked around to get his bearings before noticing the metal staircase going up. Without hesitating, he took the stairs two at a time, not bothering to be quiet. Moving quickly from the top of the stairs and down a carpeted hallway, he picked out the room with the light coming from beneath the door. Without a moment's hesitation, he burst into the master bedroom.

There was a woman in the king-sized bed across from the bedroom door. Riddle recognized her as the woman from the Liberty Arms billboards and TV commercials. She was sitting up, in mid-stretch as he kicked the door open, and she barely had time to turn and look at him before he fired. Once. Twice. A fan-shaped pattern of red and gray appeared as if by magic on the wall behind her and she fell across the expensive-looking sheets. He stepped into the bedroom, scanning back and forth with the pistol in his outstretched arms.

A door opened into the bedroom. He swung the gun to bear on the figure who stood there. It was a woman with short blond hair, dressed in a light gray robe. She was brushing her teeth. She stopped as she caught sight of him and her eyes widened.

"Don't move," he said.

Her hand, still holding the toothbrush, dropped to her side, but her mouth still gaped open soundlessly as she turned toward the bed. She saw the body sprawled there, the spray of gore across the wall, and blinked stupidly for a moment. That was all it took for him to cross the room, grab a handful of the woman's short hair, and jam the gun into the side of her neck. She gave a startled cry and dropped the toothbrush, still rooted to the spot by uncomprehending shock. He leaned over and whispered in her ear.

"Scream."

She screamed.

T HE SOUND OF THE SCREAM jolted Keller out of sleep. He was rolling out of bed and crouched on the floor before he was fully awake. He waited there, listening. He heard nothing at first, then the sound of steps on the stairs. It sounded like two people, but descending clumsily. He strained his ears, trying to catch some noise that would tell him what the hell was going on. A thought made him lean back and slide open the drawer in the bedside table. Of course there was a pistol there. It was a 9MM Glock, of a model he was familiar with. He pulled the gun out and checked it. Loaded but not cocked. The footsteps were coming closer, down the hallway toward his room. He could make out another sound approaching with them.

It was the sound of a woman weeping.

Keller gritted his teeth and racked the slide on the pistol to chamber a round. The footsteps stopped outside his door.

"Mr. Keller?" a male voice said.

Keller didn't answer.

"I know you're in there, Mr. Keller," the voice said. "She told me." The sobbing grew louder. Keller waited.

"I'm going to open the door," the voice said. "She'll be in front of me. If you try anything, she'll die."

Which she? Keller wondered, then realized the import of the man's words. It was most likely that everyone in the house was dead except for him, the unknown voice, and whichever of his hosts was still alive. He looked over at the windows, wondering if he could break one of them and get out that way. But where would he go? Across the desert? Whoever this was could pursue him across the open space and shoot him down like a dog. He straightened up slowly, gun held out in front of him, as the door swung gradually open.

A man was standing there, with his forearm across the neck of Erin Alford, holding her in front of him. He was taller than she was, his face partially exposed. His eyes were hidden behind mirrored sunglasses. Keller measured the chances of taking the head shot, dropping the unknown man, and getting them both out of here. The man's next words stopped that speculation.

"I'm not alone. Kill me, and it won't make a bit of difference in what happens to you. But it might have an effect on what happens to her."

He looked at Alford. Her eyes were red rimmed and tears rolled down her face. "He killed Becca," she sobbed. "He shot her, Jack."

The man acted as if she hadn't spoken. "In about two minutes, a group of men are coming in here. They work for some people down in

Mexico. Some people you've managed to really piss off, Mr. Keller."

"You'll have to be more specific," Keller said. "I piss a lot of people off."

The man smiled. "I heard you were kind of a smart-ass. We'll see how funny you are when Jerico Zavalo's people get hold of you."

"Sorry," Keller said, "I can't place the name."

"Seems his brother Andreas had a nice little smuggling operation going. Across the border. I hear you screwed that up. And then someone killed Andreas."

Keller shook his head. "Still not ringing any bells." But he was beginning to get an idea what this was about. He'd helped his closest friend, Oscar, find his sons, kidnapped by a white-supremacist cult who'd been capturing illegals coming across the border and redirecting them into a slave labor camp in the swamps of South Carolina. The FBI, the Border Patrol, and a mysterious group of operatives who appeared to have no official existence had dismantled the operation. A lot of people had died, including the man responsible for getting the illegals into the US.

"Jerico stepped into the power vacuum that was left after his brother and Auguste Mandujano got killed," the man said. "Frankly, I think Jerico ought to thank you. But he apparently thinks you're partially responsible." He shrugged. "Thing is, one way Jerico established his hold over the old operations is by hiring a guy that used to work for the Sinaloa cartel. They called him the Soupmaker. Ever hear of him?"

"No," Keller said, still looking for an opening, "but I guess you're going to tell me."

"The Soupmaker got rid of enemies of the cartel by putting them in a big tub of acid. If they were really lucky, the cartel boys would shoot them first. I don't think you're going to be that lucky, Mr. Keller."

Keller could hear the sounds of people in the corridor outside, voices raised in Spanish.

"In here," the man called back. He looked at Keller. "Set the gun on the floor and I let her live."

"I think you're lying," Keller said. "I think the plan is to leave a trail of dead bodies with me disappeared, so I get blamed. That doesn't work if she's alive to tell a different story. So whatever I do, you're going to kill her."

The man smiled tightly. "You're a pretty smart hombre. But there's different ways to die. Some a lot worse than others. She could always go into the soup first, while you watch."

As the import of the words sank in, Alford began to struggle wildly. "NO!" she screamed. "NO! NO!"

The man clouted her on the side of the head with the gun. "Shut up," he snarled.

The momentary distraction gave Keller his opening. He fired once, aiming over her shoulder to the man's face, but Alford's desperate thrashing caused her to jerk sideways at the wrong moment, and the bullet struck her in the throat. Blood, bone, and gore exploded out of the back of her neck in a spray that drenched the face and upper body of the man behind her. Her body began to convulse and the man dropped her to the floor, raising the gun and snapping off a shot at Keller. The bullet went wide, but so close Keller could hear the snap as it passed. He flinched to one side and pulled the trigger again as the man threw himself to the side and out of the doorway. The babble of voices grew louder; whoever the man had brought with him was coming down the lower hallway. It sounded like a good-sized group.

Keller stayed in a crouch, but moved slowly toward the door, hoping he could at least close it. He didn't know what he was going to do then. All he'd be was trapped inside with an unknown number of armed men just beyond the door. One of the unidentified Spanish voices was raised in what sounded like a question. The man he'd just seen answered back in the same language.

There was a shuffling of feet, as if people were getting into position. Keller tensed. He was probably going to be gunned down, but he preferred that fate to the one the unknown man had described. Maybe he could take at least one or two of the bastards with him. He looked at Alford's body lying in the doorway, eyes wide and staring as if in shock. "I'm sorry," he whispered. "I should never have come here." There was no answer. There was no way to shut the door with her body blocking the doorway. Keller looked up. There was no sound from the hall. He waited. *First one to move*, he thought, *will be the first to die.*

It didn't work out that way. All he saw was an arm coming around the edge of the doorjamb. The arm jerked back, but not before tossing a small cylindrical object into the room. Keller had only a moment to register *grenade* before it went off, blinding him with a brilliant flash and deafening him with a dull concussion that he could feel in his whole body. He staggered to one side, trying to keep his hold on the gun.

The doorway filled with bodies as men poured into the room, brandishing long guns and shouting at him. He couldn't hear them through the ringing in his ears but he saw the mouths working spasmodically, the dark eyes narrowed in hate and anger. He tried to raise the pistol with an arm that suddenly felt like it belonged to someone else, the seemingly unconnected hand raising the weapon in slow motion. A hand snatched the weapon away and Keller looked up to see a brown wooden gun stock swinging toward his face.

The explosion of pain didn't knock him unconscious, but stunned him into immobility. He barely resisted as he was yanked to his feet. The man who'd struck him swung the gun again, jamming the butt of the weapon into Keller's solar plexus. He doubled over in agony, gagging as last night's dinner threatened to come back up. The third blow to the back of his skull drove him to his knees and finally, mercifully, into darkness.

CHAPTER
TWENTY-TWO

Whext Keller awoke, he thought at first he'd gone blind.

He was still groggy from the blow to the head, but he was aware enough to know his eyes were open. However, all that he could see was blackness. He shook his head to clear it, then immediately regretted the motion. His head felt as if might burst open. He wondered if the blow had fractured his skull and injured the vision centers of his brain. When he tried to raise his hands to his head to check for damage, he discovered a new pain in his wrists, which were secured behind him. It felt like they'd used zip ties. There was a low humming in his ears and the feeling of vibration along his body.

Gradually, as full awareness returned, he realized that he was lying on his side, bound. He was in some kind of vehicle. When he breathed out, he could feel the soft puffs of his exhalation against his face, as if they were rebounding off something. It was then that he realized his captors had put a bag over his head. He felt around tentatively with his legs until his foot encountered metal. He was in the back of a van or truck of some kind. The humming he could hear and feel was the tires on asphalt.

He didn't know how long he'd been out or have any idea where he was. What he did know was that he was taken to be killed, probably horribly. The cartels always meant for a death to be more than just a means of getting someone out of the way. They used executions like the kings of old. The deaths of enemies were meant to terrify, to teach a lesson about the price of crossing the ruler. Keller didn't like the idea of being a lesson.

Biting back a groan of pain, he shifted around and slowly managed to sit up. He pushed back with his feet until his back was against the wall of the vehicle and took stock. Becca Leonard was dead. Erin Alford was dead, killed by his gun. The thought of how he'd not only failed to save her, but had actually caused her death, came down on him in a crushing weight. Part of him wanted to just lie back down and let whoever these bastards were do what they were going to do. There was nothing for him to live for, anyway. Everyone he knew was gone. He'd driven them away. Marie and Angela, both of whom he'd loved and who he knew once loved him; his friend Oscar—all had had to leave, to distance themselves from the violence that always seemed to find him, and to which he always responded. *You bring death*, Colonel Harland had told him once on a burning North Carolina mountainside that he'd helped turn into a battlefield, *and Hell follows with you*. Maybe, he thought, the world really would be better off without him. But as the cloud of despair settled around him, Keller began to feel the stirrings of another, much more familiar emotion.

Fury.

He had been driven by it all his life. It had come to a white hot focus when he'd seen his men, the men who'd depended on him, killed by a stupid mistake that had been covered up, swept under the rug, just as he'd been swept out of the Army, the only place he'd found a true home. He'd wandered through his life numb for years after that, the rage from that betrayal stuffed away and repressed.

The only thing that allowed him any respite from the numbness was the adrenaline rush of the chase, the takedown, the capture. He'd found a life as a bounty hunter that had helped him channel his anger. Then he'd found friends and eventually a lover, all of whom had given him an anchor to keep him from being carried away on the black molten tide of fury that lived within him. But sometimes, when those he loved were threatened, that wrath had erupted. It had kept them — and him — alive. Then it drove those he loved away from him.

He had no anchor left. And the dark tide was rising.

He felt his lips drawing back from his teeth in a feral snarl, felt the blood pounding in his temples as the blackness rose in him. He wasn't going to lie down and let himself die. He fed the fire, stoked it like a dark shaman. As it rose, he felt oddly cold, preternaturally calm. His hearing seemed to sharpen; he thought he could hear the actual rattle of the grains of sand he'd felt under him on the floor of the vehicle as it moved. He'd never felt more alive. Somewhere, in the back of his mind, a still, small voice reminded him how deeply unnatural that was, but there wasn't any part of him left that cared.

The vehicle slowed and he swayed as he could feel it turning. There was a brief pause, then the sound of a door in the front of the vehicle opening. He could hear muffled voices speaking Spanish, a bark of sharp, cruel laughter, but he couldn't understand what was being said. He heard the back door, the one nearest him, being yanked open. A rush of hot, dry air blew over him. Hands clutched at him, dragged him out the back door of the van. He staggered to his feet just as someone yanked the hood from his head.

He was standing outside an enormous metal building, the paint flaking and the metal beneath scoured and pitted by sand-blasting desert winds. There was a pair of large metal roll-up doors in the side of the building. The man who'd pulled off his hood stood behind him.

Another man stood in front of him, about ten feet away, flanked on either side by gunmen holding semi-automatic long guns pointed negligently at the ground. The man in the middle was shorter than Keller, slender, balding, and apparently very pissed off. His ugly scowl looked as if time had etched its lines into his face. He wore black jeans and a white shirt with piping and pearl buttons. There was a black pistol stuck in his waistband.

"Do you know who I am?" the man demanded.

"No," Keller said, "but if I had to guess, I'd say you were Jerico Zavalo."

The man's smile made Keller wish for the scowl. "Correct. And you know why you're here?"

Keller looked him in the eye. "Because whoever was back at the house suckered you into doing his dirty work for him."

Zavalo laughed. "You're wrong. This is something that has needed to be done for some time. For business, and" — the smile grew wider and nastier — "for pleasure, I admit."

"I didn't kill your brother," Keller said. "Last I heard, his boss did that because your brother double-crossed him."

The scowl was back. "None of that would have happened had you and your bitch not stuck your noses into my family's business."

"I was just trying to help out a friend."

"Yes. A friend. I know all about him. The one who's run to Colombia with your woman."

"She's not my woman," Keller said. "She's my friend's wife."

The man stepped closer. "I'm currently talking with some of the people I know down there. They're very touchy about outsiders operating on their territory, but I think they'll do me a favor and let me do this one little thing. I'm just sorry you won't be alive to see what I will do to your friend, the woman he took from you, and his two brats when I'm allowed to go get them." The smile was back. "It's enough for you to know I'll make sure it takes each of them weeks to die. One by one. While the others watch. And I will let them know, every minute of every day of those long, long weeks, that their suffering is entirely your fault."

A red mist seemed to drop across Keller's vision, blurring his view of the faces around him. His wrists strained against the zip cuffs as his hands clenched and unclenched with the irresistible impulse to wrap themselves around Zavalo's neck. "I'm going to kill you, Zavalo." His voice came out in a low growl. "With my bare hands if I have to."

Zavalo's response was to turn his back and wave carelessly over his shoulder at Keller. "Bring him."

The man behind him put a beefy hand on Keller's neck and propelled him forward toward the metal doors, walking behind Zavalo and the gunmen who'd fallen in behind him. As the group approached the metal doors, the one on the right rolled up. A man was standing there, dressed in a Tyvek hazmat suit. A gas mask dangled from one hand. The baggy suit concealed the lines of his body, but Keller could see he was a small man. He had dark hair, a wispy moustache, and eyes deader than a mannequin's. He looked Keller up and down as if measuring him before saying something to Zavalo in Spanish.

"Yes," Zavalo said and glanced back at Keller. "This is the man. And speak English. I want him to hear this."

The man in the hazmat suit looked impatient. "He still alive," he said in heavily accented English.

"Yes," Zavalo said.

The man shook his head. "I take care of bodies. You bring the body to me. Do the…you know…someplace else, where I'm not a witness."

"No," Zavalo said. "We put him in alive."

The Soupmaker looked exasperated. "You joking, right? You put a man into the chemicals alive, he thrash around. Scream. Stuff goes everywhere. All over you"—he gestured at the gunmen—"all over them. Everybody gets burned."

Zavalo looked frustrated. "Show me where you do this."

The Soupmaker sighed and muttered something under his breath. He turned and started to walk back into the warehouse. As he did, Zavalo drew the gun from his waistband and shot the Soupmaker in the back of the head. He staggered forward a few steps then fell to the concrete floor of the warehouse. There was a sickening crack as his face hit the floor.

"We do this my way," Zavalo said to the dead man. He turned to the three gunmen around him, who were staring at the corpse in shock. "Bring him," he snapped. He turned to the one who appeared to be the youngest. "Get the camera out of the truck," he said, before heading into the dimness of the warehouse.

Inside was a cavernous space, lit only by the sunlight coming through the opened rollup door. Keller could see blue plastic drums stacked at the back of the room. Each one had a yellow label with a skull and crossbones on it. In the dimness, he could barely make out the large letters on the label: CAUSTIC SODA. POISON. CAN CAUSE BURNS. In the center of the room was a large, old-fashioned claw-foot bathtub with one of the blue plastic drums sitting next to it. Keller caught a whiff of what smelled like drain cleaner. As the two gunmen dragged him forward, he could see the tub was half filled with milky white liquid.

"Look," Zavalo said, "your bath is ready." He chuckled at his own joke before turning to Keller. "Since you say you're going to kill me with your own hands, Señor Keller, maybe we should start with them." He turned to the gunmen on either side of Keller. "Stick his hands in first. Burn them off. Down to the bone."

The men looked at each other uncertainly. "Boss," one of them said. "What that guy said…about getting that stuff on us…"

Zavalo still had the pistol in his hand. He swiveled it around to point it at the man who'd spoken. "You want to disrespect me, too? Like that *cabron* lying on the floor over there?"

The gunman who'd spoken raised his hands. "No, boss, we know better. Just..." He looked over at the dead Soupmaker. "Can I at least get his gloves?"

Zavalo considered a moment, then nodded. "Be quick." He turned to the man standing next to Keller. "Cut his hands loose."

This one didn't hesitate. He produced a short, wicked-looking knife and sawed through Keller's zip cuffs. When they parted, the rush of blood back into his hands made them throb. He rubbed first one wrist, then the other. That seemed to amuse Zavalo. "Saying goodbye to them, Keller?"

"You know what, Zavalo?" Keller said. "Fuck you, and fuck your mother."

Zavalo's face grew dark with blood at that most ultimate of Latin insults. He raised the pistol, then relaxed. "I get it. You hope to get me to execute you quickly." He smiled. "It won't go that easily, Keller. You'll beg me for death before it's done, and people will know what it means to interfere in my family's business. Kiko," he said to the younger man, who was coming up with a small video camera, "make sure you get him begging." He turned to the gunman who'd stripped the gloves from the dead Soupmaker. "And you be sure that you—"

At that moment, Keller stepped forward, put one foot on the lip of the tub, and stepped up, propelling himself upward and shoving down as hard as he could with his right leg. The tub took his weight for a moment, then toppled over, the caustic mix of water and lye spilling out across the warehouse floor. Keller's other foot caught the far lip of the tub and he sprung forward, but he'd misjudged the leap and he went crashing to the ground on his face.

He heard a scream as the toxic brew spread across the floor toward the three gunmen, followed by a torrent of Spanish cursing from Zavalo. Keller levered himself up on his arms and got to his feet. He could see the three gunmen, one gloved, one holding only the video camera, backpedaling frantically away. The only man who still had his gun was turning to flee. Zavalo was cursing at them, his mind off Keller for a split second, and that was all he needed. He charged forward, legs propelling him with the strength that comes from rage and desperation.

Zavalo turned back to meet him a second too late. Keller was already upon Zavalo as he tried to bring his pistol to bear. He bent his knees slightly and then leaped back up, the motion providing extra force as he drove the heel of his hand up under Zavalo's chin. Zavalo's head snapped back and he gave a muffled cry of shock and pain as his lower teeth slammed into his upper ones and the muscles of his neck hyperextended.

It wasn't enough to satisfy the black desire that was consuming Keller. The only thing that would feed it was to inflict pain, pain, and more pain. He pulled his hand back and drove his fist into Zavalo's gut as hard as he could. The breath went out of Zavalo and he started to double over. As he did, Keller clenched his hands together in a double fist and hammered down as hard as he could on the base of Zavalo's skull.

This time, there was no outcry. Zavalo fell to his knees, stunned. The gun began to slip from his hand and Keller snatched it away, stepped back, and let him fall. He looked up to see the gunman who'd kept his weapon standing in the door. He'd apparently reconsidered trying to flee and was raising his gun to aim it at Keller. Keller shot him, the bullet striking him in the forehead and blowing a red mist out of the back of his skull. He dropped limply to the concrete floor of the warehouse, thrashing and convulsing.

Keller's mind flashed back to Alford's death, the look on her face as she died, and he hesitated, abruptly sickened and unsure. A sudden clatter snapped him out of it. He swiveled to see the man with the gloves, clumsily scrambling to pick up his own weapon from where he'd leaned it against the wall of the warehouse. A shot in the back shattered his spine and he fell to his knees. A second one pierced his heart and left him lying face-down on the floor. That left only the youngest of the gunmen, the one holding the video camera. He was backing away, holding the camera in his right hand, his eyes wide and shocked at the carnage in the room. Keller remembered the name Zavalo had called him by. "Kiko," he said in a flat, terrifyingly calm voice.

The young man looked up, his eyes wide.

"Watch what's about to happen," Keller said. "Record it. And take the recording back to whoever takes the place of this piece of shit. Let them know that I have only one demand." He looked at the camera held loosely in Kiko's hand. "No, I'll tell you what. Start recording now."

"Wh…what?" the young man said.

"Turn the fucking camera on," Keller said in that same calm voice. "And point it at my face. Then point it at whatever I tell you to. Or I'll gut shoot you, leave you to bleed out alone in this shit hole, and record it myself."

Slowly, as if he couldn't believe what he was doing, Kiko raised the camera and pointed it at Keller.

"Is it on?" Keller said. "Because I'm not in the fucking mood to repeat myself."

"*Sí*," the former gunman said. "It's on."

Keller looked into the blank void of the camera lens. "My name is Jack Keller. I only have one demand. That is that you leave me the fuck alone. Me, and the following people. Leonardo Santiago Rodriguez, sometimes known as Oscar Sanchez. His wife, Angela. His two sons, Ruben and Edgar. Dr. Lucas Berry. And…" He took a deep breath, considering if he should even name her. "Marie Jones of Portland, Oregon, and her son, Ben. Oh, her father, Frank, too. Because if you don't…." He walked over to where Zavalo was stirring, his eyes opening but unfocused. "This is what I'm capable of." He grabbed Zavalo by the back of the collar and dragged him toward the shallow pool of caustic liquid that was slowly spreading out in a long fan before the upended bathtub. As Zavalo began to struggle, Keller shoved him forward, then kicked him in the ass so that he landed face down in the corrosive puddle.

"SHIT!" Zavalo cried out as he tried to get to his hands and knees, shouting again in wordless agony as the chemicals burned the palms of his hands. As he tried to stagger to his feet, Keller stepped behind the blue drum full of the rest of the Soupmaker's "recipe" and kicked it over onto Zavalo. He was screaming before the chemicals hit him, but as they began to eat into the exposed flesh of his hands and face, the howls of torment rose to an excruciating level. Keller saw movement out of the corner of his eye. Kiko had lowered the camera and was backing away, his eyes huge with fear and disgust. He was crossing himself with his free hand.

"RECORD IT!" Keller bellowed, and punctuated the command with a shot that zipped by the terrified gunman's head.

Kiko sobbed with terror, but he raised the camera and pointed it at Zavalo, who was still trying to rise to his feet. The skin of his face and upper chest was a shocking red, already beginning to blister and peel. His shrieks were beyond anything that should have been coming from a human throat. His eyes were twin pools of agony and madness. He made as if to lurch toward Keller. Keller shot him in the upper right thigh. Zavalo screamed again and collapsed back into the liquid. It was beginning to burn through his clothes now to find the unprotected skin beneath. He started thrashing like a landed fish, the screams coming out now as keening whines. Keller shot him again in the other leg. He looked up at Kiko. The young man was trembling, but keeping the video camera fixed on Zavalo's death throes. Suddenly, he dropped the camera, grabbed his stomach, and vomited all over the floor. He fell to his knees weeping. "*Por favor*," he sobbed. "*Por favor*. Make it stop. Please. Make it stop."

"Whatever you say," Keller said. He walked over to Zavalo, still flopping and writhing like a caterpillar on a griddle, and shot him in the head. The man's back arched one more time in a final spasm, then he lay still. Smoke was rising from the burned and bubbling skin, and the fumes were making Keller's eyes water and burning his throat. He stepped out of the puddle, noticing that his boots were beginning to smoke as well. He got to the dry concrete and walked over to Kiko, who was bawling like a child. "What size shoes do you wear?" He bent over and began unlacing one boot with his free hand.

Kiko looked up, his eyes streaming and his nose running snot. There was vomit drying on his chin. "*Qué?*" he asked.

Keller unlaced the other boot, then stood up. "Your shoes. What size?"

The gunman was baffled by the question. "Ten. Why?"

Keller grimaced. "Too small." He stood on one leg and pulled a boot off, then switched the gun to his other hand and repeated the process. He glanced at the bottoms and saw the leather eaten away. He grimaced. "Damn. I've had these for years, too." He nodded toward the dead gunman with the gloves. He looked bigger than Kiko. "Go get me his boots."

"Wh-what?"

Keller raised his gun and spoke slowly, as if to a stupid child. "That man's boots. Go get them and bring them to me. And if he's got the key to any vehicles outside, bring me those, too."

Kiko still looked stunned, but he started to rise. "No," Keller said. "Crawl over there. I don't want you getting the idea to do anything stupid. And if I see you so much as look at that weapon he was trying to get, I'll shoot you in the spine. Best-case scenario, you'll spend the rest of your life in a wheelchair, shitting into a little bag. Now MOVE!" The last word was snapped out like a drill sergeant's command and it seemed to galvanize Kiko. He got to his hands and knees and scuttled over to the dead man.

Keller took a deep breath and took stock. The adrenaline was wearing off and he felt a sick twisting in his stomach. *What have I turned into?*

Another voice answered him, a darker one he'd been trying to silence all his life. *You haven't turned into anything. You are what you've always been. A killer.* He no longer had the strength or conviction to argue.

Kiko came back, awkwardly trying to hold onto the boots with one hand and the keys in the other as he scuttled over on his hands and knees. Finally, he rose up and walked on his knees, looking at Keller like a whipped dog. He held the boots out. "Please," he said in a small voice. "Don't kill me."

Keller took the boots. "You were about to record it while that sick fucking bastard over there dissolved me in acid an inch at a time. Give me one good reason why I shouldn't shoot you. Or why I shouldn't whip up another batch of that hell-brew and pour it down your fucking throat."

Kiko's voice was shaking. "If you do that, there'll be no one to deliver your message."

Keller nodded. "Good answer." He held out his hands. "Keys." Still trembling, Kiko handed them over. "What vehicle are these to?" Keller asked.

"Black Escalade," Kiko said. His face brightened as if he'd just remembered some good news. "And there's money in it, too," he said with an ingratiating smile. "The payment Zavalo was going to give the Soupmaker."

"How much?"

Kiko shook his head. "I don't know. A lot."

Keller looked over at the dead Soupmaker. "Why'd he shoot the guy?"

Kiko shrugged. "He talked back. You don't do that to Jerico Zavalo." He looked at the body where it still lay. "Didn't," he amended.

"Well, you go back and give my message to whoever ends up oozing his way into the top seat now. I don't want your business, I don't want your money, except what I'm taking with me. Just leave me alone. And don't try to get to me through any of my friends. Or I'll be back. Believe me, none of us wants that."

Kiko nodded rapidly. "I sure don't."

"Stay there. Where you are. On your knees. Count to one thousand, then go. If you try to follow me, I'll kill you. Understand?"

"*Sí*," Kiko said. "I understand."

CHAPTER
TWENTY-THREE

KELLER COULD HEAR THE YOUNG man counting in Spanish as he gathered up the weapons the dead men had dropped and walked outside. The black Escalade was there as promised, alongside the van they'd brought Keller in and a rusted and dented panel truck that must have belonged to the Soupmaker. Keller propped the rifles in the passenger side of the Escalade. When he looked in the back seat, he saw an aluminum case. It wasn't locked. When he popped it open, he found stacks of hundreds, banded together. He thought back to the night when he'd first met Oscar Sanchez, the night when the man who would become his best friend was holding a gun on him. "Right now, I am a man with a bag of money and a gun," Oscar had said. "Soon I will have a big truck. It is the American Dream, no?"

It seemed like a million years ago. Now he had all those things for himself, but he realized that the troubled years between then and now had stripped everyone away from him. Everyone and everything.

He was alone and empty, back where he always seemed to land. But someone had put him there. He'd been, if not totally content, at least at rest for the first time in years. This time, he hadn't been seeking trouble. Trouble had come to him, and it had torn his life apart, leaving a trail of dead bodies in his wake.

He thought of Julianne. She'd loved him, and though he hadn't loved her back, he had felt real affection for her. He might have come to love her, but his troubles had come to her first. Now she was gone, dying broken and in agony. On his account.

You bring death, Harland had said, *and Hell follows with you.*

Fine, then, he thought savagely. *Death and Hell. So let's fucking bring it.* He knew now what he needed to do. He meant to find the person responsible for fucking with him, and he meant to extract every last ounce of payment from them.

What had made Keller such a successful hunter of human beings had been his utter relentlessness, his unfailing and pitiless dedication to the chase, ending only when he'd brought his quarry to ground. Once again, there were people out there who he needed to find. And when he did, he meant to hold them responsible for the deaths they'd caused. Unlike his former life, however, he wouldn't be hauling them back to face their day in court. Despite the fact that he'd worked in the justice system, at least the edges of it, when he'd done bail recovery, he'd never really believed in it. The same people kept going through it. Nothing seemed to change, and no one seemed to get any better. And he had no faith that the kind of people who could put him on a national no-fly list would ever see a day of jail time if they were caught. There would be only one form of justice for these people.

He snapped out of his reverie and looked at the money again. If each of those bundles contained, as he suspected, a thousand dollars, then there was at least twenty-five thousand in the case. Making "soup" was apparently a lucrative business. Or had been. He stuffed one of the rolls of bills in his pocket and snapped the case shut. He slid behind the wheel of the big SUV and cranked the engine. It came alive with a roar that quickly subsided to a purring rumble.

The eight-inch glass screen in the dashboard baffled Keller for a moment, but after a bit of experimentation, he found the navigation system. He was just south of the border, east of Nogales. A second thought had him scanning through the vehicle's memory. There. There was a route, clearly marked, through the rough terrain that led across the border and back into Arizona. *Bet the immigration and DEA would give a lot for that info,* Keller thought. Then it occurred to him that they may already have known it. There was no way of knowing who might be in the pocket of Jerico Zavalo or any of the other *narcos.* Here on the border, his best bet was to stay clear of everyone.

He didn't have a plan as he started onto the rough, cracked pavement of the desert highway, but as the miles rolled out beneath him, he began to ponder what he had to do. Whoever the people were who'd been trying to get him locked up, then killed, they somehow stood in opposition to the man claiming to be his father. That man would know who they were. He would probably know where to find them. He had no love and no trust for the old man; just the opposite, in fact. But the answers he needed lay with him. And Keller had something the old man wanted. Himself. The old man wanted to see his "son"; well, Keller had the time and no commitments other than vengeance. He may not trust the old bastard, but he could surely use him. But only if he could get there before Trammell died. The thought made him frown. He'd need to call as soon as he was somewhere with a decent signal. He continued to head north.

CHAPTER
TWENTY-FOUR

MADDOX COULD SEE AS HE entered the sickroom that it was one of Trammell's bad days, the kind he always thought might be the last. The old man lay in the hospital bed he'd had moved into the sunroom, the natural light only serving to make him seem more pale. The cancer had melted away fat, then muscle, seemingly leaving nothing behind but baggy, wrinkled, nearly translucent skin lying slackly over bone that seemed ready to snap at too hard a touch. His breath came in long, wet, shuddering snores.

Maddox hated to wake him. He got so little rest these days as the agony stabbed and prodded him. Trammell had told Maddox he fully expected to go to Hell for some of the things he'd done, and now maybe the devils were getting an early start. It had been the kind of dark joke his old mentor had been fond of. Maddox, ever the faithful mentee, had usually laughed along, but that time he couldn't bring himself to even fake a laugh. He didn't believe in Hell anyway. From what he'd seen on Earth, there was no need.

Maddox had been walking as softly as he could into Trammell's room, but the old man's eyes snapped open, the piercing gaze fixing Maddox like a prison camp spotlight. Maddox froze. Trammell took a long, wheezing inhalation that ended in a gurgling cough. He tried to push himself to a sitting position with arms like twigs, then fell back with a groan. He looked up at the ceiling, panting as if he'd just run the hundred-meter dash. When he'd caught his breath, the old man lay there wheezing for a moment before he spoke.

"You got a face screwed up tight as a cat's ass," he said, the words coming out in a grating rasp. "What's the problem?"

"I'm afraid it's bad news, sir," Maddox said. "About Keller."

Trammell looked up at the ceiling, then said, with a total lack of affect, "Is he dead?"

"No, sir. He was released. Then, apparently, he went home with his lawyer."

Trammell turned his head to regard Maddox with the most interest he'd seen in a while. "I thought you told me his lawyer was a woman."

"Yes, sir."

Trammell let out a horrible strangled sound that could have been a chuckle. "Don't tell me he's fucking his lawyer."

"Doubtful, sir. She's married. To another woman."

"Huh." Trammell swallowed, with difficulty. "So what happened?"

"The lawyer, her wife, and two servants were found dead. Shot. Keller is missing."

Trammell closed his eyes. "And I suppose he's blamed for the killings."

"Yes, sir."

"Even though that makes no sense."

Maddox hesitated. "His prints were found on the murder weapons."

Trammell opened his eyes. "Weapons. Plural."

"Yes, sir."

"And that makes sense to the local police."

"I can't speak to that, sir. All I know is that a BOLO has been put out for Mr. Keller."

The man in the bed was silent, his eyes fixed in the ceiling. After a long pause, he spoke. "Of course. Blame the crazy, violent, Gulf War vet for all the local murders, then close the files. Put out a BOLO that will never pan out because the person they've accused is dead. Taken off by the real killers and buried in a desert somewhere. It becomes a cold case, but no one ever looks into it again. Very nice." He struggled again and this time he did sit up. "Get me Kathryn Shea on the phone."

"Sir," Maddox said, "it's time for your medicine—"

"Fuck my medicine," Trammell rasped. "I want that cunt on the phone. I want her to know what I'm going to do to her."

Maddox pulled out his cell phone and paged through the contacts, looking for Kathryn Shea's private number. He had a bad feeling about what was about to happen, but he had followed orders all his life, many of them coming from the man in the hospital bed. He wasn't inclined to stop now. He found the number and began to dial.

"Get the film," Trammell said. "Get it ready for release."

"Yes, sir," Maddox said. He'd finished dialing the number and was preparing to hit "send" when the phone vibrated in his hands. He looked at the screen. There was an incoming call. "Sir," he said. He didn't recognize the number, but the area code seemed familiar. "We're getting a call. I think it's from the area where Keller disappeared."

The old man smiled. "Take it."

Maddox pushed the "answer" button. "Hello?"

"Maddox," Jack Keller said. "Let me talk to Trammell."

KELLER SAT IN THE COOL of the air-conditioned SUV at the far edge of an expansive concrete parking lot, the pavement showing long cracks where it had fractured under the relentless desert sun. Across the parking lot, a huge bright yellow sign stretched across the frontage of a low-slung brick building. Giant dark-blue letters enticed visitors: THE THING? Keller had seen the signs for miles along the desert highways, advertising the mysteries of the cheap roadside attraction. There were other signs for souvenirs, T-shirts, and cheap jewelry, but it was the enigma of whatever lay at the heart of the advertised "museum" that was supposed to bring in the tourists. MYSTERY OF THE DESERT, the signs had promised. Keller didn't have time for that kind of mystery.

The man on the other end sounded surprised to hear Keller's voice. "Jack. This is unexpected."

"Yeah, Maddox. I'll bet. Let me talk to him."

"Okay," Maddox said. "Let me just say first, though, that we're glad you're—"

"Save it," Keller snapped. "Put the old man on."

There was a brief silence. Keller wondered if he'd gone too far, if he'd finally worn out Maddox's patience. Finally, a different voice came through the phone. "Jack." It was a weak, quavering voice, but tight with strain.

"Mr. Trammell," Jack began.

"I thought they'd murdered you," the old man interrupted. "I thought you were dead. But you escaped." There was a wet, gurgling chuckle. "You'll have to tell me how you did that."

"We'll sit around and swap stories by the campfire," Keller said. "But first you need to tell me who's trying to kill me. Your lapdog shows up with a DVD and suddenly…" Keller took a moment to swallow past the lump that had suddenly appeared in his throat. "You need to tell me what's going on that was worth killing an innocent girl for. And you need to tell me who was responsible. "

"Jack," the old man said, "what I sent you was only a teaser. A preview to get you interested. What I have waiting to put into your hands will be real power. Real influence." The last word trailed off into a spasm of coughing.

Keller had to force the next words out through clenched teeth. "That 'teaser' drew down a shit storm on me and someone I cared about, you manipulative bastard. Now she's dead, along with a few other innocent people that didn't do anything but try to help me. Oh, and I'm apparently being blamed for their deaths. Now I want to know what the fuck is going on, and why I'm caught in the middle of it."

"I really wish you'd call me Father," Trammel said. There was a note of pleading in the cracked voice.

Keller wasn't moved. "You really think you've earned that?"

The voice grew harder. "Maybe that's the price for what you need."

Keller felt the black tide rising in him again. He spoke before he could consider the words. "Everything is a goddamn trade with you, isn't it, you son of a bitch? Well, die soon, motherfucker, and I hope you die alone." He closed the connection and threw the phone into the floorboard of the truck. He grabbed the steering wheel as tightly as he could, put his forehead against the black plastic, and screamed. He put all of his rage, fear, and frustration into that scream.

When he looked up, he saw a boy standing across the parking lot, staring at him. The kid was about twelve or thirteen years old, dressed in jeans and a new crisp yellow T-shirt that had THE THING? printed on it in the same lurid bright blue lettering as the sign on the museum. He was standing by a dust-covered blue minivan next to the gas pumps and looking goggle-eyed at Keller screaming in the front seat of the truck. An older man who must have been the boy's father was filling the tank, and a harried-looking woman who was obviously the mother of the family was shouting something at a small girl in a white sundress who was running around in circles on the sun-baked concrete, shrieking at the top of her tiny lungs.

Keller watched the little girl for a moment, then looked back at the boy. He was still looking at Keller. As the little girl's orbit around the minivan intersected the boy's position, he scooped her up, still hollering, and put her in the back seat of the minivan, his eyes wide with terror but resolute, never leaving the truck.

So we're back to this, Keller thought. *The place where I scare children.* He was suddenly overcome with the desire to be somewhere, anywhere, other than this sun-hammered roadside gimcrack stand where normal people congregated. He broke eye contact with the kid as he cranked the engine and headed out of the parking lot. He didn't know where he was going. If he went back to Arizona, he'd be slammed back into jail, where he'd be a sitting duck. He wasn't going to deal with Trammell. He was just going to have to try to find out what he needed to know on his own. He thought of the money in the back seat. That much cash could allow him to live off the grid for a while. But he needed a place to lie up and figure out his next move. With no particular plan in mind, he got onto the first highway he found that headed east.

Toward the place he'd once called home.

CHAPTER TWENTY-FIVE

K ATHRYN SHEA WAS ON FIRE.

She stood at the podium, in front of a thousand cheering supporters, getting to the part of the speech that always brought the audience to its feet—the part about her father.

"My father," she said, her voice booming out across the cavernous space, "spent his life, from his young manhood on, defending this country and what it stands for." Applause rippled through the crowd and she paused to let it crest and die back. "He never once backed down from a fight. Never surrendered a principle." Her voice rose. "And he never, ever quit until he'd done what he believed in." More applause, this time louder and more sustained. She dropped her voice to a near whisper, only audible because of the amplification. "He was taken from us too soon." A hush fell over the room, the sudden quietness in her voice causing all ears to have to strain to pick up what she was saying over the click and whirr of the cameras. "Too soon," she said in that same quiet voice.

Cordell, standing in the curtained area alongside the stage, could see some of the members of the audience lean forward as if to hear better. *She's got them eating out of the palm of her hand*, he thought. *Timing, dynamics...she's a natural.* He was feeling better and better about this campaign.

"His work was too important to let it go unfinished. Too important to this great Commonwealth we all love, and too important to this country that is the last, best hope of mankind. We are in one of our darkest hours, under attack from all sides...and from within." She was rising to the climax, her voice picking up speed and volume. The applause began to ripple just underneath her clear, strong voice as she reached it. "And that, my fellow Virginians, is why I am running for the United! States! Senate!"

The applause exploded. The crowd rose to its feet, whistling and stomping. Cordell nodded his satisfaction. The cheering went on and on, the flashes from the cameras stuttering and strobing like lightning. Cordell felt his phone buzzing in the pocket of his suit jacket. He pulled it out and stepped further behind the curtain, sticking a finger in one ear to blot out the sound and putting the phone to the other one. "Hello."

"Just wanted you to know that our competitor was declared bankrupt this morning."

Cordell let out a deep breath. "Were there any problems?"

"Some liabilities were incurred, but they're going to fall on him."

Cordell gritted his teeth. "Are you sure?"

"Yeah," Riddle said. "I'm sure." He chuckled. "You could say our competitor's entire portfolio has been liquidated."

Cordell didn't get the joke, but he was one thousand percent sure he didn't want to. He resolved never to use Riddle again. The former DEA operative had spent so much time in "wet work" that he'd lost understanding of just how much dead bodies could complicate a situation.

"Good work," he said. *And you'll never see any more from me.*

"Thanks. Now about payment."

"You'll get it through the usual channels," Cordell snapped. "And don't call this number again." He cut the connection before Riddle could say anything else. He could hear Kathryn finishing up, telling the rapt crowd about the campaign website that had just gone up. Cordell took a second to check on his smartphone. Yes, just as promised, SheaforAmerica.com was up and running, as were the campaign Twitter and Facebook accounts. Staffers were busily putting out messages purporting to be from the candidate herself. All was going according to plan.

RIDDLE PUT THE PHONE BACK into the pocket of his leather jacket and took a sip of his coffee. He looked out the window of the diner where he'd just had breakfast and saw only desert stretching away from him. He figured they'd be just about done with Keller by now. It all depended on just how long Jerico Zavalo intended to take in exacting his revenge.

He didn't take Cordell's abrupt dismissal personally. He knew that people like Cordell had as little contact with people like him as possible. It was safer that way, and any residual hurt feelings he might be tempted to have could be assuaged by the amount of money he was about to see arrive in a shell bank account before he shifted it someplace safe and closed the account. The cheap cell phone in his pocket would also soon be gone, ground up in an industrial compactor. Everything to connect him with Cordell and his mysterious employer would be gone. He'd be like a ghost.

The phone buzzed in his pocket again. He pulled it out and frowned as he looked at the number. He put the phone to his ear. "Yes?" Then he was forced to hold the phone a few inches away as a blast of rapid-fire, angry Spanish assailed his ears. "Wait," he said, but that only seemed to make the person on the other end angrier. When he got a break,

Riddle jumped in. "So tell me how the fuck this is *my* fault?" There was a pause, then a more subdued, but still furious reply. "Look," Riddle snapped. "He was your problem once I delivered him. Anything after that is on you."

Suddenly recalling he was in public, he looked around. The waitress was talking with the cook through the kitchen pass-through and no one else seemed to be taking any notice. He broke the connection anyway. *Shit*, he thought. This was bad. Keller had escaped, apparently killing Jerico Zavalo and three of his men. The cartel was in an uproar. Heads were going to roll, most likely literally, as contenders battled for Zavalo's position.

Riddle didn't see how he could get blamed for Zavalo's ineptitude, but some of these *narcos* weren't famed for logical thinking, and others would be looking for a scapegoat. He was the one who'd brought the tiger to the party, and he might get some of the blame for the damage caused when the beast got out. Then there was the fact that he'd failed in the mission Cordell had given him.

Riddle took a sip of his coffee, keeping his face expressionless. He needed to get out in front of this. He had to tell Cordell that the situation had gone sideways, but he'd rather do it when he'd already rectified the problem. Keller's death at his hands might placate the Mexicans as well. He grimaced. First, he had to find Keller. It would be difficult to do; according to the man on the phone, Keller had taken enough folding money to go to ground for a while. But there was no one who couldn't be found. He'd proved it himself.

He called for the check.

CHAPTER TWENTY-SIX

"I SCREWED THAT UP, DIDN'T I, John?"

Maddox hesitated, but the rare and unexpected intimacy of his first name invited honesty. "You may have pushed too fast, sir."

Trammell coughed, the effort causing his face to screw up in agony. When he was done, he lay gasping for a moment. "What will he do now, you think?"

"I don't know, sir. He can't go back to Arizona. He'd be arrested immediately."

The old man nodded almost imperceptibly. "Anything we can do about that?"

"I'll see, sir." There had been a time when Trammell's name and his network might have been able to shut things like that down with a phone call, but the power of both had waned with his health.

"So where would he go?"

Maddox answered immediately. "He might go back to Wilmington.

It was home to him for a lot of years."

"He had a home before that," Trammell said. "Charleston."

"Yes, sir."

"That's where he'll go first. Check there."

"Yes, sir."

Trammell's eyes narrowed to near slits, the way Maddox had seen him do a thousand times when he was strategizing. "Whoever Kathryn Shea or her people have put on this will probably figure that out as well. Sooner rather than later."

"Probably."

Trammell grimaced. "Can we protect my son, John?"

Maddox hated what he had to say. "Not directly, sir. We don't have the reach we used to. And he won't talk to us."

Trammell turned his head to look at the man who'd served him for decades. "My son hates me."

Maddox was glad that it wasn't a question, so he didn't have to answer it honestly. Trammell turned his eyes back to the ceiling. "We still have the film," Maddox said.

"Should we release it now? Teach them a lesson?"

Maddox pondered for a moment. "A deterrent like that is a one-time thing. Not for teaching lessons. For complete destruction. A nuclear bomb's usefulness ends when it's dropped."

Trammell laughed. "Well put, John. Very well put. So there'd be no point in releasing it now, unless all we wanted was revenge. Not that I have anything against revenge, mind you. Quite satisfying."

"Yes, sir."

"Do Kathryn's people know that Jack Keller is still alive?"

"I don't know, sir. I'm sure Ms. Shea would deny any knowledge of what you're talking about."

"Of course." Trammell thought for a moment. "Who's her chief of staff?"

"A man named Frederick Cordell. Career political operative." He said the last words with an expression that looked as if someone had placed something foul on his tongue.

Trammell's lined face convulsed in disgust. "Cordell. I know him. Wormy little bastard. I can't believe she trusts him."

"He's reportedly very good at what he does, sir."

"What he does, John...what he and people like him have done for years, is get people like you and me killed. Or indicted for their crimes. While he and his cronies walk away whistling and move on to the next cluster-fuck." He shook his head. "Set up a meeting with Cordell. And have the film ready to show."

"Sir?"

"I don't know that Kathryn has told him what we have on her late and sainted father. I want him to see it. I want him to see what they'll have to deal with if they don't leave my son alone."

"Do you think that's wise, sir? Showing him what we have? It may give him a chance to prepare for the damage the film might do. Mitigate it somehow."

"He could try. But set up the meeting. And put all the sharp objects in the house out of my reach, so I'm not tempted to stick a knife in that son of a bitch's neck."

"Yes, sir."

THE PICTURE WAS JUMPY BUT clear, the colors vivid. The jungle was bright green, the flames deep rich orange mixed with the black of smoke, and the blood a brilliant red. There was a lot of blood.

Soldiers in '70s-era American uniforms moved through the village, guns at the ready. Some carried hastily made torches of gasoline-soaked rags wrapped around branches then set alight. Here and there they applied the torches to the grass huts, which caught immediately and began to burn. Other soldiers herded weeping women and screaming children to a place in the center of the village where bodies already lay face down, in a neat line. There was no sound on the film. None was needed.

The women and children were forced to their knees before the line of bodies. One soldier grabbed a handful of an old woman's gray hair and yanked her head up, forcing her to look at the dead laid out in front of her. Her toothless mouth gaped in a silent scream and she looked up at the man holding her hair, clasping her hands together in front of her chest as if praying. He was shouting something at her, and the cameraman zoomed in to catch his face, contorted in rage. Then the picture pulled back to a wide shot and panned to the right.

Two men walked into the frame. One was tall, with close-cropped blond hair and a red face already becoming jowly. He was dressed in an American uniform with lieutenant's bars glittering on the shoulder.

"First Lieutenant Michael Shea," Trammell said from where he sat slumped in his wheelchair next to the whirring projector. "Later Congressman Shea, later Senator—"

"I know who he is," Cordell snapped. He was seated in a chair positioned in front of the screen. "I suppose the other fellow is you."

"Yes." Trammell's voice sounded almost wistful. "Mike was Regular Army at the time, but the Agency already had its eye on him. I was…well, there wasn't actually a name yet for what I was doing. That came later." He chuckled. "No one was making movies about us then."

The man walking beside Shea—Trammell—was slender and wiry where Shea was broad and fleshy. Trammell wore green fatigue pants, Army jump boots, and a green boonie hat pulled down over his eyes. He had bandoliers of ammunition crossing his chest and he carried a black submachine gun that was different from the M-16 rifles carried by the soldiers. He said something to Shea, who turned and yelled something to the soldiers. One of them snatched a young woman up from the line of kneeling people and hauled her over to stand in front of Shea. He pulled a black pistol out of the holster on his hip and held it under the woman's chin. He shouted into her face, obviously demanding some sort of information.

"He's asking where the young men of the village were," Trammell said. "The unit we were shadowing had just been hit hard by Viet Cong. It was inconceivable that these people didn't know where they were. And let's just say tempers were running high."

Either the woman didn't have any information, or more likely just didn't understand what the angry American was yelling at her. Trammell hung back, but the cameraman caught the smile on his face. It was a grim rictus, devoid of humor or mercy. He took another step back as Shea pulled the trigger. The young woman's head snapped back, the bright red blood arcing through the air. The line of kneeling people began to wail, their mouths dark and wide in soundless anguish.

Trammell moved forward, said something else to Shea, then his eyes turned toward the camera. He shouted something as the lens zeroed in on him and caught his face. Then it zoomed back to encompass both men, headed toward the camera. The picture jiggled as the still-unknown cameraman began to move backwards away from the two men advancing on him. Shea raised the pistol. Suddenly, the view arced upwards, until it was pointed straight up into the sky. After a second, the camera fell over, and all that could be seen was the tall, bright green grass. Then the screen went dark.

"The cameraman," Trammell's gravelly voice came out of the darkness, "was named Remy Duplassis. He was a French stringer for Reuters. He'd heard rumors of some sort of firefight going on a few klicks from where he was." Trammell coughed painfully. "He should have stayed where he was."

"The film is faked," Cordell said. "It's easy to do."

"I could have experts test it. Determine its authenticity. Oh, wait, I already have."

"Experts can be bought. Besides, all of this was, what, forty years ago?" Cordell's voice sounded weak, even to himself.

"Forty-six. I'm sure you'll make all of those arguments, and more, when this comes out. Pity I won't be around to see it. But Kathryn Shea is using her daddy's legacy as the foundation for her whole campaign. How will that go over if it's revealed that her father was a war criminal who murdered not only helpless women, but newsmen? One who could have exposed him? One thing I've learned, those media scumbags get very unhappy when you kill one of their own."

"If he's a war criminal..." Cordell began.

"Then so am I?" Trammell finished for him. "Of course. The difference is, Mr. Cordell, that I've never pretended to be anything else. I've done things over the past forty years that make that look like a Cub Scout meeting. All for my country, of course."

Cordell heard the wheels of the chair on the hardwood floor, approaching from behind him. He turned around. Trammell's gaunt appearance and the dim lighting made him look like an evil spirit, a revenant who'd risen from death and come to extract vengeance. "I have no reputation to lose. All of my commendations and medals are classified so deeply they'll never see daylight. Some of them I got thanks to Mike Shea."

Cordell shifted his chair around to face Trammell. "So why try and destroy his daughter?"

Trammell shrugged. "Shits and giggles. But it doesn't have to happen that way."

"Now we get down to it. Leave Jack Keller alone."

Cordell sighed. "You have this obsession about Kathryn and your son. It's insanity. Whatever problems he has, he brought on himself. He needs to turn himself in." He was startled to see that Trammell was actually smiling. "What?" he said.

"It seems that you, or whoever you retained to kill my son, fucked up. He's alive."

Cordell felt like he'd been punched in the gut, but he tried to keep his face impassive. The look of glee on Trammell's face let him know he was failing. "Didn't expect that, did you, Mr. Cordell?"

"You need to have your medications adjusted," Cordell said, "if you think that Kathryn Shea tried to have your son killed. It's a fantasy. "

Trammell spoke as if he hadn't heard. His voice was subdued as he said, "I feel partially responsible. When I contacted Keller with a video, how was she to know that it wasn't the one she was worried about? But someone"—his eyes narrowed—"probably you, Mr. Cordell, overreacted. Tell me, did you know what was on that film before you came in here today?"

Cordell shook his head. His mouth was dry. "No."

Trammell sighed. "We keep secrets. From everyone. We tell ourselves we need to keep everything on a need-to-know basis. But the people who really need to know, don't. And bad things happen."

Cordell couldn't disagree. He stayed silent.

"So," Trammell said at last. "That's the price. Call off your dog. Whoever he is. Or they are." He raised a hand to stop Cordell's next words. "I know. There is no dog. Call him off anyway. And see what you can do with those charges in Arizona. Because if Jack Keller gets so much as a sprained ankle or skinned knee, copies of that film go to every major news outlet and a few of the minor ones. And the original goes to the one person in the world who most wants to see it and can make use of it. Along with all the information I have about the efforts you've made to suppress it. Efforts that have resulted in the deaths of several people. The person I'm thinking of would be extremely happy to have that."

Cordell was baffled. "Who? Other than Keller?"

Trammell still wore that infuriating smile. "That's something you don't need to know." He turned the wheelchair in a gesture of dismissal. "Mr. Maddox will see you out, Mr. Cordell. Please give my regards to Kathryn."

Cordell stood up as Maddox appeared at his elbow as if by magic. "This way, sir."

Maddox led him through a house as quiet and gloomy as if its occupant was already dead. As they reached the front door, Cordell said, "There is no conspiracy, Maddox."

Maddox didn't answer. He merely opened the door and stood impassively by it, waiting for Cordell to leave. As he stepped out into the sunlight, Maddox spoke. "Safe travels, sir."

Back in his car, Cordell waited to start the engine. He took out his cell phone and dialed the number he had for Riddle. He needed to shut this mess down, and quickly. It had already gotten out of hand. The line rang three times, then Riddle picked up. "Yeah?"

"Keller is alive," Cordell said.

"I know."

"Then you know you screwed the pooch on this one, Riddle. You need to stand down. I won't even ask for the money back. But this operation is over. You need to disappear."

There was a brief pause. Then, "Sorry. That's not an option."

Riddle felt his body go cold. "What did you say?"

"Keller's seen my face. I killed someone he cared about. More than one, I think. *He's* not going to stand down."

"Riddle—"

"Your problem, Mr. Cordell, is that you don't understand men like Jack Keller. Or me, for that matter. He's not going to rest until everyone connected with what happened is in the ground. You know that old line about 'termination with extreme prejudice'? The words 'extreme prejudice' were *invented* for guys like Jack Keller. One of us is going to disappear, all right, but it's not going to be me."

"He doesn't know how to find you—"

Riddle broke in. "Jesus, Cordell, did you even *read* his file? Finding people is *what he does*. He's done it for *years*. And he never, *ever* quits. I'm not taking the chance that he's going to walk up behind me five, six, or ten years from now and put a bullet in me."

Cordell's voice was nearly cracking with hysteria. If Riddle succeeded in murdering Keller, Trammell would release the film. Not only that, he knew about the machinations they'd engaged in against Keller to get it back, not knowing the video he had was not the one they were looking for. The first revelation might destroy Kathryn Shea's candidacy; the second could send them all to federal prison. "Mr. Riddle, I'm ordering you to *stand the fuck down.*"

"Sorry," Riddle said. "No can do." He broke the connection.

Cordell stared at the phone in shock. No one hung up on him. No one. He hit the redial button. The call went immediately to voicemail. The phone was off.

The Hellhound was off the leash.

Cordell resisted the temptation to scream and pound his forehead on the steering wheel. There was a way out of this. There had to be. He didn't know what it was. But he would think of something. Failure was not an option.

Failure is not an option. He'd told himself that on many occasions. He'd told staffers that on many more. Never in his life had he believed it less.

CHAPTER
TWENTY-SEVEN

KELLER WAS HEADED EAST TOWARD Charleston on Highway 17, the Savannah Highway, before he fully came back to himself. His mind had begun registering the old familiar names—Jacksonboro, Parkers Ferry, Osborn—but it wasn't until he saw the sign for Jericho that he was shocked back into full awareness. Everything since the border had passed as if in a dream, the miles passing in the same kind of numb fog that had comprised so much of his life after the war. He understood on a purely intellectual level that that was something he needed to be concerned about, that losing long stretches of his life like that was a symptom of a problem that might need to be addressed. Someday. But not right away. It had less urgency for him than the desire to get back home.

Home. He didn't know why he associated the word with a place where he'd always felt a stranger, an outcast, moving from place to place as his mother obtained and lost one job after another, went from one wrong man to another, until she'd finally despaired — or gotten tired, Keller could never decide which — of hauling him along in her wake and dropped him off with his maternal grandmother.

That last memory gave him the direction he'd been lacking. He saw the exit he'd been looking for without really knowing it and took it. It was late afternoon, but the slowly growing cloud cover darkened the sky until the dusk seemed to have been moved up on the schedule. The back roads that connected to the main highway led him through the swamps and creeks of the South Carolina Low Country and finally to a small white wooden church hemmed in on three sides by thick green vegetation until it seemed like an outpost in some savage jungle. To one side was a low, rusted iron fence surrounding a tiny graveyard, the stones white and stark in the gathering dimness. Keller stopped the truck and looked at the graveyard. He got out slowly, almost unwillingly, squinting up at the threatening sky. He wasn't sure why he had come here, but once here, he had to see it through.

The gate in the fence creaked as he swung it open. It took him a few minutes to find the three graves, side by side. Two names shared a single broad stone, engraved at the top with a pair of angels facing one another, marble heads bowed and wings extended so that they nearly touched. Keller's grandfather had bought the stone years before either he or his wife had died. At least that was the story his grandmother had told him, with the same tightening around the lips that occurred whenever she mentioned any of the many things the old man had done which she regarded as foolish or extravagant. His inscription was on the far left: DANIEL JACKSON KELLER 1919-1970.

Keller had never truly known the old man, except through his grandmother's stories. He had a vague memory of gnarled, rawboned knuckles, the smell of a Marlboro cigarette, kind eyes, yellowed teeth, and the rich smell of whiskey fumes. The tobacco and whiskey had done for his grandpa when Keller was two. The inscription on the right said BEATRICE STONEMAN KELLER, BELOVED WIFE AND

MOTHER, 1922-1991. The woman who'd raised him had died while he was in Iraq, shortly after he'd lost his squad and then his mind. He hadn't made it back for the funeral.

The third grave bore a less ornate stone, a plain slab bought by his grandmother that read simply CHRISTINE KELLER 1948-1990. He stood in front of that one for the longest time, trying to feel some emotion. There was nothing there. His mother had been what his grandmother had called "flighty." She would make plans with her son and break them, or show up then cut the visit short, or sometimes go months without ever calling at all. She was as much given to drink as his grandfather had been, but without the cheery disposition.

Lucas Berry had told him once that it sounded like Keller's mother suffered from bipolar disorder, but by that time, all Keller could do was shrug. He'd learned before reaching his teens to put walls around his feelings where his mother was concerned. It was easier not to get hurt that way. He hadn't even cried when he'd gotten the word that she'd died from mixing alcohol and pain medication. Some said that the death had been a suicide. He'd stood by the grave, building his interior walls higher and stronger as the preacher droned on, and when the funeral was over, he'd turned and walked away. Safe, if not sound.

Keller had grown tall at an early age, with good looks that his grandmother said he'd gotten from her side of the family. He hadn't lacked for companionship, but his reserve and the anger that most people could sense just below the surface kept most people at arm's length. He'd always felt like a stranger in a strange land. On his eighteenth birthday, he'd joined the Army, and his life had changed. There was structure there, and at least some degree of reliability, although what you could mostly rely on was that each day was going to suck in its own particular way. He thrived on it, and the tough physical regimen gave him an outlet for his rage. He learned quickly and rose through the ranks. He'd finally found a place where he felt at home.

Then had come the desert, and a night where fire had come from the sky and killed the men who'd trusted Sergeant Keller to get them home. No one in the Army would admit the obvious: that an American helicopter crew with bad intel and worse leadership had fucked up and fired on a lost American patrol. They'd turned on him, told him he was crazy. The fact that he'd snapped and begun firing at an American helicopter flying nearby hadn't helped. They sent him to the loony bin to await being cast into the outer darkness to fend for himself, or to be sent to prison.

It was there he'd met Lucas Berry, who was the doctor on his ward. Slowly, with infinite patience, he'd gotten Keller to open up, to put himself back together at least to the point where he wasn't expected to shoot at people randomly. He'd held out some hope that he'd be sent back to duty, to the only true calling he'd ever known. That's when the Army had cut him loose with a discharge for "Designated Physical and Mental Conditions." The final rejection had shattered him.

In the years after, he'd wandered, secure and wrapped in the numbness, punctuated by episodes of rage, which Lucas had told him were common symptoms of post-traumatic stress disorder. He thought he'd found some outlet when he'd gotten a job running down bail jumpers. The chase, the takedown, the sheer adrenaline of the hunt had made him feel alive again, and the relationship he'd developed with his boss, Angela, had been the kind of connection he'd not known he'd missed until he'd found it.

He'd fallen in love with Marie, the police officer he'd met while running down a demented redneck bail jumper named Dewayne Puryear. In that same chase, he'd met his friend Oscar Sanchez, now Angela's husband. He thought he could make a life with Marie, have friends in Angela and Oscar, live something resembling a human life. But the violence that seemed to dog his life had driven them all away, even as he tried to save them from it. The cure had truly been worse than the disease. Lucas had once observed that it was hard to treat someone for PTSD when they got shot at all the time.

Lucas. Keller shook his head. He should call the last true friend he had in the world and at least let him know he was alive.

He trudged back to the truck and got in. Lightning was flashing in the descending sky. He pulled out the prepaid cell phone he'd purchased for cash at a forgotten convenience store somewhere in Alabama and looked at it. It took him a moment to recall the number. He wanted to hear his old friend's voice more than anything at that moment, but he hesitated with his finger over the dial-pad. He'd brought Hell down on everyone he'd brought into his life. What if whoever was after him was watching Lucas, even tapping his phone? Given what they'd accomplished up to now, it was a pretty good bet they were watching everyone he ever knew. It's what he would have done when running down a jumper. He couldn't put another friend at risk.

He put the phone back in the center console. As he did, he thought of someone who might hide him, at least temporarily. Not a friend. Someone in his debt. Someone he didn't know if he could totally trust, but he was out of options. He started the truck. As he pulled away, the wind picked up and it started to rain.

CHAPTER TWENTY-EIGHT

THE BAR WAS LIKE A thousand other back-road taverns, a crumbling cinderblock structure set back behind a gravel parking lot along a two-lane blacktop that had faded to a cracked gray track between nowhere and nowhere. A pair of neon beer signs—one flickering and sputtering, the other still burning bright—provided the only dim illumination. A faded wooden sign over the doorway said SPANISH MOON. The lot was packed with pickup trucks and beat-up American sedans as Keller pulled in in his commandeered SUV. He didn't bother to lock the vehicle when he got out. The storms he'd driven through to get to the bar had moved off toward the sea, leaving behind a clinging humidity that made the night feel like a heavy weight everyone carried with them as they moved through it.

As he approached the door, Keller could feel the eyes on him, people who'd been talking or engaging in drunken clumsy foreplay in the shadows between the vehicles, stopping what they were doing to suss out the new and unfamiliar arrival, like animals at a waterhole noticing an intruder.

Just inside the door, on a stool under a naked white bulb, sat the doorman. He was, of course, a big man, and painfully stupid. The small and mentally quick didn't last long doing security in a place like this; their mouths tended to get them in trouble with belligerent drunks and those suffering from an excess of testosterone. No, what was needed to keep order in a place like this was a mountain, a bouncer who not even the most clueless drunk or wannabe badass would take on.

This one fit the bill perfectly. He wasn't muscular, but he had the kind of bulk that intimidated. He gave Keller an elaborately nonchalant glance through small piggy eyes as he shifted his weight on the stool, which creaked dangerously beneath him.

"Private club," he said to Keller as he strode up. "You ain't a member."

Keller gave him back a tight smile. "You sure?"

The doorman shifted again, coming up slightly off the stool as if rising to the challenge he sensed in Keller. Keller didn't move, and the smile never went away. "I'm looking for the Magic Man."

Seeing that Keller was going to neither back down nor advance, the mountain settled back down onto the stool. "Magic Man? This ain't no magic show, buddy. Now fuck off."

Keller kept smiling. "Sure. Just tell Karl that Jack Keller wants to see him. About that favor he owes me." Before the doorman could answer, Keller turned and walked away. "Hey," the doorman called weakly into the sodden darkness. Keller ignored him. He walked back to the truck and climbed in. Laying his head back on the luxurious headrest of the truck, he settled in for what might be a long wait and remembered the time he'd met and arrested Karl "Magic Man" Zaubermann.

It had been a pretty routine bust for Karl, an ounce and a half of weed found during the kind of traffic stop a guy on a motorcycle with no leathers, tattoos covering both arms, and long hair could expect from

curious cops. His baby mama had contacted Keller's old employer at H
& H Bail Bonds, Angela had written his bond, and he'd gotten out of jail
to await trial or plea, depending on a number of things. Then an eager
young prosecutor noticed that when you ran the name through the
computer as "Carl" Zaubermann with the same birth date and Social
Security number, a whole lot of other convictions popped up, enough
to indict Karl/Carl on "the bitch" — North Carolina's Habitual Felon
law, which kicked his low-level drug charge into the stratosphere of
felony sentencing. Under "the bitch," someone with three prior strikes
on their record could get as much time on the fourth for a crack rock, or
for over an ounce of marijuana, as he could for manslaughter.

Upon being informed of this new and much more serious
indictment, Karl Zaubermann did the only logical thing from his
perspective: he disappeared. This brought Keller into the picture, since
Keller's boss, Angela, had her company's name on the bond to secure
his appearance. If Zaubermann didn't show for court, H & H would be
out thousands of dollars.

Keller had done his usual checking, talking to Zaubermann's known
associates, checking out places where he was known to hang out, even
checking a new online site called MySpace, where he'd previously
discovered more than one bail jumper who'd thought no one but his
friends could see the posts that broadcasted his picture and his location
to the world. Against all expectations, Zaubermann had been smarter
than that.

Finally, during a visit to Zaubermann's ex-girlfriend, he'd noticed
gift-wrapped packages sitting on the dining room table, along with
packages of balloons and other party decorations. A quick check of
public records showed that Karl Zaubermann had a son, Kodie, who
had a fifth birthday coming up. On the big day, Keller walked up to the
festively decorated house just as Zaubermann was exiting a dented but
anonymous-looking white van. He recognized Keller right away. He
balled his fists and rolled his shoulders to show he was ready to make

an issue out of going back, then he'd looked into the house and heard the happy shouting and music. His shoulders sagged and he relaxed his hands. "Not in front of my son, Keller," he'd said quietly.

Keller kept his voice even. "I won't make a problem of this if you don't, Karl. Just come with me."

Zaubermann shook his head. "Look. I know I'm going away. I know it'll be for a long time. I'm ready to do it. I just want to see my kid one last time. Come on, man, just give me an hour."

Keller stopped a few feet away. "Right. And I come back after an hour to find you're halfway to Mexico."

"No, man, I swear it. You want me to beg, Keller? Okay, I'll beg." The big man sagged as if he was going to his knees.

"For Christ's sake, Karl," Keller said, embarrassed. "Stand up. Don't humiliate yourself."

Zaubermann straightened up. "I ain't got no pride left, Keller. You can even come in, keep an eye on me. I'll say you're a friend."

"You know I'm not."

"Yeah, no shit. But just let me do this one thing. I swear, man, I'll owe you. Big time."

Keller was wavering. He knew it was stupid, knew it was a better than even chance that Zaubermann would bolt out the back door as soon as Keller looked away for a moment. But the pain in the man's eyes was genuine. "You're going to have a hard time paying back a favor in prison."

"I been in before. I know I'll be out. You never know when you might need a favor. Even from a guy like me." Zaubermann reached into his pocket. Keller tensed, then relaxed when Zaubermann pulled out a key ring. "Here. Take my keys."

Keller sighed and took them from him. "Okay. One hour. But if you try to run, I'm taking you down, cuffing you, and driving you back in my trunk. I don't care if your son is there."

Zaubermann nodded. "Deal. And I mean it, man. I owe you one.

Anything you need, you ask for the Magic Man."

"I'll keep it in mind."

Zaubermann introduced Keller as his buddy Jack who'd given him a ride. Zaubermann's ex-wife, Denise, recognized Keller and was looking daggers at him. The children took no notice. Denise walked over with a cup of punch spooned out of a plastic bowl on the table. He thought for a moment she was going to throw it on him. She had a fake smile pasted on her face as she whispered, "You need to get the fuck out of my house."

Keller pitched his voice low. "If I leave, I'm taking Karl with me. I gave him a break to see his kid before I take him in. Don't make me regret it."

Her smile faltered a bit. Keller took the cup of punch, drained it in one gulp, then handed it back. "Thanks." She didn't answer, just turned and walked away.

The next hour felt surreal to Keller. He hung around the fringes of the party, feeling like a ghost, watching the children play and the young mothers gossip. A few of them gave him tentative smiles, but he was too focused on watching Zaubermann to respond. To his credit, Zaubermann didn't seem to be looking for a way out. He was totally focused on his son, a pale red-haired kid with a loud, braying laugh that would probably get annoying if he kept it to adulthood. He did a lot of laughing with his father, especially when he opened the present marked "from Dad"—a toy Harley Davidson motorcycle. They were having so much fun that Keller let the hour go by.

Finally, Zaubermann stood up and nodded at Keller. Keller nodded back and moved toward the door. Zaubermann spoke a few quick words to Denise, handed her an envelope from a jacket pocket, and gave her a kiss on the cheek. She reached up, threw her arms around his neck, and gave him a hard squeeze before letting him go. The boy was too focused on *vroom vroom*ing the motorcycle on the carpet to notice. Zaubermann met Keller at the door, with Denise at his side.

Keller pulled out the van keys and handed them to her. "I guess you'll need these."

She took them, not meeting his eyes. "Thanks." She gave a small sigh and looked up. Her eyes were moist. "Sorry I was a bitch."

"You weren't," Keller said. "It's okay." He turned to Zaubermann. "Let's go."

In Keller's car, Zaubermann was subdued. "He's going to look up and I'll be gone," he said in a choked voice. "And I won't be back till he's a teenager. It's tough on a kid growing up without a dad, you know?"

Keller didn't answer.

"I meant it," Zaubermann said. "What I was talking about earlier. Anything you need, man. Any time. If I can swing it from inside, I will. Or when I get out."

"Okay," Keller said. "I'll keep it in mind." But he hadn't thought about it. Not until now.

CHAPTER TWENTY-NINE

THE CRUNCH OF BOOTS ON gravel pulled Keller out of his reverie. Zaubermann walked up to the window of Keller's truck.

"Keller," he said. His face was expressionless. He'd cut his hair shorter, but he still had his long sideburns and some new ink on his neck. "Long time no see."

"Not as long as either of us thought," Keller said.

"Yeah. Well. I made some deals. Got 'em to back off on the bitch." Zaubermann looked up. "It's startin' to rain again."

Keller motioned to the passenger side. "Get in."

Inside the truck, Keller could see that the years had worn new lines in Zaubermann's face and speckled his hair with gray. "So to what do I owe this honor?" Zaubermann said. "I'm pretty sure you don't have any paper on me. I'm a regular citizen now."

"Not what I heard," Keller said. "But no, I don't have any bonds on you. I'm out of the business, actually. I'm calling in that favor you promised."

Zaubermann frowned. "What favor?"

"When I gave you time with your kid before I took you in. You said anything I needed. Any time."

"Yeah," Zaubermann said ruefully, "I guess I did say that."

"Well," Keller said, "I need a place to stay. Somewhere off the grid."

Zaubermann's eyes narrowed. "Someone after you?"

Keller decided not to try and bullshit his way through it. "Probably. Not sure, but probably."

Zaubermann looked at him for a moment, then chuckled. "That's some karmic shit, right there."

"Yeah. Ha. Ha. The universe is laughing its ass off. Can you help me?"

Zaubermann grew serious. "Maybe. But like I say, I ain't the Magic Man no more. I'm just a guy who owns a bar."

Keller had heard differently while he'd been asking around for Zaubermann's location. He'd heard that Zaubermann was still neck deep in drugs, guns, women, and any kind of illegal activity that could be run out of a bar. He'd just gotten more careful. Keller decided not to call him on it, though. If he tried to puncture the facade, the man might bolt, favor or no favor. "Well, maybe you know some people."

"Maybe." Zaubermann was staring straight ahead at where the rain was running down the truck's front window. "I can maybe work something out with some people I know." He looked back at Keller. "It might cost. More or less, depending on who's after you."

Keller nodded. "I can pay. If it's reasonable."

Zaubermann tilted his head and looked at Keller, eyes narrowed appraisingly. "Can you work?"

From the tension in Zaubermann's voice, Keller could tell the "work" would most likely not be legitimate. Still, he didn't really care at this point. "Yeah. As long as it's not likely to draw attention."

The answer seemed to satisfy Zaubermann. He grinned, his teeth white in the dim light. It looked like he'd gotten his teeth fixed in prison. "Okay, then. Come on in the bar. First round's on the house while I rustle you up a place to stay."

"Okay, then," Keller echoed. He opened the door and stepped out into the night.

CHAPTER THIRTY

LUCAS BERRY SAT BEHIND HIS desk and scowled at the paperwork piled on it. He'd had a long day, and the evening substance-abuse group had been more contentious than usual. He really didn't feel like wading through a pile of insurance reimbursement and VA forms. But without them, he wasn't going to get paid, and as much as he loved his job as a counselor, he wasn't quite ready to do it for free. He could go broke at home with his feet up if that's what he wanted to do. He steeled himself and picked up the first file. The phone buzzed, and his finger leaped to the button like that of a man waiting for a stay of execution. "Yes?"

"Dr. Berry?" the voice of his receptionist said tentatively, as if she still wasn't sure who might be sitting in the office.

"Yes, Crystal?"

"Someone here to see you."

Berry frowned. "I don't have any more appointments, do I?"

"No, sir." The young woman hesitated. "He says it's about Jack Keller."

"Does he now," Berry said. He slid the top desk drawer open to make sure the loaded .357 revolver was there. Given what Keller had been up to recently, it made sense to be careful around anyone who claimed to be looking for him. "Well, send him in." He slid the drawer partially shut.

He didn't know what he was expecting; he only knew that the mild-looking, balding man who his receptionist was letting into the office wasn't it. He stood up and offered a hand. "I'm Lucas Berry," he said.

The man put his briefcase down and took the offered hand in a surprisingly strong grip. "John Maddox," he said.

Berry released the hand, his eyes narrowing. "Maddox," he said in a voice cold enough to turn metal brittle.

Maddox smiled apologetically. "Yes, sir. I suspect from your tone that you've heard the name."

"I have. State your business."

Maddox gestured to one of the client chairs in front of the desk. "May I sit down?"

"No," Berry said. Maddox's only reaction was a disappointed look that made Berry feel as if what he'd done was petty and small. Grudgingly, he motioned to the chair. Maddox nodded his thanks and sat down. "I know you have no reason to trust me now. But I'm asking you to hear me out. For Keller's sake."

"You represent the man claiming to be Jack's father?" Berry demanded.

Maddox nodded again. "Yes."

"Then no, I have no reason to trust you. Or him."

"Granted. But there are people looking for Jack Keller that pose a greater threat to him than his father or I could. He needs to know what he's up against."

"Well, I can't help you. I don't know where he is."

Maddox nodded. "I know. But has anyone else tried to contact you regarding his whereabouts? Or maybe tried to contact some other friend of his?"

Berry leaned back and regarded Maddox through narrowed eyes. He'd gotten a call from Marie Jones, Jack's former lover, now living in Portland, Oregon. Someone had come around asking her about him, trying to find out if she'd heard from him. She'd wanted to know if Keller was in trouble. He'd told her that he didn't know for sure. They'd had a long talk after that.

Maddox read Berry's silence and leaned forward. "Doctor Berry," he said earnestly, "the people looking for Jack Keller are not above putting people he cares about at risk to try to draw him out. Including yourself." He leaned back, his expression mild. "You know him better than anyone. Wouldn't that motivate him more strongly than anything to come out of hiding? If you don't help us find him, the people after him may resort to extreme measures." He nodded at the drawer at Berry's right hand, which Berry realized was still partially open. "Whatever you have in that drawer may help protect you from them. It may not. It would be better if we could give Mr. Keller the means to protect himself better than any weapon ever could."

Berry shook his head. "You're good, Maddox. I'll give you that. You know what buttons to push. I'm thinking maybe you were Agency. A recruiter. A handler. I'll bet you were a good one."

Maddox smiled. "I can neither confirm nor deny..." He smiled wryly. "You know the rest."

"I do," Despite himself, Berry was actually beginning to warm to the man. "But I can't help you. I don't know where Jack Keller is. Yes, someone he was close to called me. Someone had been asking..." he hesitated, "her about Jack. She didn't know anything either. And no one has contacted me."

Maddox leaned back. "Not directly, no. But may I ask a favor, Doctor?"

Berry tensed. "You can ask."

"May I check your office for listening devices? It will take a few minutes."

Berry let out a disbelieving laugh. "Really? You think someone might have bugged my office?"

Maddox shrugged. "It's a possibility." He smiled. "If I turn up nothing, you can make as much fun of me as you like."

Berry gave a negligent wave of his hand. "Knock yourself out."

"Thank you." Maddox reached into the briefcase and pulled out a black box with two silver antennae poking out of the top.

"Seriously," Berry said. "I'm supposed to believe in that thing?"

Maddox fiddled with the controls, looking intent. "This will only detect RF—radio frequency—devices," he said. "Crude and obvious, but people do sometimes use them, if they're in a hurry or if that's all that's available." He stood up, device in hand, and walked around the room. "Do you often discuss important matters in any other room?"

"We hold group sessions in what used to be the front parlor," Berry said. "But that wouldn't have anything to do with Keller. If he were to call, I'd take it in here."

"Ah." Maddox lowered the black box. "How about the secretary's office?"

"Maybe." Berry realized that he was beginning to get sucked into this craziness.

"May I?" Without waiting for permission, Maddox walked out. A moment later, Berry heard Crystal's voice. "Hey! What the hell are you...hey!" She appeared at the office door, a look of indignation on her pretty face. "Doctor Berry! That guy's messing with my phone!"

"Indulge him a little," Berry said, trying to keep the amusement out of his voice. "He'll be done in a minute."

At the end of that long minute, however, Maddox walked in, looking like a doctor delivering bad news. He was holding the black box in one hand and a small piece of metal in the other. As Berry watched in disbelief, Maddox dropped it on the desk.

It was a tiny cylinder, slightly pointed on both ends, with a stubby wire projecting from one. "RF bug," Maddox said. "In your secretary's phone."

Berry frowned. "I'll be damned." He looked up at Maddox. "How did they—whoever they are—get that in here?"

"Wait a minute," Crystal interrupted. "How do we know you didn't just bring that in with you?"

Maddox nodded approvingly. "Cautious. Very good. You're a smart young lady."

"Yeah," she said. "Well, you might say I got trust issues. Has to do with my history. Right, doc?"

Berry's face was a carefully composed mask. "You know I can't talk about that."

She smiled grimly. "Thanks, doc. But I can." She turned to Maddox. "Before I met Doctor Berry, I was a junkie and a whore. So no, I don't much trust anyone." She looked at Berry. "Except him. And Jack Keller." She turned back to Maddox. "Both of them helped save my life. So just let me say this, Mr. Maddox." She advanced on him until they were face to face. "I may be just a hick from the sticks and you're some big important guy. But if I think you're tryin' to hurt either of those men, I will find some way to fuck. You. Up."

"Crystal!" Berry snapped.

Maddox pushed his glasses up on his nose where they'd slipped down. He didn't break eye contact with Crystal. "I assure you, my principal and I aren't trying to hurt Jack Keller. Just the opposite, in fact. We think that there might be people out there who are, though. And we'd like to stop that."

They stared at each other for a long moment. Finally, Crystal looked away. "Okay," she muttered. "Sorry to get in your face like that."

"No apologies necessary," Maddox said. "He's lucky to have friends like the two of you." He reached into his jacket pocket and pulled out a business card. "If Mr. Keller does call you, please get in touch with us immediately."

"If he calls or contacts either of us," Berry said, "we'll discuss with *him* whether or not to get in touch with you."

"Right," Crystal said.

Maddox inclined his head slightly in acknowledgment. "That's fair. Just let him know about what I said. He may be in great danger."

Crystal laughed. "Have you actually *met* Jack Keller?"

Maddox nodded. "Briefly."

"Then you should know that you ought to warn whoever's after him," Crystal said.

"Yes," Maddox said. "But I think they know. So if anyone else contacts you about finding him, please let us know as well. Thank you for your time. I'll let myself out."

BACK IN HIS CAR, MADDOX took a deep breath. He'd expected a confrontation with Lucas Berry, who lived up to his reputation as a formidable man. But the ferocity of the young woman's reaction unsettled him. He started the vehicle, conscious of the eyes on him behind the curtains of the restored Victorian home where Berry had his offices. He drove through the tree-lined streets of the neighborhood, marveling at the contrast with the tacky commercial strip and struggling downtown that defined the rest of Fayetteville, North Carolina. When he saw a Wendy's, he pulled into the parking lot, pulled out his phone, and punched in the numbers. The phone rang seven times, and Maddox felt a shiver of apprehension. Surely, the person he'd reluctantly brought in to look after Trammell in his absence would have followed his orders to notify him if the old man had taken a turn for the worse. Finally, Trammell picked up. "Sorry for the delay," he said in his rasping voice. "When a man in my condition can actually take a decent shit...well, you know."

"Yes, sir."

"So. How did it go?"

"They either couldn't, or wouldn't, say much. Jack Keller seems to inspire a great deal of loyalty in people, sir."

Trammell's chuckle devolved into a weak cough. "Apple didn't fall far from the tree, did it?"

"No, sir." There was a pause. "Are you being looked after, sir?"

"I'm fine," Trammell said. "Did you find anything? Any bugs?"

"No, sir," Maddox replied. "I think I may have misdirected them from the devices I left. Dr. Berry's secretary is a suspicious type, but I think I may have won her over."

"Good, good," Trammell said. "You haven't lost your touch, then."

"No, sir."

There was a long pause. "So, did you find any devices?"

Maddox sat up straighter in the seat, tensing with alarm. "No, sir. We just discussed that."

"We did? Oh. And…" The voice trailed off.

"Sir?" Maddox said. "Is Dr. Petrovitch there by any chance?"

The voice grew stronger. "That bastard? Hell, yes. He won't get out of my goddamn hair."

"May I speak with him, please?"

"What the hell for? What's he going to tell you? And when are you going to tell me if you managed to place anything in Berry's offices?"

"I did, sir. Please call Dr. Petrovitch."

"Oh, all right. Fine."

There was a brief silence, then another voice came on the line. "*Da?*"

"Petrovitch. What's going on?"

"Wait a moment." There was a pause, then the Russian's thickly accented voice came back on the line. "How can I help you, Maddox?"

"Can you talk freely?"

"I can now."

"Then tell me what Mr. Trammell's condition is."

There was a brief pause. Then, "Condition is not good. Actually, am amazed he's still alive."

Maddox felt his heart pounding in his chest. "That's why you're there, isn't it?"

Petrovitch had been a doctor working for the now defunct KGB, laboring in the bowels of the notorious Lubyanka prison. It had been his job to keep tortured prisoners alive, even though wounded and mutilated, until the time when all information had been wrung from them and they could be disposed of. Trammell and Maddox had found him in Moscow, used his own self-loathing to turn him, and eventually brought him to the US as a defector who knew, literally, where a lot of bodies were buried. Trammell, with his finely developed sense of irony and black humor, had directed Maddox to bring Petrovitch out of the exile Trammell himself had dragged him into.

Petrovitch's voice was sulky. "I am not God, Maddox. I cannot prolong life forever. He is staying alive for reasons."

Maddox closed his eyes and leaned forward to rest his head on the steering wheel. After a moment, he composed himself and sat back up. "He's waiting for his son to return."

"Well, son should probably hurry."

"Just keep him as comfortable as you can," Maddox snapped, then cut the connection. He needed to find Jack Keller, and soon. He reached over into the passenger seat and pulled out a slim laptop computer. After he'd placed it on his lap and booted it up, he accessed the program that monitored the surveillance devices he'd placed on the phones and computers in Lucas Berry's office. There was no activity. He checked the program he'd used to hack Berry's own cell phone. Nothing there either. He leaned back and looked at the headliner of the car as if it might give him some answers. It didn't. Jack Keller had gone to ground, and the only people who might have some idea of his whereabouts had gone silent. There was nothing to do but wait. And Maddox was running out of time to wait.

CHAPTER THIRTY-ONE

"IT AIN'T MUCH," KARL ZAUBERMANN said, "but it's about as far off the grid as you can get."

"I can see that," Keller said. They were standing in the yard of a low-roofed wooden house that looked as if it was about ready to collapse back into the primordial swamp that surrounded the higher ground on which it sat. The warped outside planking was faded to gray stained green with mold, and any windows that weren't boarded over were streaked with grime. Keller had driven his stolen vehicle behind Zaubermann through what seemed like an endless maze of twisted gravel, then dirt roads, before reaching this desolate clearing.

"You want to lay up," Zaubermann said, "you can't find a much better place. Only one road in and out, and it runs through a mile and a half of swamp. It's got a generator that'll run the fridge, a fan, and a couple of lights, but don't push it too hard."

Keller nodded. "I wasn't complaining. I've lived in worse."

"I reckon you have." Zaubermann handed him a key. "Place is yours, for as long as you want it."

Keller took the key. "Thanks."

"You need anything else?"

Keller went to the truck and reached into the cargo compartment of the black Escalade. He took out the pair of AR-15s he'd taken from Zavalo and his men and slung one over each shoulder. "I could use some more ammo for these, if you can get it. And I can pay." Briefly, he described what he was looking for.

Zaubermann's eyes widened, but he nodded. "Yeah. I can swing that."

Keller nodded at the Escalade. "I need to get rid of that, too. Replace it with something cheap and boring. It's a nice ride, but I don't recommend driving it around. Maybe chop it up for parts. The former owners might come looking for it. I think I may have discouraged them, but you never know."

Zaubermann grimaced. "Jesus, Keller. Just who the fuck is after you? Feds? Cartels?"

Keller shrugged. "Not feds, exactly. Maybe someone pretending to be a fed. And the cartels? Probably not. I hope I brushed them back a little."

"Brushed them back. The cartels." Zaubermann shook his head in disbelief. "Jesus. You're kind of pushing the envelope on this favor. I want you to know that."

"I know. And I won't be here long. I just need some breathing room. Some time to figure out what to do."

"Fine. Just don't take long. You're startin' to sound like trouble I don't need."

Keller nodded. "I get that. But Karl?"

Zaubermann had started walking back toward his own truck. Now he stopped and looked back.

"If you're thinking of asking around for whoever's looking for me, and shopping me to them—"

Zaubermann interrupted. "Man, you know I wouldn't—"

Keller cut him off. "Just remember. I'm very good at finding people."

He and Zaubermann regarded each other for a long moment. Then Zaubermann said, "You've changed, man. And not for the better."

"I know." Keller reached into his pocket and pulled out a roll of bills. He peeled off several hundreds and held them out to Zaubermann. "Just get me the ammo and the vehicle."

Zaubermann took the money, still looking dubious. "Yeah. Okay. I'll be back tomorrow."

"Alone," Keller said.

Zaubermann nodded. "Absolutely."

Z AUBERMANN WAS AS GOOD AS his word. He pulled up shortly after nine the next morning in a small white Ford pickup. The truck had rust showing at the corners of the bed and a minor dent in the front bumper. Keller had been up since before dawn, his sleep troubled by mosquitoes and uneasy dreams. He met Zaubermann on the front steps.

"You wanted something no one would notice," Zaubermann said, nodding at the truck. "Around here, that fits right in. Runs good, though. Dropped a new motor in just last month."

"Thanks," Keller said. "And the ammo?"

"In the back." The two men walked to the bed of the truck. A pair of olive drab army surplus ammo cans sat side by side. "Two hundred rounds," Zaubermann said. "Five point five six, just the mix you asked for. Hundred full metal jacket, fifty hollow points, fifty tracer rounds. Think that'll do ya?"

Keller nodded and hauled the heavy cans out of the truck bed. "If it doesn't, I'm probably fucked anyway."

"I heard that."

"Thanks," Keller said. "And you can keep the change."

Zaubermann grinned. "I was planning to."

"Here's the keys to the Escalade." Keller handed them over. "Remember, you may want to get rid of it."

Zaubermann took the keys. "Seems a shame to cut up such a nice ride."

Keller shrugged. "Your choice. But it didn't bring much luck to the last guy who had it."

"Understood. Hey, have you thought over what we talked about yesterday? About maybe doing some work?"

Keller picked up one of the ammo cans and walked toward the house. "Depends on the work."

Zaubermann picked up the other can and followed. "Nothing heavy, I promise. I was thinking about a meeting I have coming up. I could use a little extra security."

Keller walked up the rickety steps and opened the front door, which squealed on rusty hinges as it swung. "You expecting trouble at this meeting?" He put the ammo can inside the door.

"No, not really." Zaubermann handed his can to Keller, who put it next to the first one and shut the door. "But trouble'll be even less likely the more serious we look. Hey, all you'll need to do is stand in the corner and look mean. You're good at that, right?"

"I guess. Is this some kind of sit-down?"

Zaubermann shook his head. "Straight delivery. In and out. Won't take ten minutes if it's done right."

"So why extra security? What's the delivery?"

"Best that you not know about exactly what the delivery is. Not yet. But like I said, the extra security is just for show. This is a new, ah, partner we're dealing with here. Everybody wants to, you know, look their best."

"New partner, huh? Anyone I might know?"

Zaubermann raised both hands, palms out. "Not cartel. At least not on this level. Maybe a couple links up the chain, I dunno. But the people I'm meeting with represent an MC out of Tallahassee, Florida."

"Bikers," Keller said.

Zaubermann nodded. "Tough motherfuckers by reputation, but I checked them out with reliable sources. They're all about business. No drama."

"Good to hear," Keller said. He thought it over. "When and where's the meet?"

"At the bar. Tomorrow night. After closing. Be there about one thirty." Zaubermann shrugged. "Who knows, you might meet some new friends. And I'll make it worth your time. That bankroll of yours isn't going to last forever, Keller. Not at these prices."

Keller looked off into the distance. Finally, he said, "Yeah. Okay." Something inside him told him it was a bad idea. He still didn't know if he completely trusted Zaubermann. But a night spent by himself had left him feeling as if he was slipping back into the fog, the numbness that wrapped around him if he didn't get out ahead of it. He needed the burst of adrenaline he used to get by chasing and taking down bail jumpers. Standing watch over a drug buy might well be a poor substitute. But it was something.

"Okay, then," Zaubermann said with satisfaction. "See you there." He walked to the Escalade and got in. Keller stood watching as he drove away down the narrow rutted drive. He waited five minutes, then got into his own new ride and drove out the same way. He had some shopping of his own to do. Some items that Zaubermann didn't need to know about.

CHAPTER THIRTY-TWO

KELLER PULLED INTO THE BAR parking lot as promised at 1:30 AM. There were still a few stragglers leaning against cars and pickups, and there seemed to be a low-pitched but intense argument going on between two vehicles between a man and a woman. As Keller walked through the parking lot, the pair stopped and glared at him. He passed without making a remark and heard the fight start up again behind him. As he approached the front door, the bouncer who'd greeted him that first night stepped out. He squinted at Keller. "Hunh," he grunted. "You."

"Yep. Me."

The bouncer gave him a hard stare. Keller gave one back. The other man broke first. The bouncer's eyes slid away as he held out his hand. "Hey," he said. "Sorry about the attitude the other night. Didn't know you was a friend of Karl's."

Keller took the hand. "I'm not. But it's no problem. You were just doing your job. My name's Jack Keller."

The bouncer didn't try to crush Keller's hand. Keller hoped that meant they were beyond the tiresome dick-measuring stage. "My name's Will," he said. "But people call me Tiny."

"Of course they do," Keller said, his smile letting the man know there was no mockery intended. "Which one you prefer?"

The man grinned. "Tiny's fine. But thanks for asking." He looked past Keller into the parking lot. "Go on in while I get rid of these last few losers. Get yourself something to drink. On the house."

"Thanks." Keller stepped inside.

The only people left inside were Zaubermann and a skinny woman with a deeply lined face and long frizzy blond hair who was wiping down the bar. Zaubermann was pulling a pair of small bar tables together. He looked up and nodded at Keller. "Right on time," he observed. He turned to the blond. "Okay, Trina. You can take off. We'll finish up."

Trina was looking at Keller appraisingly. When she spoke, it was in a voice roughened by liquor and cigarettes. "Sure you don't need me to stay? And who's your friend?"

"Jack," Keller said.

Zaubermann was smirking. "Maybe some other time, Trina."

The woman shrugged. "Okay. Night." There was a door behind the bar and she walked to it, pausing as she reached it and looking at Keller. "Nice meeting you, Jack."

"Nice meeting you." But she'd already gone.

When he looked back at Zaubermann, the man was grinning. "I think she kinda likes you, Jack."

"Maybe," Keller said.

"She's got some miles on her," Zaubermann went on. "But she knows some tricks. She can make you forget your name, let me tell you."

"I'll keep it in mind," Keller said. "This meeting still on?"

"Yeah." Zaubermann motioned toward the bar. "Why don't you

stand back there?" he said. "I'll have Tiny watch the door."

Keller felt a crawly feeling up his spine. "Only three of us? How many are the other guys bringing?"

Zaubermann rolled his eyes. "Will you relax? Like I said, these guys aren't into drama."

"That's great. But what if they decide to change their minds?"

Zaubermann's grin was like a wolf baring its teeth. "Then there's a twelve-gauge scatter gun behind the bar. Loaded with double aught."

Keller stepped back and found the shotgun lying on a shelf above the bar well. He hefted it and looked it over. He jacked a round into the chamber.

"There," Zaubermann said, "you feel a little more secure?"

"Yeah," Keller said. "I'd feel better if you and Tiny were carrying, too."

"Don't worry," Zaubermann said. He reached down to his boot and came up with a stubby little revolver. "Charter Arms Bulldog snub nose .44. Can't hit a fucking house with it at range, but close up, it'll blow a big enough hole to do the job."

"What about Tiny?"

Zaubermann shrugged. "Tiny's Tiny." He chuckled. "Anyone shoots him, he'll fall on them and crush them. Seriously, man, will you just relax? I know these guys. They're brothers."

"Brothers?"

"You know. Bikers. Like me. We get one another. Everything's going to be fine."

Tiny came back in. "All clear, boss."

"Excellent," Zaubermann said. "Jack, why don't you pour us some drinks while we wait?"

Keller looked at the well, saw the bottles of cheap liquor there, then thought *what the hell* and turned to the shelves behind the bar. He pulled down a bottle of Gentleman Jack and took out three glasses. "How do you take it?" he said.

"How do you think?" Zaubermann said.

Keller nodded and poured two fingers of the amber liquid into each of the glasses. He slid two to the edge of the bar and kept the third for himself. Zaubermann stood up and Tiny came over to collect his. Zaubermann raised his glass and the other two followed suit. "To new business," Zaubermann said. "New bidness," Tiny echoed. Keller was silent, but they all drank.

There was the sound of a car engine outside. Through the door, it sounded like a big vehicle. Zaubermann was still smacking his lips. "Tiny," he said, "go on and let them in." He turned to Keller. "There's a briefcase over there by the fridge. Hand it to me, will you, Jack?"

Keller located the case and handed it across the bar to Zaubermann, who walked over and put it onto the impromptu conference table he'd made by pushing two bar tables together. He turned to the door. Keller couldn't see his face from where he stood at the bar. The door opened and Tiny came in. The look on his face made the hairs rise on the back of Keller's neck. *Something's wrong.*

A man followed Tiny in. He was slender, dressed in an expensively tailored suit. He looked to be in his mid-fifties, and his short, neatly trimmed beard was a mixture of salt and pepper. His head was shaved.

Keller saw Zaubermann's shoulders tense. "Wait a minute," Zaubermann said. "Who the hell are you?"

The man smiled as he stepped inside. He was joined by two other men, each of them a match in sheer bulk for Tiny, but they seemed in much better condition, muscles bulging against their tightly cut suits that looked at least as expensive as their leader's.

"My name is Vasily," the man said in a silky Russian accent. "I am your new partner."

CHAPTER THIRTY-THREE

SLOWLY, SO AS NOT TO draw attention, Keller reached down and laid a hand on the shotgun. He sized up the two guys who'd come in with Vasily. They gave him the same careful regard.

"Wait a minute," Zaubermann said. "Where's Hardway? I was supposed to be talking with him."

Vasily shook his head. "Mr. Hardway took, how you say, early retirement. We'll be fulfilling his contracts. How do you say it? Stepping into his shoes." He grinned, showing a couple of gold teeth. "Don't worry. Our product is better than that motherfucker's. You'll see."

He saw the table Zaubermann had set up, with the briefcase on top, and nodded approvingly. He walked to the table as if he owned it and sat down. His two bodyguards followed and stood behind him. Zaubermann hesitated, then went and sat down as well. Keller could see the sweat that had broken out on his brow. Tiny was still standing by the door, looking from Zaubermann to Vasily and back again, confusion evident in his small, deep-set eyes. He looked like a hog who'd just been asked to split the atom.

Vasily looked at Keller standing behind the bar. "Could I trouble you for a drink?" Vasily said with elaborate courtesy.

Before Zaubermann could react, Keller answered. "Sure. Let me guess. Vodka?"

Vasily smiled. "I don't like stereotypes." He nodded at the bottle on the counter. "I will take some of that whiskey, though."

Keller looked at Zaubermann. "You'll have to ask the boss."

The words seemed to jolt Zaubermann out of the funk that seemed to have paralyzed him. "Yeah. Sure. And pour me another one."

Keller nodded at the two men behind Vasily. "What about your pals there?"

Vasily looked back. "Kolya? Luka?" Each of them shook their heads almost imperceptibly. Vasily turned back. "None for them. They are driving tonight."

"Okay then." Keller poured the whiskey and delivered the glasses to the table on a tray.

"*Spasibo*," Vasily murmured as he took his. He arched an eyebrow at Keller. "And you are?"

"Jack," Keller said.

"He's new," Zaubermann volunteered.

"Hmmm." Vasily took a sip. "Interesting."

"How so?" Keller asked.

Vasily made a dismissive gesture with his free hand. "Nothing."

Keller had poured a drink for Tiny, who was still standing by the door, looking confused. He took the glass over and delivered it. "Get your head out of your ass," he whispered. "Whatever's happening here, it's not good."

Tiny looked at him uncomprehendingly for a moment, then nodded. He downed the glass in one gulp. Somehow, it seemed to bring him focus. He nodded again at Keller, more strongly this time.

Keller walked back to take his place behind the bar. He put his hand back on the shotgun. Vasily was speaking. "You brought the money, yes?"

"Yeah." Zaubermann seemed to be getting his own composure back. He patted the closed briefcase on the table. "So let's see the product."

"Sure," Vasily said. His smile was as phony as a stripper's. He raised a hand. "Kolya. Go get the cooler."

The bodyguard to Vasily's left walked to the door, stepping past Tiny without acknowledging the man's presence. Vasily took the briefcase and turned it around. He reached for the catches.

Zaubermann placed a hand on the lid. "When we see the product."

Vasily leaned back, an amused look on his face. "Mr. Zaubermann. It's like you don't trust me."

"I just met you," Zaubermann said.

Vasily nodded. "Fair enough. But I think when you see…ah, here is Kolya."

Kolya came back into the bar, hefting a large red Igloo cooler. He placed it on the floor next to Zaubermann, who shifted in his chair to lean over. As Zaubermann reached for the latch, Keller saw the gunmen Luka and Kolya tense, then reach under their suit jackets. He reacted without thinking, grabbing the now half empty bottle of Gentleman Jack by the neck and hurling it at Luka, the nearest gunman. Zaubermann was backpedaling from what he'd seen in the cooler, a gagging sound coming from his throat. He stumbled and went down on his ass. Luka, focused on that spectacle, didn't see the thrown bottle until it exploded against his right temple. He shouted in pain and reeled backward, the gun he was in the middle of drawing falling from his slack fingers.

Keller had the shotgun out by then. He saw Kolya, who'd drawn a black semi-automatic pistol, turning to draw a bead on him. The blast from Keller's shotgun caught him in the chest and knocked him back over a table. Keller swung the shotgun to where Vasily was rising from his chair, pulling an identical pistol from beneath his own jacket.

"Don't do it," Keller barked.

The Russian locked eyes with Keller for a moment. Keller's finger tightened on the trigger. Then, to Keller's amazement, Vasily smiled. He placed the pistol carefully on the table. "You got me, Jack Keller," he said. "You got me good."

"Damn, Keller," Tiny said, "that was—"

"WATCH THE GODDAMN DOOR!" Keller bellowed.

Tiny turned just as the door slammed open and a man burst in. He was slimmer than the other gunmen, dressed in jeans and a leather jacket, but he was carrying an ugly black Uzi submachine gun. He got off a quick three-round burst from the weapon that blasted several of the bottles behind the bar into shards and filled the air with the stench of mingled liquors. Keller ducked away and his own shot went wide, punching a tight pattern of holes in the wall beside the door.

The man in the leather jacket raised the gun for another burst as Keller tried to pump another round into the shotgun. The man's head snapped back as Zaubermann fired his boot pistol from where he was rising up from the floor and hit him just under the jaw.

Another man was coming through the door, this one firing an AK-47 on full auto. The rounds stitched a line across the wall behind the bar before Tiny finally brought his own pistol into play, a cheap silver .40 caliber model that nevertheless managed to put a steel-jacketed round into the side of the man's head. He stumbled and fell sideways, crashing to the floor of the bar.

Then there was only silence, reverberating with the echoes of gunfire and reeking with the sharp choking smell of expended rounds. Keller popped up from behind the bar, training the shotgun on Vasily. The Russian had picked up his pistol again, but as he looked around, he could see not only Keller's shotgun, but Tiny's .40 and the .44 Zaubermann held on him as he got up from the floor. He smiled and placed the pistol back on the table.

"Okay," he said. "I give."

"You *give*?" Keller said, "What, you think this is fucking grade school?" He advanced around the bar, shotgun pointed at the Russian. He could feel the blood pounding in his temples. Vasily's mocking smile slipped a notch. "Get on your fucking knees," Keller snarled, "while I decide whether or not to blow your goddamn head all over this floor."

"Keller," Zaubermann said as he picked up Vasily's gun. "Dude. He's giving up."

Keller turned to him, pointing the shotgun at his face. "STOP USING MY FUCKING NAME!"

Zaubermann stepped back, holding his hands up. It would have looked like surrender if he wasn't still holding the two guns. "Easy, man," he said. "Take it easy."

"Yes," Vasily said. "Take it easy. We can still make peace, Mr. Jack Keller."

Keller moved across the bar, toward the cooler that still sat on the floor, bringing the shotgun to bear alternately on Vasily, then Zaubermann, then an increasingly confused-looking Tiny. He spared a glance down into it, long enough to register the open, dead eyes of the severed head that rested inside in a half-congealed soup of drying blood. "Mr. Hardway, I presume," he said. No one answered. "Tiny. Get the other guns." Tiny blinked in confusion, but he did as he was told.

It would be so easy, he thought, to just cut loose. Kill them all. Paint the walls with blood and brains and viscera. It wouldn't just feel good. It was the smart thing to do. There was no one in this room that could be trusted to keep his name and whereabouts secret as long as they were alive. *Death*, a voice whispered to him. *You bring death.* But there were other voices inside his skull, pulling him back from that chasm filled with fire and darkness that had beckoned to him for so long. Lucas. Angela. Marie. Julianne. *You're a good man, Jack Keller*, they had all said at one time or another. Despite everything that had happened, everything he had done, he still wanted to believe it.

He stopped at the door, his weapon trained on the kneeling Vasily. Luka was stirring and moaning from his position on the floor next to him. "You said my name like you know it," Keller said. "Tell me how. Maybe I'll let you and your boy Luka there live."

Vasily shrugged. The effort of repressing fear seemed to thicken his accent. "Word is out. Find a man named Jack Keller."

"So who wants to know?"

Vasily's laugh was remarkably relaxed for a man staring down the barrel of a twelve-gauge shotgun. "Come on, Jack Keller. You know how it is. One man works for another man, who works for someone else."

Keller nodded. "Okay then. Let's do this." He turned to Zaubermann. "I know Boris Badenov here has the idea to shop me to whoever's looking for me. After he killed you, of course."

Zaubermann shook his head. "I already told you, man—"

"Skip it," Keller said. "Leave him alive, he'll just take a blowtorch to the soles of your feet until you tell. Kill him here, he'll just be replaced by another asshole who'll do the same. Right, Vasily?"

Vasily's face was turning dark red with anger, but he managed a nod.

"So give him what he wants," Keller said. "Tell whoever's looking for me where I am. And tell him I'll be waiting."

"What?" Zaubermann said, clearly not believing what he was hearing. "But I thought—"

"Change of plans." Keller walked over to where Vasily was kneeling on the floor. His stare as he looked at Keller was hard enough to cut diamond. Keller reached over and patted the Russian on the top of his head. "But tell them to come himself. Not send someone like this piece of shit here." He was still holding the shotgun in his right hand. He shifted it to his left and delivered a stinging slap to Vasily's face. The Russian rocked to one side, then recovered. His eyes were blazing with hate. "You think you can deliver that message, bitch?" Keller said.

"Oh, yes," Vasily said. "I deliver message. And someday soon, I deliver message to you."

"Looking forward to it, shithead." Keller didn't lower the gun as he backed out of the door. He didn't turn around until he was halfway across the parking lot. Then he turned and bolted back to his truck.

CHAPTER
THIRTY-FOUR

THEY CAME THE MORNING OF the next day. There were four men in the lead SUV, Vasily and three handpicked gunmen, with Riddle riding in a separate vehicle, a faded and creaky Jeep CJ-7 with open sides and a soft top, driven by Zaubermann.

Vasily Lazarenko had called Riddle (whom he knew as Hank Jessup) as soon as he had left the bar. It was five PM by the time Riddle pulled up outside the bar. A hand-lettered sign on the door said CLOSED FOR REPAIRS. Riddle had knocked anyway. Vasily was inside, with an unhappy-looking Zaubermann and a man with a heavily bandaged face. Negotiations were quickly completed, aided by the fact that Zaubermann's alternative to a negotiated settlement was a lingering death at the hands of the Russians. Riddle/Jessup turned over information on how Vasily could access the money he'd been promised for the information, and Vasily volunteered his men for the strike team. He also let them know that Keller probably had a large stash of currency that he'd taken in Mexico. That, too, would be theirs once their quarry was dead. "I know you want to teach Keller a lesson," Riddle had said. "But don't. Just kill him."

"I do what I can," Vasily said, but not convincingly. He gestured to the man with the bandaged face. "But look at what that bastard did to poor Luka. And I have to tell Kolya's mother, and Andrei's, and Kyril's..." He shrugged. "These men were friends. Close as family. Closer even. I can't promise."

"Promise," Riddle said. "Or you'll regret it. Not because of me. Because of Keller. I know what this guy can do, given an opening. And he knows you're coming."

"Sure, sure," Vasily said. "But he is only one man. We can handle."

Riddle let it drop. "Get your people together."

"More men will be here by midnight," Vasily said. "Good men. Better than this Keller. We can move then."

"You don't want to be in that swamp at night," Zaubermann said. "Gets so black you can't see the man two feet away from you. And there's snakes. Maybe even a gator or two."

Vasily looked like he was about to say something, but Riddle cut him off. "Dawn, then."

Now, as they approached slowly up the dirt road, the sky was growing lighter in the east. Tendrils of low-hanging fog writhed across the road at fender level on the beige sedan Riddle and Zaubermann were in. Riddle had his pistol out and kept it pointed at Zaubermann's ribs. The wheels slammed into a rut with a teeth-rattling impact and Zaubermann sucked in his breath in sudden panic.

"Relax," Riddle said. "I never shot anyone by accident. I'm not even going to shoot you if your information turns out to be bullshit."

Zaubermann stole a glance at him. "You're not?"

"No. I'm just going to let the Russians have you. Believe me, you'd rather have the bullet. I think they're a little pissed at you." He looked at the back of the SUV, crawling up the increasingly rough road like a tank. "I'd make sure this whole thing goes well. Maybe then they'll get over it."

Zaubermann swallowed. He reached down and flicked the lights once, twice. The SUV ground to a stop. Men started getting out. Zaubermann took a deep breath and got out as well. Riddle followed, gun held down by his side.

Vasily and his gunmen were all dressed in black: black jeans, black T-shirts, and heavy black boots. All carried new-looking AK-47s, and each had a pistol in a shoulder holster. One of the men was Luka, with his bandaged face. In addition to his shoulder holster and AK, he had a bandolier of grenades slung across his chest. All four of the men were looking around uneasily. The rich, fetid smell of the swamp hung over everything and the cypress trees were black and ominous in the growing light. There was no breeze and the Spanish moss hung down limply, like tattered curtains. Somewhere off in the swamp an owl hooted loudly. The men jumped, and one raised his AK and pointed it into the swamp. Vasily cuffed him in the back of the head, snarling something at him in Russian. He turned to Zaubermann. "How much further?" he said, his eyes like flint.

"About a hundred yards," Zaubermann said. "The ground gets a little firmer on either side of the road. You can spread out some."

Vasily nodded and barked instructions to his men. They formed up into two short columns of two each, keeping to opposite sides of the road. Riddle prodded Zaubermann in the back with his pistol. "Get going."

"Me? I don't even have a gun."

"You're going to go up and knock on the door. Tell him to come out."

Zaubermann halted. A harder prod with the pistol got him moving again, slower. "He's gonna know what's going on. He'll kill me."

"Maybe. Maybe not. Especially if you're unarmed. Either way, we'll know where he is."

"Man," Zaubermann said. "I didn't sign up for this."

Riddle's voice sounded almost sympathetic. "I know. It sucks. You just backed the wrong horse, is all." His voice hardened. "Now move."

As they came to the clearing where the little house stood, the Russians seemed to disappear, fading into the thick brush on either side of the road. Zaubermann could hear the rustle of them moving and hear the soft squish of boots in the thick mud. One of the men muttered a curse, quickly shushed by another. Then there was silence. Zaubermann turned to say something to the man he knew as Jessup, but he wasn't there. He raised his hands and faced the house again. Walking slowly, hands raised, he approached. The white truck was still parked in front of the house. "Keller!" he called out, as he passed it. "Hey! Keller!"

There was no answer.

He reached the bottom of the steps and stopped, hands still in the air. "Keller!" Frowning, he put his hands down. He looked back to where the gunmen were waiting. No one was in sight. He put a tentative foot on the bottom step. It creaked under his weight. When he reached the door, he hesitated, then gave it a solid knock. "Keller?"

Still, no answer.

Zaubermann looked down at the doorknob. He inched his hand to it and grasped it lightly as if he was afraid it might bite him. "Keller?" he said, more softly. Then he took a deep breath, turned the knob, and opened the door. It swung wide, revealing the main room.

There was no one there.

V ASILY LAZARENKO CROUCHED IN THE stinking, chilly mud just inside the tree line and watched Zaubermann enter the house. After a few tense moments, he came back out and turned to the men waiting in the trees. He gave an exaggerated shrug with his hands spread wide.

Vasily rubbed his chin. He looked around for the man he knew as Jessup, but the mysterious stranger had vanished. "Luka," he said. "Take Fyodor and check it out. If nothing else, see if the money is in there."

Luka nodded, his eyes twin pits of fury over the bandages that wrapped his face. He motioned to his cousin Fyodor. The two advanced on the house in the fashion they'd learned as recruits in the Russian Guards Rifle division before getting their chance to desert, come to America, and work for their distant relatives the Lazarenkos. Luka went first, running in a crouch to take shelter behind the white truck while Fyodor scanned the area over the sights of his rifle, looking for threats. When Luka was safe behind the truck, he took the job of overwatch as Fyodor scurried to join him. They looked over the scene with the paranoid focus of men who know there's an enemy waiting but don't know where. Luka bolted from behind the truck, running for the front door, weapon ready. He barely noticed Zaubermann going as fast as he could in the other direction. Luka bounded up the steps and through the open door, his rifle held to his shoulder, his eyes alert.

The front door opened on one room that seemed to serve as a combination living room, dining room, and kitchen. There was a counter along the back wall with a metal sink and cabinets beneath. There were two doors to Luka's left; one open, one closed. Through the open door, Luka could see the edges of what looked like a bathroom sink. He couldn't see anyone in the house, and the place was absolutely silent.

He heard footsteps on the outside stairs and moved to the side, out of the way of Fyodor, who came through the open door, rifle held to his shoulder.

"Nothing," Luka said in Russian.

Fyodor nodded to the closed door. "What's there?"

"Bedroom?"

Fyodor shrugged. "One way to find out."

As Luka approached the door, he smelled something odd. "Cousin," he said, "you smell that?"

Fyodor looked puzzled, then shook his head. "Smell what?"

Luka hesitated. Then, with Fyodor pointing his rifle at the closed door, he kicked it as hard as he could. The door burst open and Luka stepped aside, giving his cousin a clear field of fire. Nothing happened, but that smell was more pronounced. Luka finally recognized it. The smell of gasoline. He saw Fyodor's eyes widen as he straightened up. "Luka," his cousin said. "Look at this."

Luka moved to the door. The only light in the room was provided by a window that was left open. But what drew their attention was the floor. It was covered with hundred-dollar bills. It looked as if someone had picked up handfuls of money and cast them around the room with reckless abandon. Luka frowned in confusion.

"Phew," Fyodor said. "What a stink."

He was right. The smell of gas was making Luka's eyes water. He looked up and saw a large glass jug sitting on the windowsill. His English wasn't good enough to read the label, but he could see the pictures of apples on it. He frowned. The liquid in it didn't look like apple juice.

Suddenly, Luka's blood went cold as he realized what he was looking at. He turned to Fyodor to shout a warning, but he saw his cousin drop to the floor, clutching at his leg and crying out. Luka reached for him and saw with horror that the wound that had appeared in his leg as if by magic was smoking and sputtering like a holiday sparkler. He barely had time to open his mouth to scream before the second tracer round coming from outside shattered the jug and ignited its contents. The flaming gasoline spilled into the room and touched off the gas with which Keller had soaked every surface. The last thing Luka heard was a low sighing sound that filled the room like the moan of an angry ghost as the flames drew all the nearby oxygen to them. In a split second, the cabin's small bedroom became a blast furnace.

CHAPTER
THIRTY-FIVE

KELLER SAT ABSOLUTELY STILL, PERCHED in the tree stand he'd bought at a sporting goods store he'd found on the outskirts of Charleston. He stared down coldly, dispassionately, like a killer god, through the scope he'd acquired for the AR-15. First one, then the other, of the Russian gunmen he'd seen enter the cabin come stumbling out, wrapped in flames and screaming.

Burning, they're burning…

Let them burn. Let the fuckers burn.

The dark voice that had haunted him for years, skittering and slinking around in the back of his mind, was coming to the forefront, becoming more insistent, and sounding more and more like the voice of reason. That voice wanted to luxuriate in the screams, revel in the sound of men burning to death in agony. He'd heard that sound before, on a night he couldn't help but revisit again and again. But it was something else in him that moved his hands, his eyes, his trigger finger to focus, breathe out, feel the trigger break under his curled finger and send the merciful bullet down into the clearing to end the suffering of first one, then the other of the men who'd come to kill him.

He pulled his eye back from the scope and took a deep breath. He didn't have but a moment to think about what he'd just done before the return fire from the tree line across the clearing was splintering the bark of the tree next to and beneath him.

"*EBANATYI PIDARAZ!*" VASILY SNARLED AS he saw his men come running out of the cabin, on fire and thrashing wildly. He was raising his own AK to end their agonies when the tracer rounds came slicing down like bolts from the sky to lay them out, twitching and convulsing, but hopefully insensate, in the grass next to the white truck. He instinctively shifted his aim to fire on the place where the rounds had come from.

Beside him, the newest member of his squad, Viktor, who'd gotten off the plane from St. Petersburg only two days before, did the same. The *durachit* was actually grinning. Vasily considered ordering the man to charge against the tree line where he knew the enemy waited, just to see if he could wipe the stupid grin off his face.

He didn't need to. Viktor stood up, aiming at the figure Vasily could see moving in the branches of a high tree at the far edge of the clearing. He fired once, a quick three-round burst. He started to stand up, still aiming the weapon.

"*Nyet,*" Vasily barked. It was too late. Vasily saw him topple over backward, a smoking hole in the center of his forehead and a spray of blood arcing behind him. Vasily screamed with rage, flicked the selector switch to full auto, and opened up on the figure he saw descending the tree at impossibly high speed.

HELLHOUND ON MY TRAIL

KELLER HAD ANTICIPATED RETURN FIRE, just not so quickly. He slung the AR-15 on his back and pulled on the heavy gloves he'd stuck in a crook between two branches. Grasping the rope he'd secured to the tree two days ago, he slid as rapidly as he could to the ground. The enemy's fire followed him, tearing chunks of wood and smaller splinters from the live-oak tree he'd been hiding in. His boots hit the ground and he crouched for a moment, catching his breath, before moving away, keeping the larger trees between himself and where he thought his enemies might be.

In the clearing, the bodies continued to burn.

CHAPTER
THIRTY-SIX

THE MAN VASILY KNEW AS Jessup seemed to appear out of nowhere and knelt next to Vasily. "Where the hell is Zaubermann?" he whispered.

Vasily was watching the bodies in the clearing. He could feel his nerve deserting him. "He ran. Back down the road."

"God damn it. That means it's just the two of us. We need to split up. Go to either side, catch Keller between us."

At that moment, the grenades that Luka had been carrying strapped to his chest began to cook off. The dull thumps came one after the other, each one blowing bloody pieces of Luka into the air.

"Jessup" smiled grimly. "Guess he gets a closed casket."

Another dull thud and what looked like an arm went arching up and landed on Fyodor's limp body. The smell of gunpowder and cooked meat drifted down to them on the wind.

That was Vasily's breaking point. "Fuck this," he said. "Enough." He began working his way back to the road, trying to keep as many trees as he could between himself and where he thought Keller was.

"Where are you going?" "Jessup" demanded.

Vasily turned on him. "Fuck this Keller. Fuck this place, this South Carolina. And fuck *you*." He turned and went back to working his way through the trees.

R IDDLE GROUND HIS TEETH IN frustration. These Russians were supposed to be such bad motherfuckers, and this guy Keller had played them for chumps. He had to admit, he was feeling a certain admiration for the crazy son of a bitch. He was showing a willingness to go to extremes that Riddle couldn't help but appreciate.

But he wanted something. Everyone did. And the secret to killing a man was to lure him with the thing he wanted most in the world. And he knew what that was for Jack Keller.

"Vasily," he called out. "Wait."

The Russian stopped and looked back, his face stormy. "What?"

"I'm going to get Keller out in the open. When I do, kill him."

The scowl deepened. "How?"

"Watch. But stay under cover. And you'll only get one shot. Make it count." He raised his hands above his head. One was holding his pistol. He began to step out into the clearing. He looked over to where the flames were consuming the cabin.

"Wait," Vasily said. "He'll kill you."

Riddle didn't turn around. "Not right away. He wants to find out who I am. Why I'm looking for him. It's why he told Zaubermann to tell me where to find him. Wait for him to break cover. Then shoot him." He stepped out into the clearing. "KELLER!" he shouted, lowering his gun hand to the side and letting the pistol fall to the ground. He began walking toward the opposite tree line, hands still raised. "KELLER! YOU'VE GOT QUESTIONS! I CAN ANSWER THEM!"

There was no response. Riddle continued to advance. "YOU WANT

THE PEOPLE WHO SENT ME? I CAN GIVE YOU THE NAMES. WE CAN MAKE A DEAL. LET'S TALK." He walked past the still smoldering bodies of Luka and Fyodor, breathing through his mouth so the stench of roasting flesh wouldn't make him gag. "KELLER!"

A figure stepped out of the trees. He was dressed head to toe in jungle camo, and his eyes were points of bright blue in a face painted black. He held a rifle trained on Riddle. "I'm unarmed, Keller," Riddle called out. "I just want to talk." He kept walking, waiting for Vasily to take the shot. If he missed, things were going to get messy. He saw a rifle lying in the tall grass. Luka's or Fyodor's, he figured, cast aside in their final agonized rush. He returned his gaze to where Keller was standing silently. *Come on, you Russian bastard*, he thought. *Take the goddamn shot.*

Even though he was anticipating it, the report of the rifle startled Riddle. What was even more startling was that Keller didn't move. He didn't fall, he didn't fire back, he just stood there like a statue. Riddle stopped, frozen in confusion. After a moment, he turned around.

Karl Zaubermann was standing there at the edge of the clearing, holding a rifle across his chest, a look of satisfaction on his face. He raised his chin and looked past Riddle. "We square now, Keller?" he called out.

For the first time, Keller spoke. "Yeah," he called back. "We're square." Zaubermann gave a sketchy salute and started walking to the road.

Riddle turned back to Keller, still standing there. "I didn't think Zaubermann had it in him," he said.

Keller walked forward, still holding the rifle on him. "Look how wrong you can be. You push someone to the edge, you never know what they'll do."

"You got that right," Riddle said. He dove for the rifle lying in the tall grass. As his hands closed around it, he rolled to his back and fired. He saw Keller fall backwards, his rifle spraying a three-round burst into the air.

Riddle staggered to his feet. He heard the sharp crack of another rifle coming from down the hill. He turned and fired back by instinct. The first rounds missed Zaubermann, who dodged away. His foot caught on something and he went down. Riddle advanced, taking aim at the body lying in the grass. Some instinct caused him to turn at the last minute and look back.

Keller was up on one knee, taking aim. Riddle was close enough to Zaubermann that he could hear him struggling to his feet, cursing.

He was caught between two fires. Everything seemed to take on an unusual clarity: the blades of grass rustling softly beneath his feet, the shaft of light from the rising sun that fell across his heaving chest, the slight breeze that brought the stink of burning meat to him. The choice came to him with crystalline certainty. He spun and fired two rounds, not at Zaubermann's head or chest, but into his legs. The big man went down, screaming in agony. Riddle didn't try to turn back and fire; he took off at maximum speed, zigging and zagging like a running back. He heard the report of Keller's rifle, felt the wind of the first shot as it went past his ear. The second struck him a staggering blow just below his right shoulder blade. He stumbled and nearly went down, but caught himself at the last second. He clenched his teeth against the pain and kept going. Then he was into the tree line and running down the path toward the parked vehicles. Zaubermann's screams echoed behind him.

CHAPTER THIRTY-SEVEN

"**G**OD DAMN IT," KELLER SAID aloud as he headed down the hill to where Zaubermann lay, his howls of pain and fear trailing off to low whimpers. The place where the gunman's round had struck the Kevlar vest beneath Keller's shirt was bruised and aching. He dropped to one knee and took aim at the running man.

"KELLER!" Zaubermann bellowed, the sound startling and distracting Keller so that the shot went wide. "I'm shot, man. Help me."

Keller ground his teeth as he saw his quarry stumbling into the trees. Everything in him ached to go after him. But now there was a wounded man on the ground, a man who'd saved his life. Keller couldn't just leave him. That, of course, was the plan. The man he was after knew that Keller would leave a corpse behind him in his pursuit. But he wouldn't leave a wounded man behind to die.

Zaubermann was lying on his side, panting like an animal. His pant leg was soaked with blood. "It's bad, Keller," he moaned, his eyes wide with the terrified recognition of mortal damage. "It's real bad."

Keller knelt and rolled him to his back. Zaubermann wasn't far wrong. One of the bullets had nicked the left femoral artery, and the bright red blood was coming in spurts. Keller knew wounds like that, especially ones high up and close to the groin, were rarely survivable.

Zaubermann clutched at Keller's arm with desperate strength. "Help me, Keller. Please, man. Please."

Keller heard the roar of a big engine starting up. His prey was getting farther away from him by the second. He wanted to pound the earth and scream in frustration at the sky, but he turned his attention to the wounded man. "Okay, Karl," he said. "I'm going to try to make a tourniquet. I'm going to try to stop the bleeding. Okay? I'm going to need your belt."

Zaubermann nodded. His eyes were already going glassy. Keller undid the big silver buckle and yanked the belt free. He wrapped it around Zaubermann's blood-soaked leg and tried to fasten it above the place where the blood was jetting out against his hands. He finally got it worked high enough and pulled it tight. Zaubermann let out a low moan. Keller looked at his face. He'd already lost consciousness. His face was nearly bone white. Keller tried to get an arm under him to carry him to his vehicle. The big man was dead weight. Keller had to struggle to get to his feet, and when he did, the limp body began to slide from his grasp so that he had to take him back down, slowly, to avoid dropping him.

"When we get you home, buddy," he said, "we're putting your fat ass on a fucking diet. Come on, help me out here." He shook Zaubermann to try to bring him around. Zaubermann just gave a little shiver and drew a rattling breath. Keller looked at the distance between them and the truck and realized there was no way to traverse the distance with that load. He'd need to bring the truck to him. By the time he got back, however, Zaubermann had stopped breathing. Keller sat down on the grass next to the still body, leaned over and felt for a pulse. There was nothing. Keller fell back into the grass and looked at the sky, exhausted. Once again, he was the last man standing. But he'd failed. There was no way to find out who was behind what had happened to him.

No. There was one. He hated it, but that was the way it was going to have to be. This had to end. Sooner or later, Keller's luck would run out. He was out of options.

Keller got up. It was time to move. He trudged back to the campsite he'd established in the woods, with the tent, sleeping bag, and other gear he'd bought with the Soupmaker's money. He gathered up his few belongings and loaded them into his truck along with the guns. The cabin fire was burning itself out, and the bodies of the two Russian gunmen had stopped smoking.

Keller looked up into the trees, where the buzzards were beginning to gather. He shaded his eyes against the morning sun that cast them into dark silhouettes in the cypress trees. He considered taking the shovel he'd brought from the campsite and burying the men who'd fallen, but decided that the buzzards had to eat, too. He thought of the bodies he'd seen throughout his life. Too many to count. Maybe too many for any normal man to bear, but Keller had seen so much death, he'd long since passed from any normal frame of reference.

He raised his hand to the gathering carrion birds. "Till next time, fellows," he murmured.

The birds stared back with glittering, merciless eyes, waiting. Someday, they'd be waiting for him. But not today.

JOHN MADDOX WAS SITTING AT Trammell's desk, working through a mound of insurance paperwork, when the phone rang. He recognized the number and answered immediately. "Mr. Keller."

"Is he still alive?" Keller sad.

Maddox looked through the open door of the office into the

sunroom. He could hear the rasp of Trammell's breathing. "Yes. But if you're coming, you'd better hurry."

"I'll be there before dark." Keller broke the connection. Maddox sat in the dimness of the office for a long time, thinking. Then he got up and walked into the sunroom. Trammell's eyes opened as he approached the bed. He didn't speak.

"He's on the way, sir," Maddox said softly. "Your son."

Trammell swallowed, the effort clearly causing him pain. He didn't speak. He just nodded and closed his eyes again. Maddox watched him for a moment. He checked his watch. Too soon for more pain meds. He walked slowly back to his desk and sat down. He took several deep, controlled breaths, trying to empty his mind.

He'd always been a calm, unemotional man. It had served him well in his profession, even as it had cost him two marriages. But calm was coming harder and harder to him these days as he saw the man who'd mentored him for so long coming apart. He thought about Keller, finally making his way here, and experienced a brief flash of an anger that was almost alien to him.

It wasn't fair. He'd certainly been more of a son to Trammell than Jack Keller had. He'd taken the older man's advice for years and reached the point where he could offer his own and know he was respected enough to be listened to. He'd laughed at Trammell's jokes and listened to his stories, even the ones he knew by heart and the ones he knew the old man was embellishing.

Keller was a stranger. And yet, Trammell had grown more and more obsessed with the son he'd abandoned as death closed its bony fingers around him. It had caused him to lose all perspective. Keller was a loose cannon, volatile, prone to explosions of violence, at least if their research was accurate. Maddox didn't imagine that recent events had done much to calm him down.

He pursed his lips and drummed his fingers thoughtfully on the desk top. He reached into the desk's top drawer and withdrew the old

Army .45 caliber pistol that rested there. It was the sidearm Trammell had worn in Vietnam, the one he'd killed the reporter with. Moving with the thoughtless assurance of long practice, Maddox pulled out a fully loaded magazine and slid it home. He racked the slide, seating a round in the chamber, before replacing the pistol in the drawer. He hoped he wouldn't need to use it. But you never knew. Not with someone like Jack Keller.

He felt calmer now, the anger replaced with a sense of purpose. Among the many lessons he'd absorbed from Clifton Trammell, one of the most profound was that complaining about what was fair or unfair was a game for fools. He could only imagine his mentor's derision if he'd tried to tell him his obsession with the son he'd never met was unfair to the man who'd served him so well. There was what needed to be done, and everything else was irrelevant. He put emotion aside and went back to work.

CHAPTER
THIRTY-EIGHT

KELLER ARRIVED JUST AS THE sun was going down. He pulled into the gravel driveway in the truck he'd gotten from Zaubermann, then got out and paused for a moment, looking up at the house.

Trammell's home sprawled over almost an acre atop a steep rise. Hedged terraces rose in four levels from the graveled parking area to an expansive slate veranda in front of the house. Keller slowly ascended, noting how each set of steps to the next terrace was offset several feet from the one below, so that a person approaching the front door had to ascend one stairway, then walk several steps to the right or to the left to find the next one up. Each level was walled off from the one beneath with a thick hedge, so that someone going up couldn't charge straight up the hill, even if he was so inclined. For a suburban Virginia home, it was constructed remarkably as if someone was expecting a siege.

As Keller reached the top of the last staircase and stepped onto the veranda, the door opened and Maddox stepped out. His face was expressionless.

"Thank you for coming, Mr. Keller," he said. "But I'm afraid it's a bad time."

"Well," Keller said, his voice harsh, "this is the time I could get here. So let's get this done."

Maddox shook his head. "It's…" His bland composure seemed to slip a bit. "It's actually called 'sundowning.' People in Mr. Trammell's condition…they seem to lose mental function particularly badly as the sun goes down. Maybe you should come back in the morning."

Keller studied the man's face, saw the anguish lurking just beneath the surface. "I get it, Maddox," he said, as gently as he could. "But can you guarantee me he'll even be alive in the morning?"

Maddox's face froze. Then, without speaking, he turned and walked back into the house. Keller hesitated for a moment, then followed.

No one had bothered to turn on any lights. The only illumination came from the setting sun, shining through the tall windows of the old house. Keller followed Maddox through dimly lit hallways to the back of the house to a large sunroom. The light was better here, but only slightly, the dying rays of the sun casting an orange glow across the room. There was a large, incongruously gleaming hospital bed set up near the windows. Maddox was bending over the bed, taking a moment to wipe the brow of the figure inside it before leaning over to murmur something in his ear. Keller drew closer and stopped at the foot of the bed.

The man who lay there was emaciated, nearly skeletal. What remained of his hair lay in white wisps across a forehead speckled with age spots. His eyes were closed and he seemed to be sleeping. A clear plastic line ran from his nostrils to an oxygen tank nestled beside the bed. Another line ran into his arm from the bottle of clear liquid suspended from a silver stand on the other side.

"Mr. Trammell," Keller said, softly but firmly.

There was no response.

"TRAMMELL!" Keller barked.

The man's eyes opened. They were a clear, piercing blue, slowly coming into focus. Keller realized he'd seen those eyes before. In the mirror. If he'd had any doubt that this was his father, those eyes dispelled it. The man in the bed muttered something, blinked once, then looked at Keller.

"Hello, son," he said in a raspy voice, thick with phlegm. He reached out a withered hand. Keller hesitated, then took it. It felt like he was holding a bundle of sticks wrapped in paper.

"I'm glad you came," the old man said. "Have you spoken to your mother?"

Keller looked over at Maddox. The man stood in the shadows, a few feet away. Keller couldn't see his expression. "I'm sorry, sir," Keller said. "She passed away. A long time ago."

Trammell looked confused. Then he nodded. "Yes. I knew that." He closed his eyes. "She was an extraordinary woman, Jack. So vibrant. So full of life. She lit up a room when she walked into it."

She did. She just didn't walk in very often, Keller thought, but he held his tongue. The old man didn't speak for a long time. His hand went slack in Keller's grasp. Keller looked over at Maddox, who stood in the shadows, impassive. Keller started to pull his hand away, but Trammell seemed to rally, opening his eyes and clutching Keller's hand more tightly. "You came here for a reason."

Keller resisted the urge to pull away. "Yes, sir."

"Tell me what's happened," Trammell said. He sounded stronger, more focused. "We'll work out what to do."

Keller didn't want to go over the events of the last few days. They were still too fresh and raw in his mind. He'd lost people he'd cared for, people who were killed solely because they'd befriended him. He'd had to kill again, then again, and he'd begun to notice that that was bothering him less and less. He didn't think he could convey to anyone how lost he felt, least of all this stranger—father or no father.

But something in the dying man's gaze would accept no opposition. Keller began to speak, slowly, then more quickly as the story took over. He told Trammell about everything that had happened since Maddox had showed up at his doorstep. He told about the no-fly list and Julianne's murder, the words coming more haltingly at that point as he had to pause to collect himself, taking several deep breaths before continuing. He told about being jailed, then released, then attacked again at Alford's home. He told about what he'd done to the *narcos* in Mexico. At that point, he had to stop again.

Trammell's eyes seemed to glitter at him in the darkness. He thought the old man might be smiling, but it could just as well be a grimace of pain. He went on, talking about Zaubermann and the encounter with the Russians. Gradually, he ran out of words. He paused, then said simply, "And that's how I wound up here, sir."

He thought for a moment that the old man had gone back to sleep. He'd been nodding at times, even with his eyes closed, but now he was still. After a moment, he spoke.

"John," he said to the silent figure standing nearby, "what do we know about this person that Kathryn seems to have hired to harass my son?"

"Could be one of several people, sir. But given the connections with both the cartels and the Russians, I'd hazard a guess that it was Riddle."

Trammell's eyes opened. This time he was definitely smiling. "Riddle," he said. "*El Perro del Infierno.*" He began to chuckle, then winced at the pain the effort caused him. He looked up at Keller. "You defeated the Hellhound," he said. "I'm not even sure I could have done that." He gave Keller's hand a weak squeeze. "Good work, son."

Keller pulled his hand away violently. "Good work?" He turned away. "Jesus," he spat, "what the fuck is *wrong* with you people?" When he turned back to face the man in the bed, his face was so contorted with anger that Maddox took a step forward, one hand reaching back for the pistol he'd hidden in a waistband holster at the small of his back. Trammell stopped him with an upraised trembling hand.

"I didn't just win a fucking soccer game, you maniac," Keller raged. "I've had some assassin pursue me across the goddamn country, kill friends and people I loved, and try to have me tortured me to death. I've shot people. I *burned men alive*. That bastard is still out there, probably still trying to kill me. *And I don't even fucking know why*. Now you are going to give me some *answers*, old man. Or, sick as you are, I am going to haul you out of that fucking bed and *break you in fucking half!*"

Trammell accepted the tirade calmly. Keller wound down and stood there, breathing deeply. "I have the answers you want," he said in his papery whisper. "Answers for what's just happened, and answers you've been searching for for years. And once you have those, I can give you a weapon. My legacy. All for you. My...legacy."

Keller blinked in confusion. "A weapon?"

Trammell gestured at Maddox. "John will explain everything. Now"—he closed his eyes again—"I need to sleep. We'll talk in the morning." The dismissal was absolute. Keller stood there, unwilling to accept it.

Maddox finally spoke up from behind him. "This way, Mr. Keller."

CHAPTER THIRTY-NINE

THE ROOM MADDOX LED KELLER to was a book-lined study that looked like a set for a BBC drama. There was a desk and a sturdy leather chair sitting in front of a high window. A pair of thick paper files sat side by side on the desktop. To one side was a large flat-screen television and DVD player on a rolling stand. Keller stopped and looked at it, a feeling of dread spreading through his stomach. He never wanted to see the gun camera footage again.

"Which would you like first," Maddox said, "information about the incident that occurred in the Gulf or on what's happening to you now?"

Keller stared at the files. They were ragged at the edges and he could see that some of the paper was slightly yellowed. That would be the file on the incident that had killed his men. He wanted to see what was in it more than anything in the world. But he *needed* to know why someone had been trying so hard to kill him. "Let's start with what's going on now."

"Very well." Maddox gestured to the desk chair. "Please. Take a seat." As Keller sat down, Maddox pulled up another chair and did the same, sitting uncomfortably upright. Keller realized the reason for his unnaturally erect posture.

"You can lose the gun," Keller said. "I'm not going to try to kill you. Or Trammell. At least not now."

Maddox hesitated, then withdrew the pistol from the back holster. He laid it on the desk, the butt still facing toward him. Keller noticed he hadn't ejected the magazine or put the safety on.

"So," Keller said, "who's trying to kill me? And why?"

"The person behind all of this is a woman named Kathryn Shea. She's currently a candidate for the U.S. Senate."

"Never heard of her."

Maddox nodded. "Nor would she have heard of you, except for your father."

Keller shook his head. "I don't understand."

"Kathryn Shea's father was a U.S. Senator. Served with distinction for over twenty-four years. Before that, he was a...I guess you'd say an old colleague of your father. They served together in Vietnam."

Keller spread his hands in a gesture of bafflement. "And?"

"And while they were there, something happened. Something that Kathryn Shea very much wants kept hidden." He got up and went to the television stand. "This." He turned the TV on and pressed a button.

Keller sat in silence, watching the video. There was a man on it that he didn't know. He assumed that was Shea. The other man was Trammell, still young and in his prime. He saw the man he didn't know murder the civilian woman, and then saw him advancing on the cameraman. When it was over, he continued to stare at the blank screen before looking at Maddox.

"So my...Mr. Trammell in there has been hanging this murder over his old war buddy's head for the last...what...forty-five years?"

"Forty-seven," Maddox said. "And counting."

"I still don't get what that has to do with me."

Maddox reached over and turned off the TV. "Your father has the original film. Taken from the cameraman. Kathryn Shea wants it. She won't feel that her father's reputation, or her own, are secure until she knows she has it. When I was sent to deliver the gun camera footage to you, she must have jumped to the wrong conclusion."

"She thought you were bringing me this instead. She thought I'd have the film."

"Apparently."

"And that's why she sent those goons to mug you."

"Yes," Maddox said.

Keller shook his head. "Jesus. All of this killing. All these people dead. And it's all because I got caught in the middle of some fucking game that Trammell was playing with this Shea character."

"I wouldn't call it a game. There's a truth your father has lived by his whole life. Knowledge is power. He's leveraged the knowledge he had of what Shea did to great advantage. He's been able to accomplish astounding things for his country as a result."

Keller waved a hand to indicate the house around him. "And he hasn't done too badly for himself, either. Or for you."

Maddox scowled. "He could have become much wealthier in the private sector. Instead, he's devoted his life to serving the United States. In ways that brought him no—"

"What ways, Maddox? I mean other than blackmail? Murder? Torture? Just what other terrible shit has my *father*"—he turned the word into a curse—"done in the name of his country?"

Maddox sighed. "He thought you of all people might understand. He's followed your history over the past few years. Haven't you done some things that some people might consider 'terrible shit'? You might consider being a little less self-righteous."

Keller had no answer for that. He thought back to a burning hillside in the North Carolina mountains, to the image of a man, on his knees, unarmed. But confident. Knowing that he'd be back to torment Keller and the people he loved. Knowing that he'd be able to do that because Keller wouldn't shoot a helpless man. Keller had proved him wrong. He closed his eyes.

"You see," Maddox said. "You are your father's son. You're willing to do what has to be done, terrible though it may be. And now, your father wishes to put real power into your hands. If you're willing to use it."

Keller shook his head. "I don't want it." His voice was a raw whisper.

"Are you sure? Kathryn Shea's opponent is a non-entity. He's an empty suit. She's almost certainly going to become a U.S. Senator. You're facing some fairly serious troubles in the near future." Maddox gestured to the television. "Having this kind of leverage over a United States Senator might save you quite a few problems. And who knows what else you might be able to accomplish? Your friend Lucas, for example. I hear his drug treatment program is excellent, but it's always struggling for funding. Some federal dollars—"

Keller opened his eyes. "Shut up," he growled.

Maddox shrugged. "I'm sorry it happened this way," he said. "But things are what they are. You're on Kathryn Shea's radar. She has the power to do you...or your friends...good or to do them harm. The only smart thing to do is use the opportunity you're given to influence her decisions in a positive way."

"Jesus," Keller said. "You're really good at this. You must have learned from the Devil himself."

Maddox smiled slightly and inclined his head in the direction of the sunroom where Trammell lay sleeping. "There are certainly some that might think so." Before Keller could say anything else, he gestured at the file folders on the desk. "There's the other information you wanted to know," he said. "Including the actual name and current address of the pilot once known as Gunslinger two-six." He paused. "The pilot who killed your squad in the Gulf." He stood up. Keller was looking at the file as if there might be a striking snake inside. "I'll leave you to it," Maddox said. "What you do with that information is, of course, completely up to you."

Keller didn't look up as Maddox left the room. He continued to stare at the file. Finally, he picked it up and began to read.

CHAPTER
FORTY

THE SKY WAS TURNING FROM black to dark gray by the time Keller finished reading the file. He sat back and rubbed his eyes. It had been a fuckup, pure and simple. He hadn't been able to watch the video again, but he'd read the transcripts. Even in black and white, he'd felt the anguish of the pilot known as Gunslinger two-six when he'd realized he'd killed people on his own side. He'd gone back and given a full report. He'd indicated he'd fully expected to be court-martialed. He could have blamed or at least shared blame with his co-pilot, the man with the Boston accent he'd heard on the tape. But he'd accepted the full responsibility. It had been his finger on the trigger, he who'd fired the shot.

But there the matter had ended, at least officially. Keller didn't know where Trammell had obtained the documentation of what had happened next. He figured it hadn't been acquired legally. There were copies of handwritten memos in the file, minutes of meetings held between authorities both military and civilian, supposedly secret e-mails between officials in DC and the Gulf.

The consensus emerged quickly: *Bury this*. Nothing could emerge that might tarnish the public's perception of the First Gulf War as an unqualified victory. The official reports were changed to reflect that Sergeant Jack Keller had screwed up, gotten out of his assigned area, and led his men into an ambush by a Republican Guard anti-tank unit. Keller's meltdown after he'd been picked up, during which he'd picked up a rifle and begun firing at passing American helicopters, had only served to cement the official line. Keller was a screw-up. A nut case. A washout. His exemplary record up to that time notwithstanding, Jack Keller was to be detached from the U.S. Army as unfit for military service for psychological reasons.

Keller looked for a long time at the psychological report upon which that decision had been based. That report had made all the difference. It had cast him into the limbo from which he'd fought to extricate himself ever since.

There was a phone on the desk. He picked it up and dialed a number he knew by heart. After several rings, a sleep-fogged voice answered. "Hello?"

"Lucas. It's Jack Keller."

"Jack?" The voice was suddenly alert. "My God, son, I was afraid you were dead! Where are you? Are you okay?"

"I'm fine, Lucas. I'm at..." He paused. "I'm at my father's house."

"Hmmmm." The reply from his old doctor was so familiar, it brought tears to Keller's eyes. He wiped them away. "He gave me the reports," he said in a choked voice. "About what happened to me. In the Gulf. And after. Everything. Including the debate on what to do about what happened. The debate on what to do about me."

There was a pause. "Are you sure you're ready to read those, Jack?"

"I thought I was. Then I saw the final psych evaluation. The one that recommended shit-canning me. The one that said I was 'unfit for further service.'" He took a deep breath before going on. "The one you wrote. And signed."

When the response finally came, it was so soft Keller could barely hear it. "Does it occur to you why your father might be showing you that, Jack?"

"You're saying it's a fake? That you didn't recommend kicking me out? That you didn't respond to a memo as to whether I could be brought back by saying you thought my condition was 'irreparable'?"

"No," Berry said. "It's all real. And I did say all those things. Would you like to know why?"

Keller wanted to smash the phone to splinters on the table. "You're the only friend I had left, Lucas. And now I find this out."

"I was your only friend then, too, Jack," Berry said. "And the alternative to separating you from the Army was to send you to prison."

"You know, I might have preferred that. God damn it, Lucas, the Army was the first time I ever...the first..." He stopped, the words piling up behind the lump in his throat.

"The first time you ever felt like you belonged," Lucas said gently. "Believe me. I know. I know you. I got to know you then. So well that I lost some objectivity. I started caring about what happened to you. With the rage you were feeling at that time, I didn't think you'd survive a military prison. I made a judgment call. Maybe it was the wrong one. But I..." The voice was cut off as Keller hung up the phone. He turned the chair around and looked out the window. It was growing lighter outside. A lush garden was coming into view. He remembered a similar view, out the window of Lucas's office.

Does it occur to you why your father might be showing you that, Jack?

Of course it did. Showing him the psych report wasn't completely necessary, unless one of the things his father wanted to do was isolate Keller further. Cut him off from anyone, leave him with no one in the world to turn to but the father he'd never met. And it worked. Trammell was a master manipulator, and one of the hallmarks of that was that you couldn't stop him, even as you saw what he was doing.

There was a knock at the door.

"Come in," Keller called out. He turned the chair around as Maddox walked in.

"Your father's awake," Maddox said. "He wants to see you."

THERE WAS ANOTHER MAN IN the sunroom when Keller arrived, a short, stumpy man with a face like an elderly frog's and wearing a doctor's white coat. He was leaning over Trammell, listening to his chest with a stethoscope. He pulled the chest piece away, making a *tch* sound in his throat. Trammell was awake and looking impatient. "So?"

"So," the man in the white coat said. His next words were delivered in a thick Russian accent. "Once again, I discover miracle. I discover you actually have beating heart."

"Hilarious." Trammell turned to Keller. "Good morning, son."

"Good morning" — Keller hesitated — "Father."

The smile on the old man's face had too much of an air of triumph for Keller to like it. Still, it was the closest thing to a genuine smile Keller had seen from him. "You had a lot to take in last night. I imagine you're worn out."

"A little."

"Maddox has already made up a guest room upstairs where you can catch some shut-eye. But first, I want your impressions." He grimaced at the doctor. "When Dr. Death here stops fucking with me."

The doctor flushed a deep red. "Will be done in minute."

He was as good as his word. He replaced the IV line with quick, deft movements, taping it to Trammell's bony wrist with strips of adhesive tape he clipped precisely with a pair of long silver shears. "Now," he said. "You are fine for another day. If you do not die."

"That, Doctor," Trammell said, "is the kind of incisive diagnosis that justifies all the money I pay you. Now go."

The man left without looking back, his head held high with wounded dignity. Trammell ignored him. "Now," he said to Keller, "what do you think you could do with that information?"

"I don't know," Keller said. "There's a lot of it. But I do have a question."

Trammell's face reminded Keller of a bird staring at a morsel on the ground and preparing to snatch it up. "Ask away."

"That film of you and Shea. It's a bomb, all right."

Trammell nodded.

"Say I wanted to drop it. How would I do it? Is there someone specific you'd send it to?"

Maddox had caught the last bit as he walked into the room. "There's a woman named Margeaux Nguyen," he said. "Half French, half Vietnamese. She's an investigative journalist. Or was, before her newspaper cut back and laid her off. Now I guess you could say she's more of a blogger. Has one of those conspiracy sites on the Internet."

"And she's got an interest in the war?"

Maddox shook his head. "Just this part of it. The cameraman who was killed was her father."

Keller looked at Trammell. "She must not like you very much."

Trammell coughed out a short, grim laugh. "She'd love to see me dead. Well, she can take a fucking number. In the meantime, I've strung her along. Dropped hints. Steered her toward things I wanted her to find out." He sighed. "It's too bad there are so few real investigative journalists anymore. They do come in handy."

"I'd think investigative journalists would be your least favorite people."

"You'd think that," Trammell said, "but you'd be wrong. Those people are some of the easiest to play. They're so hungry. They all want the big story. You can use that."

Maddox was peering intently at Keller. "But you can only use it once," he said. "Once you do, all your leverage is gone. It's..." He smiled thinly. "I guess you could say it's a kind of doomsday weapon. You only win if you don't actually deploy it."

Keller shook his head. "I guess I don't have the gift for manipulation that you two have."

Trammell smiled. "You'll get better at it. John will advise you."

Keller turned. "That right, Maddox?"

Maddox didn't look happy, but he nodded. "Anything I can do to help."

"Okay," Keller said. "Well, as you say, it's been a long night. I'm going to grab some sleep. Maddox, do you have the original of that film?"

Maddox nodded, his face expressionless.

"Package it up for me. And give me the contact information for this Kathryn Shea, and for Margeaux Nguyen."

"All right," Maddox said. There was something in his total lack of affect that bothered Keller, but he truly was dead on his feet. "Now," Keller said, "if you'll show me to that guest room."

CHAPTER FORTY-ONE

I F THERE WAS ONE GOOD thing about all of the shit that had happened in Keller's life in the past few days it was that he'd gotten to sleep in some of the best beds he'd ever experienced. The antique four-poster bed in the upstairs guest room was huge and almost obscenely comfortable, and he was exhausted beyond all reason, but this time, he could not get to sleep. He could drift off to a half-alert, half-dreamlike state that seemed somehow familiar, but true rest eluded him.

Part of what was keeping him awake was that it was light outside, the bright sunlight leaking through the old and yellowing venetian blinds. Another part was the turmoil in his mind from what he'd just learned.

But in the back of his mind, something even more compelling was keeping him from achieving more than a light doze. When he heard another, louder voice, raised in anger or shock, followed by a sharper, more emphatic impact than he'd heard before, he realized what it was that was keeping him awake. It was the always-on-edge awareness of a soldier who knew there was an enemy out there, a soldier who was expecting an attack at any moment. Now, he realized as the house's unnatural silence was broken, the attack had come.

Keller felt the adrenaline rising with that knowledge, at the same time that the eerie calm that always came upon him at such moments wrapped him in its embrace. He checked the drawer in the eighteenth-century table beside the bed, just to be sure. There was no gun hidden there, nothing he could use as a weapon. He looked around the room. Nothing. He walked as softly as he could to the bedroom door and opened it slowly, trying to force it by sheer effort of will not to squeak. It swung silently open; Keller was facing the stairs. He moved slowly down the narrow wooden steps. Faintly, he could hear the sound of an agitated, upraised voice. He couldn't make out the words.

Keller found Maddox lying at the foot of the stairs, his head bleeding profusely from a deep scalp wound. He felt at the throat for a pulse and found it, fluttering weakly against his fingertips. The voice he'd heard earlier was louder now, more insistent. It wasn't Trammell's voice, but it seemed to be coming from the direction of the sunroom. "Where is it?" the voice was saying, and now Keller recognized it. It was the voice of the man Keller had seen directing the action in South Carolina. Riddle, Maddox had called him. Trammell had provided the nickname. *El Perro del Infierno.* The Hellhound.

Keller stepped into the sunroom. The early morning light slanted through the high windows, casting an incongruously idyllic light on the scene. The man he now knew as Riddle was standing over Trammell, holding a silver revolver to the dying man's throat with his right hand. The other held Trammell's oxygen line pinched shut. The old man was gasping and struggling for breath, his back arching, his body writhing in agony.

"Tell me," Riddle was saying, this time softly and insistently. "Tell me where the film is. Tell me what's in it." He released the line and

Trammell fell back onto the hospital bed and began sucking in air like a bellows, the frantic inhalations collapsing into a fit of hacking. It sounded as if his lungs were trying to be expelled from his body.

"Just tell me, old man," Riddle said. "Tell me and I'll end all of this. Quick. Clean." He gestured with the gun, taking in the hospital bed and the IV pole. "This isn't how men like us should die. You've put up the good fight. At least that's what I heard." Trammell was panting, looking up with narrowed eyes at Riddle, who went on: "Hell, if only half of what I've heard is true, I give you a lot of respect. But now it's time to accept the fact that—"

"Shut the fuck up, Riddle," Keller said.

Riddle looked up, his eyes narrowed. "Keller." He smiled, but the look in his eyes made it more like a baring of teeth. Keller noticed his pallor, the sweat that stood on his brow. He remembered the man staggering after he'd fired. He was wounded, perhaps badly. But that only made him more dangerous.

Riddle shook his head. "Goddamn, son, you must have nine lives." He trained the gun on Keller.

"I could say the same thing about you."

"You need to back off, though. You've caused me a lot of trouble. More than I was paid for, that's for goddamn sure."

"Yeah, well, sorry," Keller said. "I tend to be troublesome to people who are trying to kill me."

"Nothing personal. But there's some film that the people who hired me really didn't want you to have."

"Yeah, I know. Apparently Kathryn Shea thinks it could do her some damage."

Riddle's brow furrowed. "Who?"

"You've got be kidding me," Keller said. "You don't even really know who you're working for?"

The baffled look turned into a scowl. "It usually doesn't matter who I'm working for. I get a job, I get it done."

"Kathryn Shea's a candidate for the U.S. Senate. That's who you're working for."

"Wrong. Right now, I'm working for me. So if this Shea bitch wants something this bad, let's see what else they're willing to trade for it."

"Idiot." The word came in a strangled wheeze from the bed.

Riddle's pale face twisted in anger at Trammell. "You shut up, old man."

Trammell ignored his words. His laugh was a ghastly croak. "You wouldn't know what to do with power. You're an attack dog. An animal. Your paws aren't made to hold the leash."

"I said *shut up*." Riddle's hands were shaking as he shoved the gun against the side of Trammell's head hard enough to break the skin.

"Cut it out," Keller snapped. He moved toward the bed, fists clenched. The barrel of the pistol snapped up to bear on him. At that moment, Trammell's hand came out from under the sheet that covered him. Something silver gleamed in the morning sunlight. With a grunt of effort, Trammell buried the shears that the doctor had left behind into Riddle's belly, just beneath the navel.

Riddle screamed with pain and shock, looking down in disbelief at the handle of the shears protruding from his abdomen. He reflexively swung the barrel of the gun against Trammell's forehead with a sickening crack. Then he staggered back, pointing the gun at the old man. Keller was charging, but he wasn't fast enough to stop Riddle from firing. The sound of the gunshot was enormous in the small space. Then Keller was upon him, swinging a fist as hard as he could against Riddle's jaw. The blow knocked him sideways, but he staggered and straightened, trying to point the gun at Keller.

Keller wasn't going to give him the chance; he closed as fast as he could, his left hand grasping the wrist holding the revolver and pushing it aside as he reached down and grabbed the silver shears with his right. He gave the blades a savage twist. Riddle shrieked with agony and his hand tightened convulsively on the gun. It went off again and again, the bullets shattering the tall windows. Glass cascaded to the floor, glittering in the sun. Riddle's free hand was clawing at Keller's, still fixed around the shears. He was roaring like a wounded bear. He snapped his head forward, jaws snapping, and got a chunk of Keller's cheek between his teeth.

Keller screamed with the pain as Riddle began worrying the flesh like a dog. He pulled back, taking a chunk of Keller's face with him. His mouth was covered in blood. The pain was so intense that Keller's grip slackened and Riddle pulled his gun hand free just as Keller yanked the shears out, wrenching another howl of pain from Riddle's throat.

Both of them were spattered with each other's blood by now. More had dripped onto the floor and was spreading in a thin slick on the wood. As Keller stabbed downward with the shears, aiming for Riddle's neck, the other man tried to step backward and his foot slipped in the crimson puddle. He stumbled and went down on his back, swinging the gun around and firing as he fell. The shot went wild, but it nearly parted Keller's hair before impacting in the ceiling, sending a fine spray of plaster dust cascading to the floor. The back of Riddle's head hit the floor with a dull thud. Keller followed him down, landing on his chest with both knees. He raised the shears again, his mind filled with a red haze of fear and rage, ready to stab and stab and stab again until his enemy's face was nothing but a bloody mess of chopped meat.

"Do it," a voice croaked from the bed. "Finish him off."

CHAPTER FORTY-TWO

THE WORDS STOPPED HIM. HE looked down at Riddle's face. The man was unconscious, finally knocked cold by the impact of his head hitting the floor. The gun was lying a few inches away from his outstretched hand.

"Do it," Keller's father said again, his voice a faint wheeze. "Do it."

Keller slowly got to his feet. He wiped the blood from his face as best he could, gritting his teeth at the pain from his ripped cheek. The blood throbbed in it, bringing tears to his eyes as he bent and picked up the gun.

"What are you doing?" Trammell's voice was a little stronger.

Keller blinked at him, his vision still fuzzy from the blow to the head. There was blood on the sheets as well, a deep red stain that seemed to be spreading. "Are you okay?" He walked on unsteady feet to the bed. "You're shot," he said.

"No, genius," Trammell said in a fierce whisper, "I'm fucking killed. But that bastard's going to Hell with me."

"Probably," Keller muttered. A sound from the doorway made him look up. Maddox was there, leaning against the jamb, blood covering his own face. His eyes were wide with horror. "Call nine-one-one," Keller said.

"No," the old man said, but either Maddox didn't hear it or the shock of seeing his boss's blood all over the sheets overrode any ability he had to follow orders. He disappeared back down the hall.

"God damn it," Trammell muttered. He turned to Keller. "Well?" he said. "What are you waiting for?"

Keller pulled the sheet aside and grimaced. It was a miracle the old man was still alive, but the miracle wouldn't last very much longer. There was nothing he knew how to do for a wound like that.

"See," the old man said. "Like I said. Killed. And about goddamn time." He coughed and a light froth of blood leaked from his mouth.

Keller reached for a towel and wiped it away. Trammell's lips were turning blue. It wouldn't be long now. Keller hated what he had to do next. But it had to be done. He took a deep breath. "Where's the film? The original. Come on, we don't have much time." He remembered the look on Maddox's face when he'd asked for the film last night. "I think Maddox wants it for himself."

For a moment, he thought the old man had finally given up the ghost. His eyes were closed and he didn't seem to be breathing. Then he took a deep, shuddering breath and his eyes opened. "Bottom shelf," he murmured. "Table beside the bed."

Keller checked. There was a square box, like a woman's jewelry case, covered in leather. Keller snapped open the catch. Inside, nestled in red plush, was a silver film can. Keller snapped it shut. "Okay," he said.

"Riddle," Trammell whispered. "Finish him."

Keller looked over to where Riddle was still unconscious on the floor. He thought of another man, helpless, surrendering, on a burning mountain in North Carolina.

"You don't do it, he'll be back."

The words rang in Keller's mind. He didn't know if he was hearing Trammell's voice or another one, from that mountainside where he'd killed an unarmed man, a man who he knew would be back to torture and murder more people he loved if Keller had let him live. *He's got some sort of get out of jail free card*, his lover Marie had said. Keller had taken the gun from her. He'd killed the man to keep her from doing it. And in the process, he'd lost her.

"Sorry, sir." Keller turned to Trammell. "I did that once. And it cost me everything I loved."

He couldn't tell if the old man's blank look was incomprehension or the knowledge of oncoming death. But he did recognize the next expression to cross Trammell's face. Disgust. His mouth formed words that Keller couldn't hear. He leaned forward, putting his ear next to the old man's lips. "Say again?"

It was a few seconds before the words came, and when they did they were faint but clear. "Failed. No...son of...mine."

Keller sat up. "No, sir," he said. "And you know what? That's a relief."

The old man closed his eyes and let out one last breath. His chest didn't rise again.

M ADDOX REENTERED THE ROOM. HE stopped as he saw the still figure on the bed. Then he walked over, pushing Keller roughly out of the way. He picked up Trammell's wrist to check for a pulse. After a moment, he sighed and gently placed the hand back down on the bed. He showed no visible sign of emotion as he turned to face Keller. "It's over."

"Yes."

Keller was still holding the box.

"And you have the film. The original."

"Yes."

Maddox looked over at where Riddle still lay on the floor. "Is he still breathing?"

"I think so. But he won't be if we don't get him to a hospital. Did you call nine-one-one?"

Maddox walked over and knelt by the body. Keller thought at first that Maddox was going to be checking his vital signs as well. But when he stood up, he was holding Riddle's gun.

"Give me the film," he said.

"God damn it, Maddox—"

"You're going to just give it away. You're not going to use it."

"That's right. I'm not going to use it. I'm not going to start another generation of power games. People were murdered. Killed in cold blood. And all you and that sick old man lying dead over there could think of was how you could use it to manipulate other cold-blooded bastards just like them."

Maddox's voice rose. "Your father was a great man."

"Maybe. Once. Maybe I should have known him then. But he just never got around to it. By the time he got to me, he was a conniving, manipulative son of a bitch."

Maddox raised the gun. "Don't say that!"

"It's true. Shooting me won't change that. And he wanted to turn me into one too. Remember what he said? 'You'll get better at it.' And he wanted you to teach me. That couldn't have sat well with you." Keller shook his head. "Well, it's over. I'm going to give this film to the person who needs it most."

Maddox's lip curled. "Some blogger."

"No. A woman who's wondered for years what happened to her father. Just like I did. She deserves to know the truth."

"What about Kathryn Shea?"

"If this brings Shea down, I won't lose any sleep over it." Keller nodded at Riddle, still lying next to Maddox on the floor. He couldn't tell if the man was still breathing. "But that guy stands a better chance of bringing her down, all the way. If he lives. Now, I'm going to leave. I'm going to call nine-one-one. I'm going to tell them what happened here, and then I'm going to look up this Margeaux Nguyen. And I'm going to bring her the truth." He turned to go.

"Stop!" Maddox snapped. "You're not going anywhere."

Keller turned back and looked Maddox in the eye. "You're going to shoot me?" he said. "You ever actually killed anyone before, Maddox? Or did my dad there not teach you how?"

"It should have been me." Maddox's voice was shaking. "I should have been the one he gave the film to."

"I know. You were more of a son to him than I was. You damn sure were more of one than I wanted to be. And you're probably the son he deserved. That's not a compliment, by the way."

"Shut UP!" Maddox screamed.

As he pulled the trigger, Keller realized how badly he'd miscalculated. He dove to one side and the bullet blew splinters out of the wall behind him. Maddox fired again, blindly. Keller got to his hands and knees, ready to make a suicidal rush. It was the only chance he had. It was no chance at all. Maddox was still screaming, but the shouts had taken on a different tone. As he got to his feet, Keller saw him pointing the revolver down at Riddle, who had one hand wrapped around Maddox's leg in a death grip. The other was clutching the shears he'd buried into the meat of Maddox's upper thigh. As Keller watched, he pulled the bloody shears free and stabbed Maddox again. Maddox pulled the trigger on the revolver, but the hammer clicked onto an empty chamber.

Keller crossed the room in a couple of quick strides. Maddox was raising the gun above his head, trying to use it as a club to knock Riddle away. Keller grabbed his arm and punched Maddox in the gut with his other fist. He kicked at Riddle's chest, where he thought the bullet wound he'd inflicted would probably be. Riddle made a high squeal of pain like a wounded dog, and let go. He fell back, leaving the shears embedded in Maddox's leg. Maddox crumpled to the floor as Keller ripped the gun from his limp hand. He flung the weapon across the room, out the door, and heard it crash to the hardwood flooring of the hallway outside. He stood over Maddox and Riddle, both of them writhing in agony, before going to the bedside table and pulling out the roll of surgical tape that he'd seen being used earlier to secure Trammell's IV. He bound both men's hands, then their ankles. He didn't want to risk pulling the shears out of Maddox's leg, so he tore the tape with his teeth. Maddox put up only a weak resistance; Riddle had passed out again and put up none. When he was done, he stood up.

"Now, if you two will excuse me, I need to make a phone call."

CHAPTER FORTY-THREE

IT WAS A BEAUTIFUL SUNNY day, and the light glittered on the water of Baltimore's Inner Harbor. Keller sat at an outdoor table at a restaurant Nguyen had suggested, sipping a beer and watching the boats. A leather messenger bag sat at his feet. Inside the bag were the box containing the film and the file folder he'd taken from Trammell's house. People strolled about the area, shopping and sightseeing. It was a good place to meet someone you weren't totally sure about. Keller understood Nguyen's caution; judging from some of the comments he'd read on her blog, some of her readership were not what anyone would call paragons of stability, and some of the more colorful conspiracy buffs were clearly insane.

"Mr. Keller?"

The woman who spoke was taller than he'd expected, and slender. She had strong features with a slight Asian cast to them, her face mostly untouched by age except for some laugh lines around her striking green eyes. She was conservatively dressed in a just-above-the-knee black skirt and white blouse.

Keller stood up. "Jack," he said, extending a hand.

She took it tentatively and shook twice before letting it go. "I'm Margeaux Nguyen." Her voice was a warm contralto, without a trace of accent.

"Please"—Keller pulled out a chair for her—"have a seat." She complied, but the wary expression hadn't left her face. He knew he looked more than a little rough around the edges, and the bandage on his face couldn't have helped.

She set a small black handbag on the table in front of her. "I hope you don't mind meeting me here," she said. "I've found that it's a good idea to have a first meeting in a public place."

He nodded. "I understand. You're right to be careful." The waitress had appeared at her elbow. "Something for you, ma'am?"

"Just water, please," Nguyen said. She hadn't taken her watchful eyes off Keller.

"Another beer, please," Keller said.

As the waitress left, Nguyen said, "Let me just say from the outset, I don't have a lot of money to pay for information."

"I'm not asking for any money," Keller said. "I'm here because I have an answer you've been looking for."

"You said in your e-mail that it was about my father. What happened to him in Vietnam."

"Yes, ma'am."

She smiled for the first time. "Please don't call me ma'am. It makes me feel old. There are already enough things that do that."

Keller smiled back. "Okay." His face turned serious again. "I do have the truth of what happened to him."

The smile was a little more bitter this time. "You'll forgive me, Mr. Keller, if I say that I've heard that before. More than once."

"No doubt. There are a lot of scam artists out there. But like I say, I don't want any money."

"That does help your credibility. Somewhat. So what else do you want?" Her eyes were still suspicious.

"I don't know how to put it," Keller said. "Maybe I just want to right a wrong." He reached down to the messenger bag and saw her tense. She reached for the handbag, which he could see was partially open. Slowly, deliberately, he brought the messenger bag up and put it on the table. She relaxed slightly. "I'm going to reach in the bag," Keller said, "and pull out a box. Okay?"

"Okay." Keller laid the box on the table. She looked at it with a puzzled frown.

"Go ahead," Keller told her. "Open it."

She fumbled with the catch for a moment, then raised the lid. The frown deepened. "What is this?"

"Your father was a film cameraman, right?"

She nodded.

"That's his last film. And it shows the man who killed him."

She sat silent for a moment, absorbing the shock. As she looked up, Keller could see the tears in her eyes. Her voice was a raw whisper. "Who?" she said. "Who killed him?"

"A man named Michael Shea," Keller said. He paused before adding, "My father was there when it happened."

"Your..." She shook her head uncomprehendingly. At that moment, the waitress arrived with a tall glass of ice water and Keller's beer. She placed them on the table, then looked at Nguyen with concern. "Are you okay, ma'am?"

"Yes," Nguyen said. Then more strongly, "Yes." She took a deep drink of her water and smiled at the waitress. "I'm fine. Thank you." Seemingly satisfied, the waitress moved off.

Nguyen looked at Keller. "Michael Shea," she said.

"Yes."

"*Senator* Michael Shea?"

Keller nodded.

Nguyen's eyes widened in shocked disbelief. "That's crazy. How did you get this? Was it in the garage? Were you looking through the attic and stumbled on it?"

"No," Keller said. "My father gave it to me. On his deathbed. He'd been using it to blackmail and manipulate Shea once he saw Shea start to get powerful. He gave it to me to do the same. Except he wanted me to use it to manipulate his daughter, Kathryn, who I hear is the front runner for his old seat."

"But you're giving it to me instead."

Keller nodded.

The suspicious look was back. "Why?"

Keller took a sip of his beer and looked out at the water for a long moment before answering. "Because I'm not the man my father was."

She shook her head. "Are you for real?"

"As far as I can tell, yeah, I am," Keller said. He gestured at the film. "You might want to be careful with that. Keep it in a safe place. And lock your doors. Kathryn Shea, or someone working for her, hired someone to keep me from getting it. He did it by trying to kill me. Several times."

She looked at him, her eyes narrowed and appraising. Finally, she spoke. "You feel like telling that story? On the record?"

He thought it over, looking out over the water and taking the last third of the beer in one gulp.

"Yeah," he said. "Yeah, I do. Not that I expect anyone to believe it."

"You let me worry about that." She looked over Keller's shoulder and nodded. Keller was surprised to see a black man in jeans and a white T-shirt under a navy windbreaker appear suddenly at his elbow. The man sat down and nodded at Keller. He was huge, built like a football player. His hair was plaited in tight cornrows atop his head.

"This is Samuel," Nguyen said. "He's a friend."

"Good to know," Keller said. He extended his hand. The black man shook his head. "I don't shake hands," he said. "Nothing personal."

Keller drew his hand back. "So you brought a bodyguard."

"More of a partner," Nguyen said. "But you can't be too careful. No offense."

"None taken. I'm a little less worried about you having the film now. But you still need to be careful."

Samuel grinned. "I'm always careful. That's why the two of us are alive."

"So," Nguyen said. "What I propose is this. You give me an exclusive interview. On video. I hold onto it until I can check your story out. But you sign a release at the end of the interview allowing me to use it as I see fit." She took a sip of water. "If I check out your story and find out you're bullshitting me, we're done."

"How do you think you're going to check this out?" Keller said.

She smiled thinly. "I may be self-employed, as they say, but I still have sources. So does Samuel."

"Funny," Keller said to the big man, "you don't look like a reporter."

"I'm not," he said. "I just know people. A lot of people."

"Well, that all sounds very mysterious," Keller said. "But what the hell. I only have one condition."

Here it comes, Nguyen's look said.

Keller thought of the file still in his bag. "It's not money. But there's one place you don't go. It doesn't have anything to do with Shea, or my father, or the guy who tried to kill me. It's about something that happened to me, back in the Army. The Persian Gulf. We let that be for the moment."

Nguyen shook her head. "I can't promise that. If it's something that might discredit you…"

"It might. I left the Army on a psychological discharge. And my life hasn't exactly been stable since. But if you're serious about other sources, you'll be able to confirm what I say in spite of that."

Nguyen chewed her lip and looked at Keller thoughtfully. She looked over at Samuel. "What do you think?"

Samuel shrugged. "Wouldn't be the first dry well we've drilled. But if it's bullshit, all we've wasted is time." He grimaced. "And the good Lord knows we got plenty of that."

"Okay." Nguyen stood up. "Let's go."

Keller looked up at her. "Where?"

"My place."

"We're going to do it now?"

She nodded. "You have anywhere else to be right now?"

"Good point." He stood up. "Let's go."

NGUYEN'S APARTMENT WAS OLD AND small and the furniture was worn, but the place was clean, with the exception of a dining room table piled high with books and papers. A laptop computer sat at one end of the table. Nguyen sat Keller down on the couch and Samuel fetched him a bottled water.

"Okay," she said. "We'll start with you just telling your story. However you want to tell it." Samuel was bringing in a small video camera set up on a tripod. Nguyen went on. "I'll be asking questions from time to time, but for the moment, don't worry about flow. We'll be editing it down to something we can use. Got it?" Keller nodded. "Okay, let's check the sound levels and we'll get started." She and Samuel fiddled with the camera for a few minutes, conferring in low tones. Nguyen attached a microphone to a small stand and set it on the low table in front of the couch. "Can you say something for me, Jack?"

"My name is Jack Keller," he said.

"Good. Let's start with that. We're recording. Go."

He cleared his throat. "My name is Jack Keller," he began again.

CHAPTER
FORTY-FOUR

WHEN KELLER FINALLY FINISHED HIS story, it was getting dark outside. A half-dozen water bottles littered the table in front of him. He leaned back, against the back of the couch, feeling utterly drained. Nguyen was silent. Samuel had left the room several times on one errand or another. Finally, Keller sat up. "I need to use the can."

As he walked down the hallway, he passed the open door of what he assumed was a bedroom. He stopped for a moment and stared. Samuel was seated at a desk in front of what looked like a bank of computer monitors. He could faintly hear the whirring of multiple fans and the *clickety-click* of Samuel tapping away on the keyboard. Keller stood in the doorway for a moment, until Samuel suddenly became aware of his presence. He turned around quickly, his hand going to a switch that killed all the monitors and left him sitting in near darkness. "Can I help you?" he said, his tone frosty.

"Quite a setup you've got there," Keller said.

"We'll talk in a few minutes. Close that door behind you when you leave."

Keller took the hint. When he returned from the bathroom, Samuel and Nguyen were arguing. "It's all too crazy," she was saying. "I mean, the cartels? The Russians? Some crazy assassin?"

"I know it sounds nutty," Samuel said. "But there are half a dozen websites from Mexico that follow the drug cartels. They're all lit up over the murder of Jerico Zavalo. By a *gringo*, no less." He looked at Keller. "Someone even composed a *narcocorrido* about it and posted it on YouTube."

"A what?" Keller said.

Samuel smiled. "A song. Very big down there on the border. The cartel boys actually pay some of these bands to write tunes about what badass outlaws they are." The smile grew wider. "Who knows, 'Jerico and Jack the Gringo' might become a hit. I wouldn't show up asking for a cut of the royalties, though." The smile slackened a bit. "But they're also buzzing about *El Perro del Infierno*. The Hellhound. Seems he's disappeared. The scuttlebutt is that the government has him."

Nguyen was staring at Keller. "What else have you found?"

"I'm still waiting for a call-back from my guy at the DEA. He'll be able to tell me more. The thing with the Russians, that'll be your lookout. You still got someone in the FBI who'll talk to you?"

"I'll call him right now. Jack, have you got a place to stay?"

Keller shook his head. "I'll find something."

"Stay here. You can use my room." She saw the look on Keller's face and rolled her eyes. "Don't get ideas, cowboy. You can use it because we'll be working all night. You like Chinese?"

"I don't hate it."

"Samuel, call out to Peking Palace." She opened a notebook she'd been scribbling in while Keller talked. "Now, I've got some things I want to go back over."

THE MORNING STRATEGY MEETING WAS held in a penthouse suite of a hotel that boasted a brilliant view of the Potomac River. No one was looking out the window, though; everyone was intent on the data on their laptop screens or iPads.

"We're in good shape in the rural western counties," a young, curly-haired female number-cruncher whose name Cordell couldn't remember was saying, "but the urban polling's a little squishy. We may want to reach out to some of the black churches. Maybe show up at some fish fries. Stuff like that."

"Pfft," another staffer with tousled blond hair and the lazy smile of a prep school Lothario replied. "That's chasing votes that we'll never catch."

Cordell looked over at Kathryn. She was leaning forward, looking down the table at the young man. Her eyes were stormy. *Good*, he thought, she'd been distracted lately after hearing of Clifton Trammell's death. The official line was that he'd passed quietly in his sleep after a long illness. Nothing Cordell could turn up told him any different, but Kathryn had still brooded over it. Now, however, it looked like she was getting her head back in the game. Still, he didn't envy the young man who was about to get his ass reamed.

"Kevin," she said, her voice level, but dangerous. "We can't afford to think like that. We're in a fight for every —"

The door burst open and Cordell's secretary came charging in. She was holding an iPad. "Sir," she said, "I think you need to see this."

Kathryn's eyebrows went up in astonishment, then drew together in anger. "Cynthia!" she barked.

The girl's eyes were wild, almost panicked. "Mr. Cordell..."

Cordell could see Kathryn building to an explosion. He needed to get this meeting under control. "Let me see it, Cynthia." Wordlessly, she passed it to him. He took one look at the headline on the site and physically flinched with the shock that ran through his body as it leaped out at him off the screen.

SEE THE VIDEO A SENATE CANDIDATE WOULD LITERALLY KILL TO SUPPRESS!

"Everybody," Cordell said, "leave the room. Everybody except me and Ms. Shea."

"But..." Cynthia reached for the iPad in his hands. "My—"

"You'll get it back, Cynthia," Cordell snapped. The girl looked stricken, but scurried away, behind the rest of the staff. They were murmuring amongst themselves, pulling out phones and tablets, searching for whatever had put everything in turmoil. He had no doubt the story would be all over the office within five minutes. A minute after that, people would start updating and sending out resumes.

As the last staffer closed the door behind her, Cordell looked down at Kathryn. She was staring down at the screen as if it were a poisonous snake dropped on the table in front of her. She looked up at him, fury in her eyes. "You told me this was contained," she hissed. "You said it had been taken care of."

"I thought it had," Cordell said weakly.

"Liar. You thought you could keep this from me while you got it under control. Does this look like IT'S UNDER CONTROL!?" Her voice rose to a shriek and she threw the iPad against a wall. *Looks like I'll be buying Cynthia a new one,* Cordell thought.

"We can deal with this," Cordell said. "It's just some blog. No one even reads those anymore—"

There was a tentative knock on the door. Cordell turned, ready to blister whoever had disobeyed his order to leave them be. The door opened and two men in dark suits came in. "Frederick Cordell?" one said, reaching into his jacket and coming out with a thin leather case.

"Who are you people?" Cordell was afraid he knew the answer already.

The man who'd spoken first smiled as if he truly loved answering that question. He flipped the case open to reveal the credentials inside. "Special Agent Morris," he said. "FBI." He nodded to the other man.

"Special Agent Mulvahill." Mulvahill nodded and pulled out a set of silver handcuffs. "Frederick James Cordell," Morris said, "you're under arrest for conspiracy to commit murder, conspiracy to obstruct justice, and racketeering. Please turn around and put your hands behind your back."

"I can't believe this," Cordell said. "You're arresting me on the word of some *blogger*?"

"I don't know about any blogger, sir," Morris said. "But we do have a witness in custody who's telling us some very interesting things over the past few days. Now, please put your hands behind your back while I read you your rights."

Numb with shock, Cordell put his hands behind his back. Mulvahill cuffed him as Morris began the litany. "You have the right to remain silent—"

Kathryn Shea interrupted. "Wait. Do you know who I am?"

"Yes, ma'am," Morris said. "And right now, you're what we call a 'person of interest.' You're not currently under arrest, but you might not want to try and leave the country. Can I answer any further questions for you, ma'am?"

"Kathryn," Cordell said, "don't say anything else. We'll get this sorted out."

She opened her mouth as if to speak, then closed it. Morris nodded with satisfaction. "Okay, then. You have the right to remain silent...."

When they were done, they hauled Cordell to the lobby, and out the front door he saw the vans pulling up outside. CNN. NBC. FOX. He felt the ground falling out from under him. This wasn't going away. This was actually happening.

"HOLY SHIT." SAMUEL WAS LOOKING at his smartphone. The thing was the size of a brick, but it looked like a toy in the man's huge hands. "We're closing in on two hundred thousand hits. And counting."

Nguyen shook her head. "Amazing." She looked over at Keller, sitting on the couch. "Thank you."

"Least I could do." Keller stood up and slung the messenger bag on his shoulder. "I know it's shitty. What happened to your dad, I mean. But I hope it helps to finally know."

"It does." She stood up, walked over and hugged him. Keller tensed for a moment, then returned the hug. When they broke, Nguyen was suddenly all business again. "Now, you said you might have something else for me."

"I might," Keller said. "But I have to go see someone first."

She tilted her head and looked at him appraisingly. "And who would that be?" At the look on his face, she smiled. "Never mind. Had to at least try."

"I know."

Samuel walked over and put out a hand. "Be safe, man."

Keller took it. "Thanks. You, too." He left without looking back.

CHAPTER
FORTY-FIVE

Ray Parkhurst, the man whose call sign had once been Gunslinger two-six, lived in a comfortable brick ranch house in Fayetteville, North Carolina. When Keller had learned that, he'd shaken his head. All the time he'd spent in Fayetteville, hunting down bail jumpers, and the man who'd caused him so much pain in his life had been living in the same city.

Parkhurst's co-pilot, a Bostonian named Tommy O'Connell, had died a few years after the war when he'd driven his car into the Charles River. There'd been rumors that the death was a suicide, but since O'Connell had had a blood alcohol level twice the legal limit and traces of opiates in his blood, it was eventually ruled an accident.

It was late afternoon on a Friday. People were coming home from work, pulling into driveways bordered by nicely kept yards.

There was a minivan already parked in the driveway. From where he was parked across the street, Keller had seen a blond, slender, fortyish woman in jeans pull up a half hour earlier. Two teenagers, a boy and a younger girl, piled out of the minivan and ran into the house, backpacks slung on one shoulder.

Keller knew that this was how millions of people lived, but to him, it looked like a scene from another planet. He waited. It wasn't the type of neighborhood where he'd usually done surveillance, and he knew he stood out like a sore thumb. He'd already gotten some curious stares from people who'd been jogging by or walking with strollers. But Keller knew from long experience that the best way to make yourself invisible was to become something no one wanted to see. Passersby would check out the magnetic sign he'd picked up at a storefront office downtown and affixed to the side of the truck, then glance at Keller in the red ball cap he'd gotten at the same place. TRUMP 2016, the magnetic sign read, along with the same slogan as on the ball cap: MAKE AMERICA GREAT AGAIN. When they saw that, most people apparently clocked him as a political canvasser and averted their eyes, although one older man on a bicycle gave him a thumbs-up.

Finally, another car pulled up at Parkhurst's house, a new red Mustang convertible. The man that got out was an older version of the picture Keller had in his file, but it was definitely the man he was looking for. He got out of the truck, tossing the ball cap into the passenger seat. He crossed the street in a few quick strides and approached Parkhurst as he was getting a leather briefcase out of the back seat. "Ray Parkhurst?"

The man turned around with an annoyed look. He was tall, with close-cut graying hair. His face had once been handsome, but now it sagged a bit and he had the blotchy red complexion of someone who'd seen a lot of sun or a lot of alcohol, or both. "Yeah. Who are you?" The accent was less pronounced, but it was definitely the same voice.

Keller stopped. He couldn't speak for a second. This was the man who'd pulled the trigger. Parkhurst's look of annoyance became one of unease. Keller found his voice. "My name's Jack Keller."

Parkhurst backed away a little bit. He didn't offer to shake hands. "Do I know you, buddy?"

"Probably not. And I only learned your name recently. Did you used to go by the name 'Gunslinger two-six'?"

Parkhurst stood still for a moment, the color draining from his face. "Who are you?" he asked again, but this time all the belligerence was gone.

"I'm the survivor. From the Bradley. You know what I mean."

Parkhurst sagged against the Mustang. He raised the briefcase in front of his chest as if he expected it to try and stop a bullet. "What... what..."

"We need to talk. And put that down. You'll attract attention." Slowly, Parkhurst lowered the briefcase to his side. "Good. Now you want to do this here, or somewhere else?"

The front door opened. The woman he'd seen earlier poked her head out. "Ray?"

"Go back in the house, honey." Parkhurst's voice broke on the word "house."

The woman didn't. She stepped out and closed the door behind her. As she advanced down the walk, Keller got a closer look. She was a good-looking woman, with high cheekbones, a few streaks of gray in her hair, and the kind of lean body that came from hours at the gym. "What's going on, Ray?"

He straightened up. "Nothing, sweetheart. I just met up with an old friend from the Army."

Keller held out a hand. "Jack."

She took it, her dark-brown eyes still suspicious. She was striking now, but she had probably been a knockout when she was younger.

"We're going to have a couple of beers," Parkhurst said. "We won't be long. Will we?"

"No," Keller said, releasing the woman's hand. "Just going to catch up a bit. Then I've got to get back on the road."

She still looked suspicious, but nodded. "Dinner's at seven thirty." Then, with the reflexive courtesy of the well-brought up Southern woman, she turned to Keller. "You're welcome to join us." Her eyes didn't extend the same invitation.

"Thanks," Keller said. "But like I said. I'll be moving on."

THEY TOOK THE MUSTANG. "THERE'S a place I know," Parkhurst said. "It's kind of a neighborhood sports bar. I go there sometimes after work."

"That's fine," Keller said. They made the rest of the ride in silence.

O'Kelley's was a mock Irish pub in a generic suburban strip mall. Parkhurst led the way to the large fake oak door, his shoulders slumped like a man walking the Green Mile to the electric chair. A couple of barflies marked their entrance by looking away for a moment from ESPN playing on one of the bar's multiple large flat-screens. One of them raised an unsteady glass. "Yo, Ray," he said. His voice was blurred by a ten o'clock slur at five-thirty in the afternoon. Parkhurst raised a hand in reply.

A plump, pretty girl in her late twenties, with multiple rings in her ears and nose, came out from the back. She smiled when she saw Parkhurst. "Hey, stranger. You're in early." She looked at Keller and the smile widened a bit. "Who's your friend?"

Keller answered before Parkhurst could. "Jack."

"Okay, fellas." She gestured to the empty booths along the wall and the tables scattered across the room. "Grab a seat anywhere." They took a booth as far from the bar as they could get. The bartender followed, carrying a set of menus. "You guys up for an early dinner, or just drinks?"

"Jose Cuervo," Parkhurst said. "Bud Light chaser."

"Oooh," the girl said. "Looks like the boys are ready to howl tonight. How about you, Jack?"

Keller studied the beers lined up behind the bar. "Shiner Bock," he said. The girl nodded and headed back behind the bar.

Neither of them spoke until the bartender returned with the drinks on a tray that reeked of stale beer. She set the shot and the beers on the table, with a worried glance at Parkhurst, who didn't look up. He snatched the shot up, downed it with a quick convulsive movement, then smacked the shot glass back onto the table with a sharp report that made the bartender jump. "Another," he said. "Better make it two."

The bartender looked at Parkhurst, then back to Keller, her pierced brow furrowed with concern.

"Go ahead," Keller said. "I'm driving."

That was clearly not all the bartender was worried about. She gave Keller a dubious glance, murmured "Okay," then headed back to the bar. Keller took a sip of his beer and waited. He'd spent twenty-five years wondering what he'd do if he ever confronted the man who'd killed his squad, and after all this time, he was still wondering.

Parkhurst finally spoke. "Man," he said. "Just let me say." He gulped, as if he was struggling for air. "I am so, so, sorry."

Keller didn't answer. He took a sip of his beer.

Parkhurst went on. "I asked, I asked over and over. It didn't seem right, man. There was something wrong about it. They said there were two Iraqi APCs and all I saw was one. I asked, man. I really asked. And Control told me…they told me…" He trailed off. The bartender was back, with two more shots and an even more worried expression. She set the glasses down without comment and backed away as Parkhurst slammed one down, then the other.

"You really ought to take it easy on that," Keller said.

"Fuck that," Parkhurst muttered. He held up his hand to the bartender, two fingers held aloft. *Two more.* She looked stricken for a moment, then glanced at Keller. Keller shook his head and held up one finger, then held his index finger and thumb a short distance apart. *One. A short one.* The girl nodded and poured the shot before bringing it over. "You all right, Ray?" she said, but she was looking at Keller.

The first shots were starting to have their effect. "I'm fine, baby," Parkhurst said, his voice starting to get a little fuzzy. "Just having a drink with an ol' war buddy, right, Jack?"

"Yeah." Keller looked at the bartender. "Everything's fine."

"I don't want any trouble in here."

"You won't see any," Keller said. "I promise."

The girl still looked troubled, but she backed away, then went back behind the bar. She tended to the few other customers, but her eyes never left the booth where Keller and Parkhurst sat.

"So," Parkhurst said, the tequila really starting to get to him now, "what's next? You gonna fuck me up? You gonna kill me?" Before Keller could answer, Parkhurst's face crumpled like a child's. "That's it, isn't it? You're here to kill me."

Keller felt sick to his stomach. "No, Ray. No. I'm here..." He stopped. He didn't really have an answer to why he was here.

Parkhurst was practically blubbering now. "You got the right, man. You do. But I'm asking. Don't. Please don't. I got a wife and kids, man."

So did 40 Mike, Keller thought, remembering the member of his squad who'd been a wizard with the 40-millimeter grenade launcher. 40 had talked a lot about the son he'd been expecting. Now his fire-scoured bones were somewhere in the Kuwaiti desert. Maybe. Keller didn't know.

But now he did know one thing at least. He didn't want to kill Parkhurst. For years he'd dreamed of confronting the man who'd killed his squad and gotten away with it. That desire for vengeance had driven him ever since, fueled his rage, made him a relentless hunter of men. He'd told himself that his love for the takedown, that moment when he seized a fugitive and brought him back to face justice, was the only way he knew to feel alive. But now he realized that in reality, it was a way of restoring the balance, a way to make someone face the reckoning that the man who'd killed his squad had never faced. Now the actual day of reckoning was here, in a sad, mostly empty little bar in a cookie-cutter suburban strip mall. The men who'd really fucked with his life were still beyond his reach, and probably always would be. Suddenly, there was nothing Keller wanted more than to get out of there.

Parkhurst was still babbling something about his family. "Ray," Keller said. The drunken flow of words continued. "RAY!" Keller barked.

Parkhurst stopped talking, his eyes wide and frightened.

"Give me your keys, man," Keller said. "Let's get you home." Parkhurst didn't move. Keller held out his hand. "The keys, Ray. Come on, I'm not going to hurt you."

Parkhurst looked confused. "What…where…."

"I'm going to get you home. And then I'm going to leave. And you'll never see me again."

"Really?" Parkhurst's face lit up like a child being told that Christmas would come after all.

"Really. Come on, hand the keys over. If I wanted you dead, I'd let you get behind the wheel."

Parkhurst stared, uncomprehending, for a moment, then fished in the pocket of his dress slacks and handed over a keyring that jangled with a dozen or more keys of all shapes and sizes. Keller took them, downed the last of his beer, and stood up.

"Go wait by the van," he said. "I'm going to settle up the tab." Parkhurst stood up, a numb and uncomprehending look on his face, and stumbled for the door. Keller walked to the bar. "Let me get the check," he told the bartender, pulling out a wad of bills. She rang it up silently, giving Keller what she probably thought was a hard look. It wasn't. "If anything happens to him," she said in a low voice as she gave Keller his change, "I know what you look like."

"Good," Keller said. "Have a nice night."

"You too," she said, the words a reflex born of years in customer service. Then she realized what she was saying and looked angry. "Just go, okay?"

"Sure."

CHAPTER FORTY-SIX

WHEN THEY GOT BACK TO the house, Parkhurst got out of the car. He was weaving a little bit. He stood there for a moment, blinking as if he didn't know which way to go. Keller sighed and got out. "Come on, Ray," he said, taking him by the shoulder and steering him down the walk.

The door opened as they approached. Parkhurst's wife stood in it, her face grim as she took in her husband's condition. "Well," she said, "that didn't take long."

"Sorry," Parkhurst muttered. "Sorry."

She sighed. "Go wash up, Ray. I went ahead and fed the kids. They were starving. But your supper's ready. I'll be in in a minute." Parkhurst just nodded meekly and went inside. She closed the door and stood there, arms crossed. "Mind telling me what that was all about?"

"Sorry," Keller said. "Guess we both dredged up some bad memories."

"Maybe it would be better if you just didn't come back here. Like, ever."

"I don't think I will be," Keller said. He started to turn away.

"He's a good man," she said. "Whatever you might think of him."

Keller stopped. Her chin was thrust out defiantly, as if daring him to contradict her. "Does he ever talk about the war?" Keller asked.

Her voice and expression softened. "Sometimes." She grimaced. "Every now and then, a few of his old buddies come over. They drink beer, do shots, and tell stories. Usually the same ones, every time. They always end up around the grill singing that goddamn Lee Greenwood song. Off-key." Keller could see there were tears in her eyes. "Then when everybody's gone, he goes and sits in a lawn chair, under a tree. In the dark. And he cries. But it usually takes till he thinks everyone else is asleep." She shook her head angrily. "What the hell *happened* to you over there? All of you. You were children. Like...like..." She took a deep breath and got herself under control.

"Like your son," Keller said.

She wiped a hand across her eyes angrily. "Yes. Like my son. And my daughter, I guess. Now."

"Yeah. Well. I hope that doesn't happen to them. And I hope Ray finds some peace." The words just came out without Keller thinking about them. He was surprised at how much he meant it.

"Thanks," she said. "I hope you do the same."

"You know," Keller said, "I think I might. I think I'm getting closer at least. I'm getting better at putting things behind me."

She nodded. Then she smiled ruefully. "Well, judging from tonight, Jack," she said, "I do hope we're one of those things. No offense."

He chuckled. "None taken." He turned and walked back to the truck. He took the Trump sign off and threw it in the back. Before he drove away, he dialed up Nguyen on the cell phone he'd bought in Baltimore. He got her voicemail. "That other story we were talking about?" he said. "I checked into it some more. It's nothing. Never mind.

Good luck with the other thing, though." He looked out the window. It was dusk and the street lights were coming on. A few lightning bugs were flashing in the yards, in a world Keller would never be part of. He was, for once, at peace with that. At least for the moment.

"If you need me," Keller said to the voicemail, "I'll probably be a guest of the Arizona prison system for a while. I've got some mistakes of my own I need to take care of." He killed the connection and started the truck. On the way out of town, he came to a bridge over the Cape Fear River. He stopped the truck, leaving the motor running. Passing cars honked angrily at him as he got out, holding the file his father had given him in his hand. He walked to the rail, hesitated, then opened it and let the documents and photographs spill out. He watched as they fluttered in the slight breeze, down to the black water below. Some of the pages lay upon the water like flower petals for a few moments, then became waterlogged and slipped beneath the surface. Others continued to float on the current, headed down the long dark path of the river, toward the sea. Keller didn't stop to watch them. He got in the truck and drove west.

EPILOGUE

Nine months later

KELLER WALKED OUT OF THE prison on a cloudless spring day. He had a plastic bag with his few remaining possessions and nowhere to go.

Despite the pleas of his exasperated public defender, he'd rejected probation and asked for an active sentence. Whatever he did when he got out, he wasn't going to do it in Arizona, and the prospect of reporting to a probation officer and being forced to stay in the state had zero attraction for him. He wanted to just do his time and go. Finally, he'd taken the lowest active term his lawyer could negotiate for him on the auto theft.

The charges against him for the murders in Becca Leonard's house had fallen apart when Nguyen's story had caused the police and the FBI to take another look at the forensics and discover what they'd previously missed: that one of the bodies found at the scene had been killed somewhere else, brought to the scene, and staged. That, and some information regarding the death of Jerico Zavalo quietly provided by the DEA, had convinced the locals that Rebecca Leonard, Erin Alford, Marta Guzman, and Alejandro Miron were not murdered by Jack Keller. The case was officially listed as "open," but the unofficial consensus was that the killers were themselves dead.

While Keller was locked up, he'd gotten another surprise in the form of a visit from a second lawyer, a nervous-looking young associate from a notable Phoenix firm. The man obviously was more used to meeting with wealthy clients in paneled conference rooms than convicts in grimy prison visiting rooms; he'd stammered and fumbled with the papers that detailed his father's last bequest to him. Maddox had gotten the house, its contents, and most of the money Trammell had accumulated, but Keller had received a sum of cash larger than any he'd ever seen in one place. He'd also received the key and address to a safe deposit box in Miami, Florida. The young lawyer did not know what was in it, nor did he seem particularly eager to know. He'd suggested a number of options for investment that they would be glad to help him with. Keller had thanked him, but directed that the money be placed in a bank in Phoenix. They could send him the account number and a debit card. The card rested in the plastic bag; now he just needed to get to someplace he could use it.

"Hey, stranger."

He turned. The woman leaning against the white Ford Explorer in the parking lot was someone he'd never expected to see again. He stood there, shocked into immobility. She smiled and took off her sunglasses. There were a few more lines on her face, but the eyes were the same: the sharp, hard blue of the sky on a cold winter day.

"Marie," he said.

"Yep." She straightened up. "You look good. Prison food must agree with you."

"Not hardly," he said. "You look good yourself." And he meant it. Her body was still lean and hard; age hadn't softened the contours he remembered so very well.

"Need a ride?" she said.

He looked at the Explorer. "Yeah. I guess."

"Hop in." She opened the door and slid behind the wheel. He hesitated for a moment, then got in. He felt self-conscious as he set the plastic bag down.

"So, where to?" Her voice was nonchalant, but he could sense the tension in her.

"Um," he said. "I need new clothes. And a place to stay. But right now, I could murder a steak."

"You're on." She pulled out of the parking lot and onto the highway. He studied her as she drove. She'd left him, years before, because he'd killed a man in front of her and her son. It hadn't mattered that he'd done it to save them both; the experience, and the horrors leading up to it, had traumatized the boy, and she'd told Keller she needed to get him away from anything that might remind him of the event. Even Keller. He hesitated to ask after the boy, but he had to know.

"So, how's Ben?"

She grimaced. "Ben is...a handful. He's had some problems. Not surprising."

"I'm sorry," Keller said.

"It's okay. It really wasn't your fault. Any of it. Just...bad luck."

"Yeah." He didn't know what else to say.

"So, this okay?"

Keller looked up. She was pulling into the parking lot of a chain steak restaurant. They didn't speak again until they'd been seated. It was still early in the day, and the place was mostly deserted. Marie stared at the tabletop and fiddled with the silverware. Finally, Keller broke the silence.

"So. How'd you find out where I was?" *And why*, he wanted to ask, but he figured she'd tell him that, when it was time.

"Lucas," she said, then looked up. "Some guy came around, asking if I knew where you were. I had a bad feeling about him. I told him I didn't know. Which was the truth. Then I got worried. I called Lucas. He told me what was going on. About your father."

Keller sighed. "So much for doctor-patient confidentiality."

She shrugged. "Well, he's your friend, too." She reached out and put one hand over his. "And so am I. I was worried about you."

Keller didn't know what to say. The waitress, who looked no older than seventeen, brought them two glasses of ice water. Keller downed half of his in one gulp.

"Lucas was worried about you, too. And when he told me about your father, what had happened, I..." She stopped. When she spoke again, it was in choked voice, almost a sob. "I reconsidered some decisions I made. After we...after..."

"After you left."

"Yeah."

"You know I don't blame you for what you did. You had to look after Ben. He was terrified of me. After what he saw me do. He was too young to see any of that, or to process it. You did what you had to do."

"I know." She was crying now. She wiped her eyes with her napkin. "And thank you. So I hope you understand what I did next." She looked up and away, not meeting Keller's eyes. "Like I say, Ben's having some problems. Getting in trouble at school. Fighting. Smoking weed. Sometimes I think the only thing keeping him from going completely off the rails is his little brother."

It took a minute for that to register with Keller. "His..."

She'd been fumbling in the small handbag she'd brought with her. She took out a picture and slid it across the table. It was a photograph of Marie, leaning over and laughing while talking to a little blond boy of about ten. The boy was smiling up at her. He had her eyes, but his face...

"His name is Francis," she said. "After my dad. But his middle name is Jackson."

He looked up from the picture. When she saw the look on his face, the next words came out in a rush. "I know, I know, I should have told you, but everything was so fucked up and Ben was still freaking out and I didn't know what to do and it was so hard to leave, I didn't know if I could stay away from you if you were in his life because I was still in love with you but I couldn't be *with* you and…and I'm sorry, Jesus, I know, I know it's…."

Keller noticed the waitress. She'd approached to take the order but was now standing there watching, her eyes wide, unable to go forward or back. "Give us a few minutes, will you?" he said gently. The girl nodded frantically and practically bolted away.

Marie was wiping her eyes with her now soaked napkin. Keller handed her his. "Damn it," she said, "I had a better speech prepared than that."

"Well, things don't always go like we planned."

That made her laugh. It was the same laugh he remembered loving. "Ain't *that* the goddamn truth." She looked up. "So. I'm sorry. It's all I can say. Other than, if you want to be in his life, you can. I know it may be too late, but…you deserve more of a chance than I've given you. And he deserves to know who his dad is. Just like you did."

Dad. Keller had never considered the word as applying to him. But now that it did…or that it might…

He looked up at Marie. "Okay," he said. "Yeah. I'd like that."

"I was thinking, maybe you could come by, visit some with me there, then we could work into—"

He interrupted. "Something else you said. About—"

She cut in in turn. "Still being in love with you? I know. I…I wasn't going to say it, but I'm glad I did. But let's take one thing at a time, okay, Jack?"

"Okay," he said. "One thing at a time."

THE END

ABOUT THE AUTHOR

Born and raised in North Carolina, **J.D. Rhoades** has worked as a radio news reporter, club DJ, television cameraman, ad salesman, waiter, attorney, and newspaper columnist. His weekly column in *North Carolina's The Pilot* was twice named best column of the year in its division. He is the author of four previous Jack Keller novels, *The Devil's Right Hand, Good Day in Hell, Safe and Sound,* and *Devil and Dust,* as well as the novels *Ice Chest, Breaking Cover,* and *Broken Shield,* and more. He lives, writes, and practices law in Carthage, NC.

Follow him at @jd_rhoades.